THE BLOOD OF TITANS

by

C. Michael Forsyth

DEDICATION

This book is dedicated to my wife Kaye, without whose love and support it would have been impossible.

ACKNOWLEDGMENTS

I wish to thank the late Marilyn Lee, who inspired me to write the book, and the playwright J.e Franklin, whose advice was invaluable. Although the civilizations depicted are fictional, the novel includes details about African societies that are drawn from works by many researchers. These indispensable resources include *The Lost Cities of Africa* by Basil Davidson, *Golden Names for an African People* by Nia Damali, *African Systems of Kinship and Marriage*, by A.R. Radcliffe-Brown and Daryll Forde, *African Religions and Philosophy* by John S. Mbiti, *African Proverbs* by Charlotte and Wolf Leslau, *The Destruction of Black Civilization* by Chancellor Williams and *The African Origin of Civilization* by Cheikh Anta Diop.

Cover art by Mshindo
Print Layout and Copy Editor by Ruby N. Hilliard

i

PROLOGUE

Listen:

This is the story of the first man and the first woman, and how our race was born. I sing it now as I heard it from the lips of my father – just as he heard it from his, and he from his, and as the story has been passed on, unchanged, since the morning of our people.

Long ago, the great desert was green and teemed with people, cities, and living things. Mother Africa had not yet given birth to her daughter Egypt. The great cities – Thebes, Memphis, Timbuktu, and Carthage – existed only in the dreams of seers. However, there were places that were old; kingdoms whose names are long forgotten and which lie today under white dunes, steaming jungles and murky lagoons.

Among these ancient places there was a large city by the sea. Its earliest name is lost to human memory but in later generations, it became known as "Kali." Eons have passed since the oceans claimed it, but in her time, this kingdom knew an unmatched greatness.

Her temples and towers were built from coral rock and her streets were broad, straight avenues. From her ports, long ships sailed forth toward distant lands, bringing back silk and spices. Her seamen mapped the shores of every continent. Her artisans created intricate designs from copper, bronze, and iron. Her scholars mastered the subtleties of mathematics and astronomy. Her surgeons cured ailments of the heart and the brain. Her kings sat on stools of gold and ivory.

Among the last of her rulers was Babatunde, whom men called "The Good." He reigned for threescore years, ruling justly and wisely in peace and war, until his back was twisted from age and white wisps of hair clung to his chin.

He was the wealthiest of men, with coffers over-flowing with gold, silver, and ivory. The one thing he treasured more than all his wealth was his youngest daughter Halima.

They say she was the most beautiful child who had walked the earth in 600 years: an excellent creature of smooth mahogany skin and eyes bright with wisdom. So much did the king love his daughter he could not bear to be parted from her. He kept her by his side until she was well over fifteen years old and still not betrothed. Halima's love for her father was equally great; there was no place where she was happier than sitting at the foot of his throne, entertaining him with song.

Her young days had been as free from worry as an unclouded sky. Then war came and everything changed…

PART ONE

CHAPTER 1

ÞETROTHEÞ

Peals of girlish laughter rang in the open air as Halima and her seven handmaidens bathed in a shallow pool in the center of the palace garden. Amid floating lilies and dashing schools of minnows, they splashed and chased each other through the shimmering, sunlit waves.

Given license once a day to abuse their princess, the serving girls dunked Halima mercilessly, giving forth boisterous cries of victory every time she disappeared among rings of bright water.

Spluttering, water gushing from her nose, Halima broke away for a moment's peace. Taking long, leisurely strokes, she swam to the far side of the pool. Like Venus, the princess rose dripping from the water, a sleek, graceful black swan. She dropped down on the sun-baked limestone, feeling a delicious sting as the stone scorched her flesh.

Halima drank in the splendor embracing the bathers – scores of palm and mango trees and brightly colored flowers culled from the surrounding country – and she thought this was her favorite spot. If you could love a place the way you love a person, then that was how she felt about her father's garden. She shut her eyes and threw back her head, basking in the life-giving sun rays that flooded her lids with orange light.

The sounds of laughter and splashing water faded away as Halima endeavored for the third time that day to recall the previous night's strange dream. In her mind's eye, she fancied she saw emerge out of cool, silvery mist a giant of a man, who strode toward her with a lion's sure gait.

His features were indistinct, but he wore a necklace of yellow, curving lion's teeth and his body was broad and powerful, like the wrestlers who visited her father's court. She recalled his large and strong hands. Yes, if she tried, she could remember the touch of those hands.

Halima felt a splash of water as someone approached, and like a child running out of a forbidden room, she quit her fantasy.

Neema, her first handmaiden, splashed noisily over with her clumsy dog paddle. Halima groaned, but at heart, she was pleased someone had missed her. Neema, whose name means "born in prosperous times," was the closest thing she had to a real friend.

"You've lived all your life by the sea," Halima called out. "Learn to swim properly!"

"I swim well enough," Neema insisted.

Halima snorted, "Yes, for a hippo!"

Neema clambered out of the pool beside her. A fleshy girl of fourteen, proud of her full bosom and broad hips; she shook the water off her tail, jangling the mass of beads and copper bracelets that adorned her wrists and ankles. She squatted down at Halima's feet.

"We're bored, Princess!" Neema complained. "We want you to sing for us!"

Squinting against the sunlight, Halima protested, "All of you know the same old songs I do."

"But none of us sing as well as you do, Princess."

The other girls swam over and clustered eagerly around Halima, pleading for her to begin. Halima sighed, but was secretly glad for the attention. In her darker moments, she felt it was only slavish flattery, but today she believed her handmaidens genuinely loved to hear her sing.

"Well, I need accompaniment," she insisted. "Aisha, bring your *muet*."

Aisha, her youngest handmaiden, ran off, arms fluttering like little wings, and then scurried back with a small, stringed instrument that sang like a human voice. When the other girls had settled around her feet, Halima cleared her throat. Then, in a voice as sweet and clear as any bird of the forest, she sang:

> *"There is a land, a faraway place*
> *I see only in my dreams.*
> *A mountain of silver,*
> *A ghost white high mountain,*
> *I see only in my dreams,*
> *I see only in my dreams.*
> *And in this place is my lover,*
> *My dark handsome lover.*
> *I go to him each night,*
> *But only in my dreams,*
> *Only in my dreams..."*

She drifted off, feeling blood rushing toward her cheeks, suddenly aware of the wide-eyed, innocent gaze of the young girls at her feet. Little Aisha paused from plucking the *muet*.

Halima coughed and was gamely preparing to launch into the second verse when a rumble like far-off thunder distracted her. She shivered, suddenly aware of her nakedness. All at once, she felt as helpless as a kitten.

Halima bolted to her feet. Neema stood up beside her and the other girls followed.

"What, Princess?" Neema demanded.

"Hush!" Halima cried sharply. Obediently, the girls became silent, cocking their heads left and right like curious cubs. Soon they could hear it too: the low, solemn beat of a drum.

"The warriors are returning!" Aisha exclaimed, clapping her hands.

"Hush!" Neema hissed, in precise imitation of the princess.

Another girl, well versed in the language of the drum, struggled to interpret the faint sounds. "Many have died in battle... A royal person has fallen..."

Neema covered her gaping mouth. The other girls began to mumble prayers. Halima shut her eyes.

Damn, she thought. *Damn all those men and all their honor and all their wars*! She felt herself beginning to cry.

The interpreter bowed her head. "Forgive me. It is your brother, Princess!"

Neema instantly burst into a loud, braying sob and the other girls followed suit. They drew around Halima in a tight circle. She surrendered to their clammy embrace, although part of her wanted to wrench free and hide away alone.

The funeral of Bakari, the brother of Halima, was full of honor, for he had distinguished himself in battle, slaying many of the enemy before a Zimbian spear gored him.

Women washed and wrapped his body in leopard skins. Then the men, their faces painted in white clay, the color of death, carried him aloft, leading a procession toward the burial field. The women marched behind, and Halima watched the long, winding line of women – led by the dead man's wives – preceding her. The widows made a solemn dance, a joyless, shuffling step, pitching to and fro as if they were on a rocking boat. They wailed their songs of mourning:

"Our husband has left us.
Now he fights alone,
One spirit alone
Against the darkness.
Our husband is gone.
Now who will protect us?"

Other songs praised her brother as a warrior and hero, but Halima instead recalled a round-faced, bare-chested little boy running across the sand, shaking a sharpened stick, making believe it was a spear. Back then, she remembered, her elder brother had been her hero, leaping across ditches and stabbing at straw lions.

Bakari, whose name meant "noble promise," was Halima's special brother. For among her people siblings were paired and raised together, linked forever in a custom known as *gorulanya*, the first brother with the first sister, and so on. He was supposed to have been her lifelong friend and confidant. Instead, she was alone.

Halima had lost seven brothers to war. They had fallen in turn one after another. Silently, she again cursed men for having invented war, for having transformed boys' play into deadly art. She wished women ruled. Surely, women would not allow such barbarity. Teeth clenched, Halima

5

stubbornly refused to join in the dirge. Others may have noticed, but Halima was too angry to care.

At the burial field, the body was laid east to west, in line with the setting sun. Bakari's favorite weapons were positioned nearby, along with blankets to keep him warm on his journey across the river of death, and near food to quiet his hunger. Anguished horns blared and rattles as frightening as the death rattle itself shook fiercely, speeding him on his journey to join his ancestors. An awful bullroarer, which made the roar of a jaguar, bellowed as if imitating the yawning, welcoming jaws of death.

Halima and the other mourners returned to the palace, where the priests slaughtered a giant sea turtle, the symbol of their clan, then the bones were burned and mixed with wine. They passed the cup, all members of the family drinking from it, saying prayers for the departed son.

As the sun set, they went down to the blackening sea, and cleansed themselves of the stench of death. Halima stood knee-deep in the ocean, looking out over the great, stormy sea, imagining her brother wrestling with the tiny boat's sail, braving the perilous river of death.

After the ceremony, a servant of her father King Babatunde summoned Halima to his chambers.

The king's private chamber was a small but stately room filled with rolls of papyrus, ceremonial spears, and shields. Banners and masks decorated the walls, and finely crafted stone and wooden statues stood in each corner. Frankincense burned in a pot, lending the room a delicate fragrance. A single wick that floated, flickering in a bowl of oil, illuminated the chamber.

In the center was an ivory stool, into which was carved scenes from the long history of their family: from the founding father who first arrived in the land, to those who ruled in times of famine and flood and led the charge of warriors into battle. Babatunde sat on this throne, draped in a purple robe fringed with the fur of a leopard.

Halima ran and knelt at her father's feet, resting her cheek on his knee. She expected to be scolded for not having sung at the funeral, but she was not worried; she could always charm her way out of punishment.

"Father, I learned a new song yesterday," she chirped. "May I sing it to you?"

Babatunde shook his head. "Stand up, daughter," the king said gently, "you are too old to crouch at your father's feet."

"There is no place where I am more happy, Father," Halima replied, smiling and hugging his knee more tightly.

"Stand, I say," Babatunde insisted, firmly pushing her away. Halima stood up hurriedly. Her father was never cross with her and so this new tone stung.

The king took her arm. "Daughter, you know that you are a jewel I prize above all else."

Halima nodded. "Yes, Father. You are always kind to me."

The king took her small hands in his. "Halima, you are my only joy. To me you are like a new spring day. In the drought of my life, you are the gently falling rain."

For the first time, the king looked truly old to Halima. He was bent, and as wrinkled as a dry, withered fruit. Babatunde spoke slowly and chose his words carefully, as if he only had a few left.

"Listen to me. One after another, each of your brothers has perished on the field of battle. One after another, we've watched each of our brave boys go down into the earth."

Halima nodded solemnly.

"I have no more sons of age to do battle," Babatunde continued. "Our enemy, the warriors the plain, the Zimbai, cannot be defeated. We are trading people, craftsmen and merchants. They live to make war. The Zimbai are as pitiless as the beasts of the forest. If they overrun the city, they will destroy everything we love about our land – like fingers crushing the light from a candle."

His hand hovered over the candle, throwing dark shadows across the room. Babatunde shook his head, as if casting the image from his mind.

Hoarsely, he continued: "I've sat with my counselors and my diviners. They say we must ally ourselves with the people of the west, the People of the Snake. They are strong. They, too, are a warrior people. Only arm in arm can we keep the Zimbai at bay. If you wed King Olugbodi, the ruler of the People of the Snake, a bond of kinship will unite us for generations to come."

Halima dropped his hand. She felt a rush of blood to her cheeks. She could almost pitch the old man over in his chair. *How could he? How could he send me away*?!

Bitterly, she exclaimed, "You call me your precious jewel, but you would bargain me away like a plot of worthless land!"

Iron crept into the voice of Babatunde. "Every young woman must marry. 'Woman without man is like a field without seed.' That is what the proverb says, Halima."

She refused to look at him.

"Father," she said softly, with her head hung low, "I am content here, with you. And I've tried to make you content. Why must life change?"

"Life is change," Babatunde replied firmly.

Halima found herself breathing so fiercely, her head swam. She envisioned the hills and valleys, the rivers and barren plains that lay between Kali and the kingdom of the People of the Snake, and she knew she would not see her father again in life.

"If you never want to see me again, surely you can send me farther away than that," she muttered.

The king winced, as if a physical pain had lanced his heart. Halima's own bitter words echoed in her ears. She had never dared speak to her father before in such a tone of rebellion.

With a gentle finger to her chin, Babatunde raised the

girl's head, so their eyes met. She stared at her father's sad, yellow eyes. Over his shoulder, she could see death perched like a vulture. She remembered a proverb: "There is no medicine for old age."

Babatunde looked at her helplessly, as if he wished to embrace her passionately, but could not. Halima wished she could unsay her angry words. Of all the people in the world, he was the last she wished to hurt.

The king whispered, "Daughter, we of royal blood belong to the people. In times of famine, we must spill our semen into the soil; in times of war, we must give up our best blood. We do what we must for the good of the many. We have no choice in the matter. 'A man is born. A man dies. The people must live on.' There is no choice in these things, Halima."

Halima saw he would not be swayed. Quietly she said, "Forgive me, father. You've told me my duty and I will obey."

The old king nodded. He drew his daughter's head onto his lap, and ran his withered hands through her long braids. Tears trickled down the old man's face, running through the crevices of his aged skin like an undammed river pouring through a ravine.

Then they embraced as tightly as two lovers. He had always seemed like a giant to her, but now his bones felt fragile and small.

He whispered in her ear, "Brave, wise, obedient daughter. I will surely miss you."

When Neema and the other handmaidens of Halima learned of the betrothal of their princess to King Olugbodi, they clapped their hands in joy. He was a wealthy and powerful king and they all expected to find good husbands in his land. However, Halima did not feel such undiluted elation. She had never before left the serenity and comfort of her father's house. To what kind of place would this journey take her? What kind of man was her husband to be? What if he were cruel or ugly – or simply dull, worst of all to a young mind? Each passing day, one of Halima's servants rushed home with new rumors. One day he was tall and handsome, and the next day round and fat. One day he had a court of fifty wives and was a master of the art of lovemaking; the next a senile old man.

Halima spent a grim afternoon walking the beach, wet sand squishing up between her toes. She gazed out across the gray sky, and the limitless sea. Imagine, never seeing the ocean again; to never see dolphins leaping from the water, or hear the crash of waves against the rocks.

She decided to pay a visit to her great aunt Bimkubwa, her grandmother's sister and thus one of the most honored of her clan.

The venerable old woman had taken Halima under her wing when she was very small, after her mother had died. Over the years, she remained more of a mother to her than any of her father's wives. She was not an official diviner, but her parents had practiced magic arts in the land to the south, and Halima trusted her skills more than any of the court diviners.

Bimkubwa lived in an uneven old house built of small clay bricks, in the center of the city. The old woman greeted her in the doorway.

"You haven't come to see your old Bimkubwa in a long time, child," the bent old woman scolded. "I, who suckled you with these very teats."

She gestured at her bare, withered bosom. "Bah! The

old are always forgotten." Then she laughed.

Halima hugged the gray old woman, tears in her eyes. "Mother Bimkubwa, I am troubled and I need your advice."

Bimkubwa wiped away the young girl's tears with a crooked finger and led her in. The tiny round house was filled to the brim with shelves, stuffed with jars of oils and weirdly twisted roots. A strange sweet smell, the intoxicating blend of unfamiliar herbs, filled the air. The atmosphere was so rich with competing aromas and so steaming hot that the young girl felt herself almost swooning. The old woman motioned for Halima to sit with her on a mat woven from palm leaves. She stared at her young kinswoman with eyes as black and sharp as a hawk's.

Bimkubwa told her, "You are about to take a long journey. You are to be married, but you don't know your husband."

Halima's eyes widened. If anyone doubted that her great aunt had the vision of the third eye, here was proof!

The woman cackled. "Old Bimkubwa knows many things. That one, I heard at the marketplace."

Halima put her fists at her hips in mock anger. Which of her handmaidens had been trading gossip, she wondered.

"Let us see what the shells say, beautiful Halima," Bimkubwa suggested. The old woman pulled from a nearby shelf a small goatskin bag and poured out a handful of cowrie shells. She bade Halima to arrange them. The young girl cautiously shuffled the shells about on the floor. Several times, she changed the positions of each shell, mindful of the old woman's penetrating stare. Finally satisfied, she stopped and leaned back.

Bimkubwa nodded and squinted as she studied the configuration of the shells. She blew out a mouthful of air, as if perplexed. She scratched her chin with two gnarled fingers. Then she shook her head, muttering.

Halima felt a trickle of sweat run down her temple.

"What do the shells say?" she whispered nervously.

The old woman's eyes twinkled as she revealed the meaning of the shells:

"The man you marry will have the heart of a lion. He will be strong, but to you he will surrender. He will be wise, but for you he will throw wisdom to the wind. He will be rich, but for your love he will lose everything."

CHAPTER 2

THE PEOPLE OF
THE SNAKE

alima and Neema, perched on the city wall, peered down as the caravan containing the wedding gifts from King Olugbodi appeared at the city gates. They were not the only rapt spectators. The streets below were packed with women carrying baskets on their heads, filled with shark meat, cassava melons, and other wares they had brought to market. Along with hordes of barefoot children, they stopped and lined the streets to watch the spectacle, hands at their fat hips.

A gaily dressed band of musicians led the procession. Their wrists and ankles were covered with a shower of grass and jangling bells. Marching to the beat of drums, they filled the air with intermingling sounds: high-pitched whistles and sweetly singing flutes and oboes and harps, the crystalline ring of the xylophone. Ivory trumpets, carved with charging elephants, shouted out triumph and joy.

Yet beneath the clamor, there was another sound, nearly drowned out yet always vaguely present. Halima could not see what instrument produced it, but it was a low hiss, like steam rising up from between rocks, or a snake slithering over dry grass.

"Look," Neema cooed. Halima leaned forward. Ten elephants, each as white as the shell of an ostrich, their faces costumed in bronze masks, lumbered through the city gates each holding the tail of the one before it. The two girls leaned so far over the wall they nearly toppled over. It was impossible for Halima to suppress childish wonder at the scene.

Next came one hundred prize bulls, whipped along by young boys in kidskin, along with rams and oxen for the slaughter. Fifty sleek black stallions, nostrils flaring proudly, trotted behind. Following the animals, bearers marched toting barrels of honey wine; chest after chest of ivory and jade; crates of silk and velvet. The crowd roared in approval at each new arrival.

Well, thought Halima, *at least he isn't cheap.* She leaned her chin on her fist as more gifts arrived.

Then strode row after row of warriors, long and lean young jaguars. Each shook his spear above his head as they marched and sang, their boisterous chant mixing with the triumphant voice of the trumpet:

"We are the People of the Snake.
We will always conquer.
When we march
The earth trembles!"

The girls leaned forward in unison at the sight of the young men. Each warrior carried a large oval shield of buffalo hide adorned with two painted intertwined serpents, one red and the other black. The young men's hair was long and braided, decorated with ostrich feathers. Chins jutted proudly and thick, strong arms strained against bracelets of buffalo horn and wood. Upon closer inspection, Halima could see a line of tattooed scars dotted their broad shoulders like buttons.

How brave they must be to endure those scars, Halima thought in awe. Neema wrinkled her nose in disgust at the sight of the scars, and then craned, squinting for a better look at the foreign warriors. After a moment, she glanced at Halima, who watched the arriving spectacle without comment.

"So, your gloriousness, I suppose you see this kind of thing every day."

"It's quite a show," Halima admitted, noncommittally.

"Well!" Neema sniffed. "No one will ever make a fuss like this over my wedding."

Halima pinched Neema's chubby arm. "And why should they, you good-for-nothing child of a fisherman!" she laughed.

Neema shuffled a few steps away, rubbing the sore spot.

Halima put an arm around her shoulders and drew her back.

"I don't know why I tolerate your insolent tongue!" the princess scolded affectionately.

Six drummers marching abreast announced the arrival at the gate of an important person. A ram's horn blared and Halima held her breath, waiting for her husband-to-be to make his appearance. To her embarrassment, she found her knees knocking rapidly together, as if she had to urinate.

Come, show yourself now, she thought impatiently. *Show yourself, damn you. Enough fanfare!*

At last, borne by six burly men, came an elegant carriage draped in black cloths hiding the person inside. No princely banner rose above the carriage.

Neema exploded with disappointment. "It's not their king. Some musty old dignitary!"

Halima sighed, oddly relieved, and pulled her hand-maiden from the wall. "Come, we must prepare to meet him."

They raced down the stone staircase to Halima's chamber. Neema bathed her in hot ass's milk, and then drenched her flesh with coconut oil. Sweet smelling leaves were pressed under her arms for perfume. She was clothed in a silk robe trimmed with brightly colored beads, and bedecked with a slew of bracelets of gold and copper, long looping earrings and other jewelry. Of all this finery, only one piece had any value to Halima: a turtle-shell necklace, on which there hung a royal pendant bearing the likeness of a sea turtle, the symbol of her clan.

When she was finally ready, they entered the King's Hall, an enormous chamber strewn with silken carpets and full of sturdy ebony furniture.

Mwendapole, the king's griot, was committing to memory a full record of the gifts they received. An army of scribes also knelt beside crates of ivory and jade, making an exact count of the contents. But his oral account of this day would be the sacred record.

Mwendapole was a rabbity, white-haired old man, meek but good-hearted. Halima had always felt a great deal of affection for him. He scurried over to greet the princess.

"My dear child, you must meet the emissary from King Olugbodi – his chief counselor and slave general, Masomakali."

A chill rushed over Halima at the name. Out of the shadows emerged a tall, gaunt man dressed in a turban and the flowing white robe of an elder. One arm trailed off to a deformed, three-fingered hand, Halima observed. But that gripped her attention far less than his eyes: the yellow, saurian eyes of a crocodile. As he slowly bowed and then raised his head, he never once took those eyes from hers. When he smiled, Halima could see that his teeth had been filed down to sharp points. And when he spoke, his voice was a soft, sibilant hiss:

"Illustrious Princess, I greet you and pass on to you the

love of my master, the noble King Olugbodi."

"I welcome you to the country of my father, wise Masomakali," she replied, bowing in return.

The emissary continued, "We regret that our ruler, the noble King Olugbodi the Trustworthy, could not greet you in person. Regrettably, the king is attending to affairs of state. He has sent me in his place to prostrate myself before your father and plead for your hand in marriage on his behalf. King Olugbodi will meet us at the Winding River that flows from the Silver Mountain. From there, we will travel on to your new kingdom."

Halima frowned and turned to Mwendapole.

"I thought my wedding was to take place here."

The griot explained, "It is a tradition among the People of the Snake that all their weddings take place at a holy lake in their land."

Halima was unable to disguise her unhappiness. To travel such a great distance in the company of strangers…

Masomakali smiled at her, his yellow eyes unblinking.

Halima considered him, and then announced firmly, "I wish my own guard to accompany me to your country." She imagined she saw a look of dismay flash across the face of the emissary, with the speed of a lizard darting across the grass.

Ignoring Halima, Masomakali turned to Mwendapole. "Does your king think we are unable to protect his daughter?" he inquired in his odd, disconcerting hiss.

The little man seemed flustered for a moment, then recovered and replied, "The prowess of your warriors is legendary, wise Masomakali. The child speaks only of an honor guard, to carry the praises of our king to noble King Olugbodi."

The emissary nodded and the tension that momentarily filled the room now eased. Finally he blinked – and Halima found herself able to breathe again for the first time since the conversation began.

That night, the emissary Masomakali was treated to an evening of feasting and entertainment, including jugglers, dancers, magicians and storytellers, Mwendapole among them. Halima watched him closely and noticed that while the visitor politely applauded each act, he seemed to take no real joy in any of it, sitting rock-still as a toad. She wondered what would give this strange man joy.

Chosen to lead the dozen-man honor guard was King Babatunde's sword bearer, Madongo, whose forefathers had served Halima's family for twelve generations. He was a broad-shouldered man of bronze, stout as a baobab tree. His clean-shaven head glistened, the style of the fishing people of the southern coast.

Madongo was a cousin of her handmaiden Neema through their great-grandfather. Although they were related, a marriage between them was possible and even prized among their people. For a man to marry a woman related to him through his paternal grandfather was spoken of with pride as "waking the hut of the father." The union was unlikely, though. Neema had always looked down her nose at the burly servant.

When he visited Halima in the palace garden, he was bare-chested and wore a short sword in a leather sheath, strapped to a rawhide belt. Her tittering handmaidens ran and hid themselves; it was rare that a man came here. Madongo dropped to his knees before Halima.

"Gentle Princess, I have been ordered by your father the king, Babatunde the Good, to accompany you to your new home, and on this journey to protect your life with my own. I have made this solemn oath at the shrine of my grandfather."

Halima looked down at the kneeling warrior. She knew him well, from childhood. He was like a tree that could not be uprooted by the most powerful storm. She smiled at the sword-bearer.

"Faithful Madongo, I do believe that while you live no harm shall come to me."

The warrior bowed shyly. Her handmaidens came out of hiding as Madongo strode off. *They are always giggling,* Halima thought slightly annoyed, *about things I do not understand.*

Three days later, a great caravan left the city of Kali. As well as the dozen-man honor guard sent by Babatunde, the grand party included the warriors of King Olugbodi: fifty horsemen, one hundred spearmen and twenty bowmen. It was well that their force was strong because their journey would take them across the plain through the country of their enemy, the Zimbai. Even more warriors would have escorted the travelers had reports not indicated that the Zimbai were engaged in a fierce battle with another tribe fifty miles away.

The bearers returned with many gifts for Olugbodi: jars of honey, banana wine and millet beer, and finely wrought ceremonial axes and spears.

Halima and her seven handmaidens rode in two golden *tipoyes* or carriages borne by men on foot. In one, she and

Neema rode, stretched out comfortably on velvet cushions playing *oware*, the game of pebbles; in the other, the remainder of her servants played with their pet monkeys and cats.

As the caravan marched away from the tall spires of Kali, Halima gazed back mournfully. If only she could stay another day, another hour, she could perhaps stand to leave.

She saw a figure waving to her from atop the city wall, a silhouette against the bright morning sun. She knew it was her father. *He looks like a ghost already*, she thought with a shiver.

Halima looked back toward the sea. She had said prayers and left libations at the tomb of her mother and forebears, making peace with them. But still, it was said that misfortune awaits those who travel too far from the land where their ancestors are buried.

"We will never hear the sounds of the ocean again, gentle Neema," she remarked sadly. Her handmaiden gave a mischievous grin and pulled out from her calabash bag a simple necklace made of copper wire run through a single large, spiked seashell. It was far less fancy than the serving girl's usual fare.

Neema told her, "My mother gave me this present. Here, hold it to your ear."

Halima did so and could hear the comforting, familiar roar of waves rushing to the shore. She smiled and returned it to her servant.

"You see," Neema said, proudly holding up the charm, "as long as we have this, we will always be able to hear the ocean."

The caravan passed through towns built of stone and others built of mud, passed neatly laid out villages of round houses and fields crowded with banana trees.

Spare, wiry men – thin from digging walls or crouching over potters' wheels – stood up as they passed. Women stopped their weaving and waved, with infants in their arms. Young boys, loincloths flapping in the wind, ran out and followed the caravan for miles, beating their own small drums and marching alongside the warriors.

The caravan climbed the steep hill country, where broad-backed smiths, her father kin, forged iron, mumbling strange incantations and mixing their blood into bubbling vats of molten ore.

They rode through valleys where proud herdsmen drove their cattle. They traveled past fields of giant stone heads; strong, helmeted faces shattered half to dust – decaying monuments to some ancient conquerors, long forgotten.

In a few days they reached the great plain, a flat endless vista of pale, yellow grass. Peeking out from between the silk curtains of the carriage, Halima gazed out over the landscape. In its own way, she had to confess, it was as magnificent as the ocean with its own limitless horizon. *It is as if it were indeed the sea*, she thought, as steady easterly winds sent a rippling wave across the grass.

The veldt was crowded with wildlife. As they rode along, she and Neema competed to be the first to spy each breed of animal. Halima first saw a herd of ostriches rushing across the plain, leaving a blizzard of feathers in their wake. Neema pointed out the tall giraffes galloping alongside the caravan, strangely graceful despite their long and bony legs. But it was Halima who spotted the lonely elephant digging sullenly for water with its tusks.

In the distance, Halima could see the Silver Mountain, rising up from the veldt like a tall, green fortress. A perfect pyramid, its peak sparkled as if crowned by colossal diamonds. Dark, stormy clouds nestled it like circling vultures.

Neema nudged her and pointed. "They say giants live atop that mountain," she whispered confidentially. "They carry off young maidens and cook them!"

Halima smirked at her fanciful servant. Curious, she

called out to Madongo, who was riding nearby. He trotted over.

"Faithful Madongo, is it true that giants live in that mountain?" Halima asked with some embarrassment. She did not want him to think she was a foolish child. The warrior considered her soberly, as if he did not consider the question in any way comical, and then looked off at the mist-enshrouded mountain.

"People say that there is a strange race of tall warriors who live there among the spirits of the mountain. There are forests where men live who are no taller than children. In caves in the north, there live men whose skins are white. Who can declare there is no race of giants?"

Halima stared at the far-off peak. She'd thought she would never again see anything in nature so awe inspiring as the great ocean. But there was an unearthly beauty to that distant mountain, vaulting so proudly into the heavens, that held her and seemed to beckon.

Halima awoke startled to find Neema shaking her, as if the carriage were on fire. She'd been dreaming about her mother, she realized, but the essence of the dream quickly fled, like water draining from a sieve.

"Look outside!" Neema cried in excitement.

"Little fool, I told you not to wake me every time you see a filthy vulture," Halima growled sleepily. They had been traveling a week now, and her handmaiden still found it necessary to point out every animal they passed.

"Don't be so grumpy," Neema said, continuing to stir her.

Her handmaiden pulled the curtain aside and pointed out to the veldt. There a lion, muscles rippling, bounded after a young antelope. Halima felt her heart leap in instant sympathy for the fleeing, doomed animal. The girls watched in fascination as the antelope turned and twisted, desperately trying to evade capture.

"Run, run!" the girls cried out. They could hear the men of the caravan crying out as well – rooting for the lion.

Finally, the big cat lunged at the antelope and brought the braying animal down. Neema screeched and looked away. Halima forced herself to look on as the lion tore and rended its prey, pulling off chunks of flesh and sinew, until all the fur of its face was smeared red with blood.

"Awful beast!" Neema wept. Halima put her arm around her friend.

"That is nature's way, Neema." Halima told her sternly. Then she shut her own eyes, trying to dispel the picture of the brutal slaughter.

That afternoon, they reached the Winding River, which flowed from the great Silver Mountain. It ran quickly and was clear as crystal. On the bottom, they could see the bones of animals as well as a few human skulls, made smooth by the running water. A few broken shields and spears rested there silently, half buried in the mud.

In the distance, the falls rumbled, sounding like boulders crashing down.

Halima sighed at the sight of the river. Here at last they were. Now she would finally meet her husband-to-be, the celebrated King Olugbodi.

Across the river, a party of about fifty warriors stood waiting. Halima craned for a glimpse of her betrothed. Squinting through her curtains, she could make out a figure on horseback, wearing a high, feathered headdress. *That must be King Olugbodi,* she thought.

The horns of the caravan blared, announcing their arrival. Almost immediately, a drum signal returned, welcoming them and inviting them to ford the river.

Madongo rode back to Halima's carriage. His brow was knitted like the face of a worried parent. "Princess, it would be safer for you to cross the river on horseback," he informed her.

Halima assented and she and her handmaidens crawled out of their carriages.

With some diffidence, Madongo put his broad hands around Halima's waist. She felt a rush of blood to her cheeks; no man ever held her before. With seemingly no effort at all, the warrior hoisted her into the saddle.

He took her delicate fingers in his broad hands and planted them on the horse's mane.

"Just hold on, Princess," he said.

Halima watched as the warrior pulled off his robes, stripping down to a slender loincloth. She noticed his broad and powerful back. *Like a rhino's,* she thought.

Taking the reins, he gingerly led the horse into the chilly waters of the Winding River. Halima looked down at the churning waters; the base of the river seemed dizzyingly far away. She was a strong swimmer, but there was something about this uncontrolled rush of water that completely unnerved her. With crystal clarity she could picture herself being swept downriver.

She clenched the horse's mane in her fist and focused on Madongo's thick neck, trying to ignore the current. Several times she was sure the powerful current would uproot the warrior. But, straining against the river, he stayed upright and continued to tug the horse's rein.

Sometimes the horse pulled away, fearful of falling, but finally it found its faith in Madongo, allowing him to guide it across the river.

At last the horse, hooves slipping and sliding on the silk-smooth mud, clambered out of the water and onto the river bank. Exhausted from his effort, Madongo bent, hands gripping his knees, panting.

Halima leaned down from the saddle and gently touched his broad, sweaty shoulder.

"Thank you, faithful Madongo. Thank you for making me feel safe," she told him.

The warrior turned and looked up at her, as if her words were a blessing from a priestess. Masomakali had already made the crossing and he stood by the horse of King Olugbodi, a milk-white mare.

King Olugbodi grinned broadly. He was a young man of no more than twenty years, with a round face, a plump, soft belly, and birdlike arms, slender as a girl's. His headdress was festooned with hundreds of brightly colored feathers, and yards of bright gold chains hung around his neck.

The instant Halima saw him, her heart sank. This was not the lion her seer had described. Then she scolded herself immediately. *How unfair to judge a man by his appearance.*

The king saluted her.

"Most illustrious, most kind, gentle, most beautiful, most radiant Princess Halima. I, King Olugbodi, who is unworthy even to wash the dust from your feet, salute you. I throw myself before you as your humble servant."

Halima covered her mouth. She almost giggled at the pompous greeting, but, biting her lower lip, she resisted. She replied, "The honor is mine, noble King Olugbodi. My father King Babatunde sends his greetings."

The young ruler spurred his mare forward. He trotted slowly around Halima, and she could sense his gaze passing across her long neck, full lips and gentle curves, burning her like the noon sun.

He faced her, eyes aglow, and murmured, "If you are as sweet to taste as to look upon, I will have found a worthy wife."

Halima whispered back, "If your courage matches the glitter of your gold, I will have found a worthy husband."

The king chuckled, then spoke loudly, so that all could hear. "I know you've traveled far. Let us rest a while here and learn about each other."

But his slave general Masomakali counseled the king, "This is not a good place to tarry, Lord. This crossing is a favorite place of ambush for the Zimbai."

"Very well," the king responded. "We will move on then."

He took Halima's hand and kissed it. "Tonight we will camp and you and I will get to know each other better."

Halima bowed.

The bearers had struggled across the river with their carriage. Halima returned to it, and found her handmaiden Neema waiting impatiently.

"He's too fat!" Neema submitted immediately.

Halima, who was in no mood now for impudence, replied, "Of course you are too childish to know the true measure of a man."

Neema snorted, "I can measure his belly from here. To me, he looks just like a pregnant woman."

Halima slapped her face. "Your foolish mouth will be the end of you," she shot back.

Tears began to stream from Neema's eyes. Immediately, Halima regretted the blow. She reached for the other girl, but Neema pulled away, folding her arms across her big bosom and throwing her head back proudly.

Halima sighed. She was furious, but not sure yet with whom.

The caravan, now reinforced by the warriors of Olugbodi, continued across the plain.

Halima and Neema slept in their *tipoye*, heads bobbing together. The heat poured through the silk coverings of the carriage, making them both sweat as if in a fever. Halima drifted back and forth from the world of dreams to reality. In her uneasy dreams, a snake as big as a man slithered around in the carriage with them, winding itself around and around her. Try as she might to slip away, the snake pursued her, sliding through her legs and thighs, intertwining with her, until she could not tell where the snake ended and she began.

"I'm hungry," Neema announced loudly. Halima opened her eyes. She shuddered, still feeling the slimy beast coiling around her.

Neema fished in a jar for some millet cakes her mother had stored for her. She passed one to Halima and took two for herself.

"I hope we'll be stopping soon. Bumping and swaying is making me seasick!"

She flicked a beetle off the cake and chowed down greedily.

Halima nodded. "Think about the poor fellows who have to carry the thing."

"I think one of them likes me," Neema said casually. "The short one."

Halima took a bite from her cake. "What did he tell you?"

"He didn't say anything. He winked at me – twice."

Halima laughed.

Then, from outside the carriage, they heard a deep bellow of warning.

A chorus of cries went up. The warriors of King Olugbodi roared in their own language and there was a sudden commotion outside.

The carriage stopped with a jerk, throwing the two girls forward. It crashed to the ground like a bird with its wings clipped off in midair, spilling the two girls on top of each other.

"What is the matter with those fools?" Neema yelped. Outside, screaming horses reared and frantic, high-pitched voices barked and jabbered conflicting orders. Halima threw back the curtain.

From out of the tall grass a thousand painted warriors rose, spears in hand. The faces were dotted with the markings of the Zimbai. Halima shut the curtain.

Neema struggled to get by. "What's going on? Let me see!" she demanded.

"Sit still!" ordered Halima.

An arrow ripped through the roof of the *tipoye* and flew into the pillow with a thunk, right between Neema's plump thighs.

Neema squealed in terror, and then began to shriek again and again, as if the arrow were an asp about to strike.

Halima caught her and wrapped her arms around the hysterical girl. "The warriors will protect us! Don't be afraid! Everything will be all right!"

She cracked the curtains half an inch and stared out. A shower of arrows rained down on the defenders of the caravan, as the Zimbai charged, yodeling out their war cry and bounding forward with long, powerful strides. The warriors of King Olugbodi took up defensive positions around the caravan, bracing themselves for the attack.

Halima pulled the curtain shut. Neema began to weep and Halima took her to her breast, as if she were a small child. She clapped her hands over her handmaiden's ears and began to pray to her ancestors for their intervention.

Outside she heard the screams of the dying and the ring of metal slapping metal as shields collided. Through the curtains she could see the shadows of warriors doing battle, as spears thrust and men fell. To her alarm, she realized the din of battle was growing louder and closer.

As if tossed from a bucket, blood splashed across the silk curtains of the carriage.

Halima heard the shrieks of young girls. She opened the curtains and saw that the *tipoye* behind them was on fire and surrounded by Zimbai warriors. One by one the girls were plucked from the burning caravan like chunks of food carried off by black ants. Each was flung over the broad shoulder of one of the Zimbai and carried off.

Halima watched in horror as each of her handmaidens vanished – even little Aisha, pounding the chest of her captor and lashing at him with her tiny feet.

Where was her proud husband-to-be, King Olugbodi? Up on a hill, Halima could see him running from the battle, his short, stumpy legs pumping fiercely. Four of his warriors followed behind, every few steps turning to fire off a volley of arrows.

The twelve warriors of King Babatunde clung close to the carriage, rearing up on their horses. The Zimbai used ropes and spears to bring down the warriors, and each in turn was quickly butchered.

Behind her Halima heard the sound of ripping cloth. Neema shrieked and grabbed hold of her arm, sinking fingernails into her flesh. A short sword rent the curtains in the rear of the carriage and sliced a long narrow slit. Halima slid back on her rump and scrambled for a spoon or knife to use as a weapon.

Before her trembling hands found anything, a bald black head covered with blood rammed its way through the ripped curtain like a child's head emerging from the womb.

Halima's heart leapt as she recognized Madongo. His broad chest heaved and he panted mightily.

"The caravan is lost," he cried. He ripped the curtain away and pointed to the tall grass a hundred yards off. "We must reach the high grass."

Between the carriage and the grass, warriors of the two sides crashed into each other, shield against shield, like rams locking horns. Wounded men, filled with arrows like pin cushions, staggered by bleeding.

"Hurry!" Madongo cried. Halima scrambled forward.

"Come!" she called to Neema. The servant girl sat paralyzed, clutching her cushion. Halima yanked her by the arm, but Neema moaned and shook her head violently from side to side, refusing to move.

"Leave her, Princess!" Madongo shouted.

"No!" Halima cried. "Put her on your back!"

The warrior groaned. He grabbed Neema and threw her over his shoulder. With his free hand he helped Halima down from the carriage. He planted her hand on his belt.

"Follow me – don't let go no matter what happens!"

Madongo charged forward like a rampaging bull into the thick of battle. She darted along behind him, barely able to keep up as he twisted left and right to avoid the gauntlet of spears – occasionally bashing broad shoulders with the combatants. They hopped over the bloody carcasses which lay broken, strewn about the clearing.

The tall grass, which had seemed so close, appeared to hang in the distance like a shimmering mirage. Halima clenched Madongo's belt and clung close to him. She screamed as a hand reached greedily for her. Madongo swung back and lopped it off with his sword. Halima shut her eyes and kept running.

At last, she felt the comforting tickle of grass against her legs. They reached the tall grass, and fell face-forward into it.

Neema slid off Madongo's shoulders and fell down on

all fours. Again paralysis set in and she knelt, eyes clenched closed. She clasped her hands and began to babble a babyish prayer to the Great One in the Sky.

Halima looked back over her shoulder for pursuers. The soldiers of Olugbodi had been put to rout, fleeing in all directions. The Zimbai, who did not believe in needless slaughter, did not pursue them. Instead, they plundered the caravan, picking it clean like vultures stripping a corpse. They passed the stores of gold and silver, hand to hand, as if they were members of a fire brigade handing along jugs of water.

Others were dancing around the caravan, chanting triumphantly and thrusting their spears into the sky. They crowed:

"We are the people of the plain.
No one passes
Without paying tribute!"

It seemed to Halima that she and her companions had escaped unseen – then a Zimbai warrior dropped his load of spoils and pointed in their direction. He let out a holler and he and several others came running straight at them.

CHAPTER 3

THE WILDERNESS

Madongo gave Neema's rear end a solid shove, sending her scurrying into the tall grass. Halima hesitated, then followed her, and Madongo, knife in hand, disappeared last into the bush.

Halima, her servant, and her loyal bodyguard ran through the tall grass crouching, hotly pursued by the whooping warriors of the Zimbai. Halima glanced over her shoulder and saw a dozen of the painted men wading towards them through the crackling grass. She almost shrieked in terror, but choked back her cry.

"Let's give ourselves up!" Neema gasped, tears and sweat spewing from her in all directions.

"Hush!" whispered Madongo, and wrenched both girls down to the ground. They nestled together hidden from sight as the enemy warriors slowly converged on them, poking through the grass and mumbling to one another.

Halima knelt, head bowed, like a rabbit hiding from some foraging beasts of prey. She bit back a hysterical laugh. *This is so strange*, she thought, *I feel like we're playing a childhood game of hide and seek.*

Beside her, Neema clutched her robe and pointed with a trembling hand at the foot of a Zimbai warrior tiptoeing only a yard or so away.

There came a low honk nearby. A moment later, the strange bellow sounded again. Halima had heard such a sound once before, but couldn't place it. There was a second of silence, then –

"Snake! Snake!" a panicked voice squeaked in the tongue of the Zimbai. A terrible ruckus broke loose in the bushes, as the startled warriors backed off, tumbling over each other, slashing at the grass willy-nilly with their spears like old women chasing after a rat with their brooms.

Halima was gripped by a primordial terror. She had always hated snakes, and now one must be just inches away. Again she had to fight the impulse to scream. The Zimbai were spitting distance away.

Neema fears snakes ten times as much as I do, she remembered. She quickly clapped her hand over the other girl's mouth, stifling the scream that was gurgling up Neema's throat.

Madongo will protect us, Halima thought. She turned to the warrior.

To her amazement, she saw that Madongo was cupping his hands in front of his mouth. He blew through his hands again, making the sound of the python, and followed it by hissing through his teeth in a perfect imitation of a viper. *He* was one making the sound! The warriors danced away from the sound, shouting at each other in confusion. Halima looked at Madongo and smiled at his cunning.

"Well done, faithful protector," she whispered. He grinned shyly in response.

Madongo pointed to some thick bushes in the distance.

"The nyika!" he whispered.

Sliding to his belly, he slithered off, truly snakelike indeed. Halima lay down and crawled after him, and Neema anxiously followed at Halima's heels.

The voices of the shouting warriors grew fainter and fainter as they crawled toward the thick bush.

They crawled for hundreds of yards under the nyika –

sharp, thorny bushes that were impassable except on hands and knees. Halima could feel the sharp claws of the nyika raking against her back, tearing away at her pretty robes.

Yet Halima was surprised to feel a guilty rush of excitement, as if they were embarking on a grand adventure. *This is the first time in my life that something has really happened to me*, she thought.

After three hours of uncomfortable crawling, they broke out from under the thorny bush and into a sparse forest. They scrambled to their feet. Neema bent over like an old woman, holding her back.

"This is the most horrible day of my life!" she exclaimed. "All that blood! I think I'm going to... going to..." She leaned over and began to retch. Halima, panting, leaned back against a tree, exhausted.

"Are we safe here?" she demanded. Madongo glanced around, getting his bearing. In the distance a column of black smoke rose from the burning caravan.

"No, Princess. We must go farther."

That night the three sat on the limb of a baobab tree as thick around as a dozen grown men, far out of reach of the animals of the forest. All around them a chorus of unfamiliar birds, lizards and insects sang.

Halima shivered. "Can't we build a fire? That would warm us and keep the beasts of the wild away as well."

Madongo shook his head. "We are still too close to our enemies." Halima nodded. Somewhere a hyena cackled.

Neema jumped at the sound, almost tumbling out of the tree. "I hate this jungle!" she spat.

" 'Do not call the forest that shelters you a jungle,' the proverb says," Madongo cautioned her.

Halima couldn't banish from her mind the picture of her handmaidens – her only friends – being plucked from the carriage like ripe fruit. She didn't even want to imagine what had become of them.

"My poor handmaidens!" Halima exclaimed. "Will I

never see them again, loyal Madongo?"

The warrior rested his broad hands reassuringly on her shoulder.

"They will not be mistreated. Any woman taken by the Zimbai in such a raid becomes a daughter to the warrior who captured her, and it is taboo for him to molest her. He must clothe her, feed her, and take care of her, just as a father would, until he finds her a husband. Each of your handmaidens will find a good husband among the Zimbai."

Neema snorted, "I would sooner lie down with a baboon then be soiled by the touch of a Zimbai." She shifted uncomfortably on the hard tree limb.

Halima and Madongo exchanged smiles at the jittery servant girl's burst of bravado.

"What now, Madongo?" Halima asked.

"Well, Your Highness," he replied, "if we retrace our steps along the tracks of the caravan, we should be back in Kali in a week."

Halima nodded thoughtfully, then asked, "And if we go on to the Land of the People of the Snake?"

Madongo's eyes widened and Neema's jaw dropped.

"Princess Halima!" cried Neema. "You can't mean us to go on through this foul enemy land, with all kinds of savage beasts around. And besides, your bridegroom is probably dead! The Zimbai probably caught him and cut off his stinking yellow hide. And if he's not dead, he's already proved himself a worthless coward!"

Halima gave her a warning look. "I'm sworn to marry King Olugbodi, and upon that marriage depends the safety of our kingdom," she said sternly. She turned to Madongo. "What do you say, faithful protector?"

Madongo looked at her solemnly, then told her, "You are at a crossroad, Princess. I will be your guard on any path you take – but only you can choose the direction."

Halima sighed. *That was so helpful!* She looked up at the star-filled sky. *Unfamiliar as our surroundings are,* she thought, *the stars at least are unchanged.*

"This reminds me of a story our griot, old Mwenda-pole, used to tell us," she said.

Madongo looked at her, puzzled, then cracked a smile.

"I think I know which one you mean. The story of Jabari and Bolade."

Halima nodded.

"I don't know that one. Sing it, Halima," Neema beseeched, perking up.

"We're trying to hide, child," Halima reminded her.

"Sing softly then. It would make me feel so at home to hear you sing again," Neema pleaded. Halima turned to the Madongo, who bobbed his head in approval.

"All right then," Halima began.

"Bolade was a princess of a small, slender people of the north. She was beautiful as a rose, but haughty and vain, like a peacock. She beat her servants like dogs, and turned her nose up at every suitor who asked for her hand in marriage because she believed they were too ugly.

"But one day a terrible famine came onto the land. The people were all starving, and would soon die.

"In desperation, Bolade's father sent a message to the Snake King, whose land was always fertile. He offered gold, he offered silver, he offered land, he offered slaves. He offered everything he had for a few cattle and some grain to feed his people.

"The Snake King sent back word, agreeing to send food. All he wanted in return was the most beautiful maiden in the land. And that was Princess Bolade. That is the price the Snake King demanded.

"Bolade's father agreed, because that was the only way he could save his people. He sent Bolade, along with wedding gifts and servants, on the path through the forest to the land of the Snake King.

"But along the way they were set upon by bandits, who robbed them of everything but the clothes on their backs.

They killed all her servants, all who were supposed to protect her, except for one brave boy named Jabari.

"So they went on together, Bolade and Jabari, the princess and her servant. Together they wandered the desert and across the plain and through the forest. Together they crossed rivers, hills and valleys. Along the way, brave Jabari saved Bolade's life a dozen times; once from a lion, once from a snake, once from drowning, once from a crocodile.

"And each time he saved her, she came to love him a little more, and he tamed a little of her haughtiness.

"But finally they arrived at the land of the People of the Snake, where Bolade was to be married to the Snake King."

"But she loves Jabari!" Neema protested.

"But her *duty* is to marry the Snake King," Halima reminded her patiently. "It is the only way she can save her father's people.

"The people blindfolded Bolade and took her to a great lake. They pointed to a great rock in the center of the lake. And they told her, 'That is where you will marry the King of the Snakes.'

"For you see, the Snake King was a great serpent that lived at the bottom of the lake. And he demanded one virgin girl, the most beautiful in the land, to be left for him each year, in exchange for keeping the land surrounding the lake fertile. The people rowed Bolade to the rock and chained her there weeping.

"When Jabari saw what the people had done, he took a spear and dove into the lake. He swam to the bottom, and there he saw a serpent with a head the size of an elephant, and a tail that stretched a mile long.

"For an hour, Jabari wrestled the horrible monster, until he was out of breath, and then he swam up for air. And again he dove down and battled the lake serpent. Finally, he slew the Snake King and cut off his head.

"He came ashore carrying the Snake King's head, and when the people realized that he alone among men had the courage to defeat their overlord, they made him their king. He promptly married Bolade and made her his queen.

"Together they ruled their new kingdom. But because the magic of the Snake King had been broken, the lake dried up for ever...

"... and that is why there is drought," Halima finished.

"That is a beautiful story," Neema sighed. She scratched her head. "But how did Bolade's land get a famine to begin with if there wasn't drought yet?"

"It's only a fairy tale," Halima reminded her.

"And yet they say there is many a truth told in a tale, Princess," Madongo said meaningfully. She smiled wryly, and looked at him for a moment. Then she made her decision:

"I think we will spare ourselves a long journey, and you Madongo, we will spare from a heroic dive to the bottom of any lake. We will not go on to the land of the People of the Snake. Tomorrow we will go home."

"Praise the Great One in the Sky!" Neema exclaimed.

"We'll need to rest then," Madongo said. "We should move out at first light, Princess."

They made ready for sleep, huddling together for warmth. Madongo sat bracing himself against the tree trunk, his broad back flat against it. Halima sat between his knees, leaning against him, and Neema huddled in her lap.

Encircled by the big man's long limbs, Halima felt protected as a small child. No man since her father could make her feel this safe. The long day's hardship had exhausted her, made her almost giddy with sleepiness.

She wondered: *Would he dare entertain fantasies of his princess? He couldn't! And yet... Hadn't Jabari lain with Bolade like this, the servant with his princess, up in the treetops, among stars?* And with those girlish thoughts she slowly drifted off to sleep.

They trekked back along the dusty trail that the caravan had made. Though they began early, they soon were sweltering under the merciless red sun.

Madongo let both girls take a sip from his gourd each hour that they walked to replace the rivers of sweat that poured off them.

"Take some for yourself," Halima insisted.

Madongo shook his gleaming bald head. "No, we passed a waterhole as we came this way, I remember. It isn't far." He strode ahead and the girls hurried after him.

Halima soon felt her legs going wobbly under her. She was not used to long walks; all that saved her from keeling over was her youth.

This path seemed a lot shorter and cooler when we were being born in a carriage, she thought. It had been a full day since she had eaten, and she was growing faint from hunger.

Soon they came upon one of the huge termite mounds Halima had noticed on their outbound journey. She marveled at the tiny creatures and their architectural skill. It seemed to rival, in miniature, the handiwork of a temple-builder of Kali.

Madongo burrowed eagerly into the mound with his spear and, after poking about for several moments, brought up a fist-size ball of wriggling white larvae. He set it on a stone and used his knife to grind the creatures into soft white goo. He tasted it from the tip of his blade, and then offered it to each of the girls.

Halima closed her eyes and took a bite of the food. It

turned out to be delicious – gummy, a bit like honey, but not as sweet. Neema held her nose and reluctantly swallowed a bite of the food, then hungrily gobbled down all that remained.

"We should dig the whole thing out and have ourselves a dinner," Neema said, licking the gooey food from her lips and fingers. Madongo smiled and shook his head.

"We've passed this way twice already – let's leave some in case we pass again."

A few hours later, they arrived at the waterhole. Halima tumbled to her knees with Neema just beside her, both nearly fainting. Madongo raced to the waterhole, and threw himself face down, lapping at the water like a wild dog. Then he scooped up water in his gourd, filling it to the brim, and trotted back to the two girls.

Halima sucked down the cool, clear water, half-emptying the gourd in one tremendous gulp, and passed it to her servant. Neema threw back her head and drained the gourd, splashing half of it on her bosom.

Madongo stopped her. "Not too much, you'll choke."

The three of them collapsed, flat on their backs. What a relief! Halima had almost been starting to think they would die of thirst.

After a few moments rest, Madongo struggled to his feet, picked up his spear, and announced he was going to try to spear some fish. He pulled off his robe, and wearing only his loincloth, waded into the waterhole. Out of the corner of her eye, Halima watched as her broad-shouldered bodyguard stood knee-deep in water, feet planted wide apart like two stout trees. He held the tip of the spear poised above the pond, ready to strike, and hunched squinting at the glimmering water, as attentive as a falcon. His broad bare back was to Halima, black and shining with sweat, muscles rippling. She felt the blood rush to her cheeks and a girlish titter tickled her throat.

Halima whispered to her maidservant. "Neema... what

do you think of him?"

"Who?"

"Madongo, fool!"

Neema turned up her nose. "He's a bit rough, I think, like all his side of our family. I know he likes me though."

Halima raised her eyebrows.

"You?!"

"Yes. He steals me a glance when he thinks I'm not looking. I expect he will ask your permission to court me soon."

Halima frowned. "Well, I certainly wouldn't give it."

Neema looked at her in surprise.

"You want to marry up, don't you?" Halima demanded. "In Kali I will find you a rich, fat old man who will give your daughters land and your sons cattle."

Neema smirked. "Thank you for your generosity, Princess." Neema climbed to her feet. "I'm going for a swim."

She unfastened her now ragged robe and dropped it, then strutted toward the water in her loincloth, swiveling her hips impudently and jangling her many bracelets. Neema waded into the water beside Madongo, who still stood in precisely the same position, frozen like a statue. He ignored her entirely, Halima noted much to her satisfaction, his eagle eyes fixed on the water.

What does she think she's doing, the princess wanted to know.

Neema bent over, scooped up two handfuls of water and splashed her underarms.

"Brazen, cheeky little trollop," Halima whispered to herself. For some reason, she felt an unfamiliar twinge of anger welling.

"Don't scare off the fish," Madongo warned Neema stiffly, without turning his head. Standing behind him, Neema cupped her hands in the water and poured the contents over Madongo's bald head. He was so startled he yelped and fell back, spilling into the water. Neema burst into robust laughter. Madongo scrambled to his feet, grabbed hold of her and shook her.

"You silly child! Stop playing games! We need food to eat! I need to catch fish!

Neema stuck out her tongue at him like a little girl. Madongo scooped the buxom teen into the air, and dumped her into the water. Neema gurgled under the water, flailing her arms. Madongo roared with laughter as the girl spluttered and sat up.

"That's what I needed – bait!" he chuckled.

Halima called out to him. "Madongo! When you're through with your horseplay, I'd like to not starve today!"

He looked guiltily up at Halima, as if only now remembering her presence. "Yes, Your Highness," he said, bowing solemnly.

By the end of the day, Madongo had caught five long, silvery fish, which he roasted for them on a stick over a small, comforting fire.

Before they left the spot, Madongo dug several traps beside the waterhole. He pointed out tiny tracks in the mud, explaining that many kinds of animals used the waterhole, and they would soon return to drink from it. Even though the pond would still stink of man a day from now, animals would risk approaching it.

The next day, they marched on across the veldt, continuing to follow the tracks of the caravan. Halima looked into the distance at the Silver Mountain, the mountain of mystery, with its halo of white at its peak. *Are those really spirits at the mountain peak*, she wondered, *and do giants truly inhabit those hills?* She recalled what Madongo had told her on the caravan:

"There are forests where men live who are no taller than children. In caves in the north, there are men whose skins are white. Who can declare there is no race of giants?"

Again she felt a strange sensation that the mountain was beckoning her.

They reached a ravine, a drop of some fifty feet. At the bottom, a meager trickle of water ran between the jagged rocks. Eons ago, a giant river must have run through here, down from the Silver Mountain, but had long been dried up. *I must've been sleeping when we passed this way before*, thought Halima.

A slender, natural bridge of rock no more than a dozen feet wide was the only way across the ravine. Before making the crossing, they stopped to rest. Neema tore some parched leaves from a dead tree, and disappeared behind a dry, stony bush. That usually signaled a long absence, Halima knew from experience. Madongo squatted down and began setting a handful of stones about the circle, in which to build a fire.

Halima knelt beside him, smiling at his efficiency. Quietly she told him, "You are very much like Jabari in the fairytale."

Madongo looked up at her, his dark eyes strangely sad.

"That was a fairytale, princess," he replied.

"And yet you said there was much truth sometimes in fairytales," she said, looking at him intently.

He shook his head solemnly.

"A princess does not marry a servant. That doesn't happen." He hesitated, then added, "Even her father's sword-bearer."

Halima felt the blood rushing to her cheeks. She bowed her head.

Madongo went on. "There is an order to things, Princess. Those who oppose that order are usually destroyed."

Halima felt her heart pounding. *Order, order, order!* She was supposed to be a princess, but she was a slave to order. First order declared she must marry a coward. Now it declares she could not have a true man.

"Fine," she said coldly. "But you cannot have Neema. I forbid you to speak or look at her on our journey."

His eyes betrayed dismay, but he spoke calmly. "As you wish, Princess." He stood. "But remember, there are some things you cannot command."

Halima felt herself trembling with fury. Neema appeared from behind the boulder, pouting.

"These leaves are rough as sand," she complained. She stopped in her tracks, and looked at the two, who were facing each other in stony silence.

"I'm going back to the waterhole to check my traps. I'll be back by dusk." Madongo said. He turned and jogged off in the direction from which they had come. Halima and Neema eyed each other warily.

The orange sun hung low in the sky and Madongo had not yet returned from the waterhole. Halima ordered her servant to hunt for firewood. It was steaming hot now, and flies the size of hummingbirds flitted about their hair and eyes, but it would be cold come nightfall.

Halima gathered wood, too; she knew Neema was too lazy to gather all that they needed. She bent again and again for the sticks, annoyed that she was reduced to the work of a common servant.

For as long as Madongo has been absent, he better bring back a plump, juicy hare, she thought. *I've never before built up such an appetite. This outdoor life is turning me into a different person altogether.*

After collecting a staggering armload of large dry sticks, she let them tumble into the middle of the circle of stones Madongo had made, and then stood stroking her worn shoulders. *I'll be happy when we get home to Kali,* she thought, *and others will take care of this type of brute labor.*

She heard gentle singing, and looked up to see Neema approaching, holding a single, greenish branch. Halima could not believe how stupid she was!

"That won't burn!" she shouted. She ripped it from Neema's hand and broke it. "I declare you must have cow blood in you. I've never seen a woman with so little sense!"

Neema bowed her head, humiliated. Then she murmured, almost inaudibly, "He prefers me, you know."

Halima turned on her. "What's that?" she demanded.

Neema met her eyes defiantly. "I said, he prefers me."

Halima scowled. She could not believe how insolent her servant was becoming – as if Halima were some village girl who had to squabble over the prettiest boy of the town!

"If he prefers you," Halima said, angrily, "It is because you give off the scent of availability, like a she-cat of the jungle. When you were brought to the palace as a little girl, from your pitiful fishing village, we thought we could make a lady of you. But I see we were wrong. A cat can live in the temple – but it's still a cat!"

Neema, turning purple, balled her fists and stepped up into Halima's face, so close their breasts nearly collided.

"Princess," she snarled, "we're not in the palace now!"

"Don't you dare use that tone with me!" Halima exclaimed. She shoved Neema away and the girl stumbled back a few feet. To Halima's astonishment, the servant girl charged her and pushed her right back. Halima stumbled backward in disbelief, nearly tripping to the ground.

This was an outrage!

She grabbed hold of Neema's meaty shoulders and hurled her back with all her might. Neema staggered back, arms swinging wildly – and she took one giant step backward off the ravine.

She screamed in terror. Halima rushed forward, and snatched Neema's wrist. She yanked, using all her weight, and hauled Neema back from the precipice. They faced each other, exchanging looks of horror over the near tragedy. Halima embraced her servant in relief.

"All this over a *man*," she whispered.

Neema giggled.

All of a sudden a male voice chortled – and it didn't sound like Madongo. They turned in unison, to see a pair of strange faces poking out of the brush.

The two men stood up from the bushes. One carried a bow, the other a spear. The bowman was tall and slender, with large, long-lashed eyes that gave him an almost girlish beauty. The spearman was short and stout, like a wild boar, with a heavy furrowed brow. The bowman smiled and spoke in the hissing tongue of the People of the Snake, King Olugbodi's people:

"Mercenaries say that in the pleasure domes of the eastern world, women wrestle in pits for the entertainment of men. My kinsman and I thought you were going to give us a show like that!"

Neema slid behind her princess.

The handsome one raised a hand in greeting. "We see you were preparing a fire. May we join you?"

I don't think so, Halima thought. She bowed her head and adopted a humble tone.

"We cannot give you permission, brave warrior. Our husbands and brothers are hunting nearby. When they return, they would be angry if we invited strangers into our camp."

The handsome one's pretty eyes narrowed, and he grinned. He set down his bow and arrows.

"You're lying," he said. "We know that you are girls from the caravan, and have no husbands. My kinsman and I were in the party guarding it."

Neema pushed forward and pointed. "Look at their cheeks, Halima! They wear the brand of the deserter." As she said it, the squat one reflexively brought up his hand as if to shield his face. Halima saw that, indeed, each man's cheek bore a freshly carved single red X. It wasn't the carefully detailed tribal scarring she'd seen before. This had been done hastily – and brutally.

Neema spat, "They are cowards who fled from the battle on the veldt, branded and banished to wander."

The squat spearman bristled. The handsome bowman merely smiled coolly, and said through clenched teeth, "Many ran from battle that day – and not all of them wear the brand of cowardice."

Halima put her hands on her hips. "If you are warriors of the People of the Snake, then you must take us to your ruler, King Olugbodi, at once," she commanded.

The handsome deserter let out a harsh laugh. He turned to the squat one.

"Do you hear that one, cousin? They want us to take them to our king? What do you say to that, cousin?"

The squat deserter spat a wad of saliva over the ravine. The handsome one stepped closer to Halima.

"Listen: We are proud to be deserters. What use do we have for kings? What do kings do for us but send us to war in foreign lands? What do kings do for us but make us shed our blood, while griots praise them? Why should we lose arms and legs, and make widows of our wives, so that kings can sit on thrones of gold? Our king ran from battle like a frightened girl! We obey no king now. We are our own kings now!"

Neema let loose a contemptuous laugh. "Yes, kings with no country!"

The handsome warrior looked more serious now. He strode up to Halima and took her arm urgently, then pointed to the Silver Mountain.

"You see the Silver Mountain?" he demanded.

"Yes," Halima answered, startled at his touch.

"Beyond the Silver Mountain travelers say there is a greater mountain still. And in those mountains a great lake – a lake of lakes that is said to be the birthplace of all mankind. From that lake flows a river that runs into a valley, and makes that valley more fertile than any land the world has ever known. That is the land we will settle."

"You two are mad!" Neema laughed.

The handsome deserter tightened his grip on Halima and stared at her, his black eyes flashing with strange desperation.

"There is no going back for us now. There is no home. We need wives to take with us. Come with us."

Halima shook her head.

"We want you as our women," he insisted.

Neema stepped forward and pulled Halima away from him. "Be gone, worm. You vermin aren't fit to stay in our sight, far less assault our ears with trash about marriage!"

The glow departed from the handsome deserter's eyes and he stepped back sullenly. He drew out a glimmering dagger.

"Come with us as our wives – or be taken here and now like beasts of the wild. That is the choice we give you."

Halima's heart began to pound. She stepped back and pointed to the turtle-shaped pendant around her neck. Mustering a voice of cool superiority she warned, "I am Halima, Princess of Kali. Dishonor me and the wrath of my father will rain down on you until you pray for death!"

The two men traded quick looks of surprise. The handsome deserter took a long step toward her.

"I have never lain with a princess. This may be the only chance I have," he purred. But he stopped short and there was a hint of cowardly indecision in his eyes.

Neema put her hands on her plump hips and laughed

derisively. "You weaklings would never have the courage to defile my princess!" she exclaimed.

The handsome deserter turned on her. "Then we'll take the servant."

"No!" Halima cried. The handsome deserter gestured to the squat one, who bolted forward like a bull elephant, and tackled Neema as she tried to run. He brought the screeching girl to the ground as easily as a cowherd taking down a young heifer for branding.

Halima screamed in protest, and the handsome deserter grabbed hold of her. She squirmed, a hellcat in his grip, while she watched the squat one wrestle Neema to the ground and pin her.

Halima looked on, frozen in horror, as the squat deserter shredded away Neema's bright robe, tearing it into strips. The serving girl let out a stream of earsplitting shrieks and curses, and pounded on his big drum of a chest with fists – all in vain. He reached between her legs with one big hand, yanked off her loincloth and flung it into the ravine.

Neema managed to wriggle onto her belly and slipped away, her long fingernails breaking as she scrabbled for purchase on the dry red earth. Before she got two feet, however, the squat deserter caught her again. Kneeling behind her, he scooted his big hands on her hips and hoisted her broad buttocks up into the air.

Snorting like a wild boar about to charge, he prepared to mount her.

"You pig!" Halima cried, her paralysis breaking. She tore away from the handsome deserter and picked up a piece of firewood, then broke it over the squat one's head. He keeled over, groaning. Halima whirled, brandishing the stick.

The handsome deserter faced her, smiling at her patiently as if she were a toothless lion cub. He stepped toward her. Halima raised the stick in warning. *Damn*, she thought, *unless I nail him with a death blow to the temple, he'll be able to take the weapon away from me as easily as a rattle from a baby.*

She brought down the stick on the handsome deserter with all her strength. But his hand caught her slender wrist in midair, like a striking cobra pouncing on a too-slow mongoose. He twisted her arm behind her back, and gently pulled the stick out of her hand. He tossed it away. *How could I have thought those eyes pretty? They are as empty of pity as a snake's.*

"Now I want to see how a princess makes love," he growled.

Just then, Halima saw a shadow fall across his face. Halima turned to see Madongo standing on a boulder, with a young antelope draped over his shoulders and his spear upraised. *Thank the Great One in the Sky!*

The warrior's broad nostrils flared angrily as he took in the scene before him. The squat deserter stood up.

Madongo looked at the two young men with contempt.

"Jackals! Is this how the People of the Snake treat their women?"

"We are outcasts," the handsome deserter replied. "No laws bind us."

Madongo looked at Neema, crouched trembling at Halima's feet, shielding her womanhood. His voice trembled with rage.

"Have you no mothers, or sisters, or daughters, that a woman's honor means so little to you?"

The handsome deserter took a step closer to his bow, which lay a few feet away on the ground. He yelled back, "We gave them a choice: Be our wives, or lie with us like beasts of the wild."

Madongo let the antelope fall with a thud, and jumped down from the boulder, kicking up red dust as he landed.

"I will give you two a choice," he said solemnly. He held his spear aloft, poised to hurl it. He gestured to the ravine. "This is your choice: Jump into that ravine, or die at the point of my spear."

The handsome deserter looked in confusion at his squat kinsman.

Madongo strode forward. "Choose, I say!" he bellowed.

The handsome deserter stepped back. "All right then – the ravine," he said. Then he ducked down and made a quick-as-a-cobra snatch for his bow. Fast as lightning, he had an arrow in place and was pulling back the bowstring.

Halima screamed "Watch out!" much too late.

Before the deserter could let loose his arrow, Madongo bounded toward him and buried his spear straight through his throat. Halima screamed as the spear point burst out of the back of the deserter's neck, and blood squirted across her robe.

The squat deserter moved as quickly as his chunky frame would allow, and he retrieved his own spear from the ground. But by the time he bent forward, the contest was over. Madongo had the handsome deserter's bow trained right between his eyes. Madongo marched determinedly toward the squat deserter, backing him toward the ravine.

The squat deserter looked around in desperation and saw he had no chance. He looked so pitiful, like a poor trapped bull. Despite all his brutality, Halima cried out, "Mercy!" She couldn't stand to see another killing.

But there was no mercy in Madongo's eyes. Another second and he would let loose the arrow right into the deserter's left eye.

The squat deserter's heels reached the crevasse, and he momentarily lost his balance, swaying there for a moment.

Then he spun, and roaring like a gored bull, leapt off across the ravine. With a running start he might have stood a chance, but leaping from a standing position? He bellowed in anguish all the way to the bottom of the ravine. When he hit, the sound was like a spoiled melon splattering.

Neema was still crouched at Halima's feet, covering her face. Her body shook convulsively as she wept with shame. Madongo rushed to her side. He rested a broad hand gently on her bare back, and she jumped as if she'd been touched by lightning.

Halima shooed him away and knelt beside her maidservant. Gently, she took Neema by the shoulders and raised her up so they knelt facing each other. Neema's face was covered with red dust and marked with tear stains. Halima took pieces from the girl's tattered dress, and wiped away her tears, cleaned off her face and tried to wipe her body.

Neema snorted back her tears. "Leave me alone. It's nothing. I'm just a servant girl. That is my lot."

Halima shook her head, silently.

Neema said listlessly, "You must beat me for pushing you, Princess. I forgot my place for a moment. I forgot what I am." She bowed her head deeply, in bitter defeat.

"No!" cried Halima. She stood up and yanked Neema to her feet. She pulled off her own robe and wrapped it around Neema. Then she hurriedly began to pull off her jewelry one piece at a time, and to carefully place them on Neema's arms and neck and ankles.

She stripped herself of every priceless ring and bracelet – all except the sea turtle pendant, the symbol of the royal clan, which hung about her neck. All of it she used to adorn Neema. Then she stared deeply into Neema's reddened eyes.

"From this day forward, gentle Neema," she said, "you are not my servant, you are my sister, my friend." She embraced the other girl. Neema hesitated, then hugged back – tentatively at first, then as hard as she could.

Madongo grabbed the feet of the dead bowman and began to drag the corpse away. Halima turned to him and they exchanged somber glances. Madongo gestured at the corpse.

"Without laws, we are nothing," he said.

"What are you doing?" Halima demanded.

"I want to bury them before the sun goes down. The hyenas will be out soon."

Neema broke away from Halima and rushed over, her eyes full of angry tears.

"Don't you dare bury them!" she screamed, and kicked the dead man's lolling head as if it were a ball. "Leave their stinking meat for the vultures."

Madongo cautioned, "Princess, if we do not bury them, their restless spirits will haunt this ravine for eternity."

Halima frowned. She shuddered at the thought of the ghosts of these two rogues plaguing every traveler who passed this way for the next 10,000 years.

"I'm sorry, Neema. We must bury them. Let's be quick."

They buried the deserters side by side at the base of the ravine and said a few quick prayers to speed their journey to join their ancestors.

The plan to follow the caravan tracks back home had hit a snag. If there were other deserters, many of them might be taking the same route to escape to Kali. There was still the roaming band of Zimbai, too. They decided the safest course was a detour skirting through the foothills of the Silver Mountain, where few traveled out of fear of the legendary giants of the mountain. They planned to set out at first light the next day.

That night, dancing before the fire, Madongo used the entrails of the antelope in a ritual to cleanse himself of the killing of the two deserters, as well as the killings of the Zimbai warriors during the ambush. While singing prayers begging the Great One in the Sky for forgiveness, he wrapped himself in the intestines of the slaughtered beast and then sliced them away. By doing so, he severed himself from the deaths he caused.

At the end of the ritual, Halima felt a deep sense of harmony restored, and a new sense of peace fall over their camp. She sat beside the fire, under the blanket of stars, watching her two companions, who knelt facing each other.

They were silent, but between them passed something that went beyond words. After a moment, Neema and Madongo both began to quietly cry. Although Halima sensed the sudden bond between them, for the first time she did not feel an uncontrollable outburst of jealousy. Somehow she understood that this is how it must be. She suddenly felt as if she were alone on the vast plain. *I've never felt more lonely than this*, she thought.

Someday there will be a man for you, she told herself. *But this is not the man; this is not the day.* Tears welling up in her eyes, she looked off to the Silver Mountain, its white peak glimmering faintly in the moonlight. And as she gazed at it, a tingle of excitement rushed over her like a quick night breeze.

CHAPTER 4

THE SILVER MOUNTAIN

Through the foothills of the Silver Mountain they tramped in single file, first Madongo, then Halima, then Neema. No one spoke; there was no more ceaseless chatter from the servant girl. Halima almost missed her complaints and silly observations. This was like a funeral march.

As the country steepened, plant life seemed to sprout up everywhere, an almost maddening overgrowth of green. Save for the ocean, Halima had never seen so much of any one color.

It was stifling hot. Even stripped to her loincloth, Halima felt herself drenched in a salty, oily sweat. Flies and mosquitoes hung in the air in thick clouds with a deafening buzz. All around was a cacophony of humming insects, shrill, screaming birds and the abiding rumble of a distant waterfall.

Through the trees high above, troops of gray and white monkeys poured, cackling, while underfoot small lizards slithered across their toes.

From time to time, they came upon a great boulder of granite jutting up from the earth, a forbidding black wall blocking their path. They would pass around it respectfully.

We are like children wandering about the feet of a giant, Halima thought.

All at once, Madongo stilled them with his hand. Halima stopped in her tracks and Neema slammed into her from behind. They stood still, watching in alarm as the warrior stood frozen, his head cocked to one side like a wild dog as he listened to the air.

"What is it?" Halima whispered. She listened, trembling, for the crashing footsteps of giants. She heard nothing except the twittering of a bird.

Suddenly the man broke into a broad white smile. He pointed upward, and Halima looked up at a branch where a small brown bird sat.

"Ladies, we will have a tasty breakfast today," Madongo said. Then he let out a boisterous whoop.

He ran toward the bird, which flitted away from the branch immediately. Madongo twisted back his head to see if the two girls were following him, but saw that they instead stood dumbfounded. He waved them to follow.

"But we will never catch that bird," Halima protested.

"Humor him – he's gone mad," Neema said, and pushed Halima on. The two girls hurried after Madongo, who, suddenly acting carefree as a boy, chased after the bird, ducking under low branches and hopping over vines.

The bird almost seemed to be teasing them. It would hop onto a branch, and wait until the panting trio nearly caught up. Then it would take flight again, soaring off and staying barely in sight. Halima began to laugh along with Madongo. She felt like a child again herself – and Neema, running alongside her, began to laugh again too. It was truly as if they were children, playing one of their palace games.

Finally, the bird came to rest on a dead, thick-trunked cotton tree, and sat staring patiently down at them from a branch twenty feet in the air.

"Anansi the spider couldn't climb that tree," Halima advised him.

Madongo grinned. "Don't try to teach the forest paths to an old gorilla," he replied, quoting a proverb. Halima raised a skeptical eyebrow and crossed her arms, waiting to see what he would do next.

She was puzzled to see Madongo gather together an armful of dead, wet leaves and stack them at the base of the tree. Ah, he was making a fire, she realized. But what for?

He broke off a dry branch of the dead tree and knelt. Out of his pouch he pulled his flint and began rubbing it furiously against the dead branch, until a spark finally lit and the wood burned.

He looked up at Halima, as if challenging her to guess what he was up to. She threw up her hands, admitting she hadn't a clue. The warrior grinned, and lit fire to the leaves. A choking column of black smoke rose up, and the two mystified girls stumbled back in confusion.

"What is he doing?" Neema asked. Halima shrugged, unable to answer.

Madongo crept toward the tree, and pulling out his knife, began hacking away at the dry, dead wood. He chopped a fist-sized hole – and out buzzed half a squadron of smoke-drunk bees, which wobbled weakly in the air and fell to the earth, tiny feet in the air.

Of course, Halima thought. *He's smoking the bees out.*

With the bees safely intoxicated, the warrior reached into the hole, and drew out a fist full of bright amber jelly.

"Honey!" Neema whispered in awe. The two girls ran forward in delight. Madongo distributed to each of them a handful of the sweet treasure. Then, on a tree stump, he set out a portion for the patient bird, which swooped down to seize its reward.

"The bird – is this possible, Madongo?" Halima asked.

Madongo nodded. "Yes, Princess. The honey guide is a friend to man, and every hunter knows him. They lead men to the hive of bees, for they know we will give them a share."

Halima shook her head in amazement. For the first time she saw why some called nature "mother," and felt safe in her bosom.

The girls gorged themselves on the honey, while Madongo sat on the ground like a bear, feeding his face with a heavy paw. Halima smiled to see him relax, let down his guard for the first time.

She threw back her head and ran her tongue over her lips, with her eyes shut, savoring the sweetness. When she opened her eyes, she saw a dozen giant men before them. All were hunters carrying bows tall as herself. They stood in a circle training weapons upon them.

Neema screamed, and stepped behind Madongo.

The men, who all wore long goatskin robes, each stood well over seven feet tall. They were purplish black in complexion, with strong, chiseled features that looked as if they'd been hacked from mahogany. On each man's forehead was painted a reddish dot that stared out like a third eye. The men stood silent and still as forest trees.

Giants, she thought in terror. Madongo sprang to his feet.

Neema buried her face against Madongo's broad back.

"Don't let them hurt me!" she pleaded. Madongo raised his spear and took a step forward.

A dozen arrows whistled through the air and kicked up dirt right before Madongo's toes.

"Stop!" Halima shrieked, stopping him in his tracks. There were too many to even think of fighting. The giant men towered over her bodyguard as if he were a boy.

"How can they have appeared so suddenly?" she gasped.

Madongo shook his head, and whispered back, "It must be true that these giants have magic powers, to move through the forest in utter silence. It is said their *mugwe*, their sayer of blessings, gives the hunters powder so they may steal up on game."

Standing stock still, the tall men stared blankly at Halima. There was something so unearthly, so noble in their quiet bearing and demeanor, that for some reason Halima felt more awe than fear.

"See if you can speak to them," Halima said. Madongo nodded, and lowered his spear. Gently shaking off Neema, he stepped gingerly forward over the line of arrows, which stood up like a hedge.

"Tell them we only wish safe passage to our land," Halima added.

Madongo addressed the hunters, attempting first one foreign tongue after another. First he tried language full of clicks and whirrs, then another with a high, yodeling sound – and finally a solemn, melodic tongue to which the tallest of the men responded. The giant hunter, who also seemed the oldest of the men, wore a graying beard and carried a knotty walking stick.

He must be the leader, Halima thought. When he replied to Madongo, his voice was deep and so mellifluous it was almost hypnotic.

He spoke slowly and calmly for a solid minute. All the while, he never took his eyes from Halima, gesturing in her direction from time to time. Finally he stopped, and stood politely back.

"What did they say?" she demanded of Madongo. He looked at her unhappily, rolling his spear in his hands as if he were anxious to use it.

"Come, tell me," she insisted.

The warrior reluctantly growled, "They say… These human giraffes say that you are wondrously beautiful – like a proud antelope, they say. They have never seen a creature of such beauty. They wish to make you a gift to their king! They say that they have seen me fight bravely, against the men of the snake; they do not wish to kill me unless they must. They ask me to surrender you to them without a battle. Here, let me cut out his tongue for his insolence!"

He started forward, and the hunters raised their bows again. Halima could envision the fight in her mind's eye. She could see every drop of blood, every valiant thrust, and she could see him cut down like a slaughtered animal. She grabbed his bulging bicep and yanked him back.

"Faithful Madongo, there are too many."

"Then many will perish," he shot back, over his shoulder.

"You will die."

"Only once."

"I cannot ask you to give your life for me in vain," she insisted. He turned back to her, keeping one eye on the giant man.

"It is my duty, Highness. It is my duty to die for you." He seemed confused now. He stuck out his lower lip, pouting like a stubborn boy. "I must fight them, and I must die!"

Halima grabbed his shoulders and faced him sternly, saying, "If you die, and yet they take me, where's the gain?"

Madongo looked at her eyes, protesting silently.

"No, I will go with them to their king," Halima concluded with certainty.

"No, Princess!" Neema cried. She rushed forward and grabbed Halima, locking her in a death grip.

A strange calm possessed Halima and she went on. "Return to our country, faithful Madongo. Tell my father what has befallen me, so that he may send a ransom for my release. When I tell this king who I am, I shall not be molested."

"I will not leave you, Highness," Madongo insisted. His broad nostrils were quivering; his eyes were full of emotion. Halima returned his gaze. In a girlish way, she wanted to see him fight to protect her – even die to protect her. But she fought off the selfish urge. She was a princess, she reminded herself. And these were her subjects, whose lives she was responsible for.

"You will leave," she said gently. "I order it." Sadly Madongo lowered his eyes and then his head.

"No, Princess," Neema protested, weeping. Halima held her friend and kissed her neck. Then she ran a hand gently over Madongo's smooth bald head.

"Madongo, take Neema and guard her on your journey as you would guard my sister – with your life."

Madongo stared at her with fierce anguish. Halima mustered all her authority. "Swear that you will do that, Madongo. That you will not follow the hunters."

Solemnly, Madongo nodded. He pried the weeping, thrashing, servant girl away from Halima. Backing away, he dragged her slowly off toward the trees.

"No! No! No!" Neema screamed, weeping.

Before their eyes broke their lock, Halima smiled, and told the pair, "My friends, I will see you again. I promise it."

Then she turned back to the quiet hunters, raising her hands in a gesture of acquiescence. The giant hunters of the forest lowered their bows.

Halima walked along behind the strange, tall men, her hands bound loosely with a goatskin strap. She was tethered to the last man of the party, a youth of no more than thirteen, but taller than any man in her native land.

The hunters had collected the bodies of four impalas that they'd left hanging from trees nearby, and now some of the men carried the carcasses hanging from long bamboo poles, with the hooves crossed and tied.

The men ambled slowly through the forest. She could only think their leisurely gait was to accommodate her, because with their long limbs, she was sure they could cover enormous distances in no time. They almost never spoke to one another, and when they did, it was in their

strange mellifluous tongue which she could not comprehend. They made no effort to communicate with Halima.

I feel like you, she thought, addressing the dead impala
that swung stiffly from the pole. *Like captured game.*

The ground steadily steepened, growing rockier, until
at last they came to a vast field of bamboo. It seemed to
stand between the men and the upper reaches of the
mountain like an impenetrable barricade. Looking more
closely, Halima could see that in places a path had been
cleared where the bamboo had been cut down, creating a
labyrinth-like trail.

Suddenly, the bearded one, the leader, took a cloth
from his belt and bent. Wearing an apologetic expression,
he wrapped it around Halima's eyes, blindfolding her.

She felt hands at her waist, and she was hoisted up into
the air and placed like a sack over one of the hunter's
shoulders. Head hung down, she could feel the blood
rushing to her brain.

Halima panicked and screamed.

What false pride I showed before, she realized. *To act
noble and pretend to be unafraid, to send Madongo on his
way.* Now she was terrified.

*Are they cannibals – worshipers of some evil god who
demands human sacrifice?* She screeched and began to kick
her feet and pound the hunter's back with her bound fists.
She kicked and screamed until eventually she collapsed,
weeping.

After hanging upside down for a bumpy hour or so, the
truth finally dawned on her: The path through the labyrinth
of bamboo and up through the jagged rocks above must be
a secret, taboo for any outsider to know. That was why she
was blindfolded. Her panic subsided and she allowed
herself to hang limp.

Even though she was blindfolded, she could tell they
were ascending. The air was becoming cooler and more
pure, tasting as crisp as spring water. The sensation was

almost intoxicating. She felt a delicious dizziness come over her and she swooned into the darkness.

They were high in the mountain when the hunters put Halima down and the blindfold was finally removed. She stumbled about on uncertain feet, like a child making its first steps, feeling the ground slope severely beneath her as she squinted against the sudden light.

They were under a canopy of enormous trees that shot many hundreds of feet into the air and formed a giant umbrella against the sun. The sky was almost entirely hidden from sight. Only a few errant rays of light poked through and dotted the hard, bare ground with brilliant spots of light.

It was like nothing Halima had ever seen, and she was overcome by wonder.

Unlike the hot, steaming country below, the highlands of the Silver Mountain were cool and silent. A fine, misty rain touched Halima's skin, as gentle as moonlight, giving her goose bumps and making her tremble. Unlike the unending chatter of monkeys and hum of insects that filled the low country, here it was eerily silent.

The hunters made camp beside an elephant-sized boulder, sharing with her some dried goat meat. It was tough and bland, but she was starving, and tore into it greedily. As they sat beside the fire, the hunters watched her eat with fascination. They traded a few comments with each other in their deep, rolling voices. Occasionally one would make a joke, and the others would give a soft, rumbling laugh.

They passed a gourd filled with a milky, fermented drink. Halima sipped cautiously from it when her turn came; it was sweet and good. The hunters watched with concern. She nodded and smiled at them, indicating her approval. They smiled back and mumbled, nodding to each other.

After a while, one of the men took out a small instrument with a single string and began to pluck it. *It sounds as gentle as the voice of a child*, Halima thought.

The other men began to hum along, a choir of bass voices so deep and resonant it almost shook the earth.

In time Halima realized it was much like a song she knew, an ancient rhyme old farmers sometimes sang as they drove their oxen. To hear something familiar now, so far from home, moved her almost to tears. She moved her lips, mouthing the words silently, and then softly sang the song, in her own language:

"Let your love be like the rain.
"Let it be like the falling rain.
"Let your love be like the rain,
"Coming softly,
"But flooding the river,
"Yes, but flooding the river."

The hunters all turned to her in surprise, and when she was done, they clapped their long-fingered hands. Halima bowed her head and thanked the Great One in the Sky for music – one language that all people speak. That one moment she did not feel utterly alone.

However strange, these are men I am with, not animals, she thought.

It was icy cool at night in the mountains. Halima had never felt such cold before, not even bathing in the sea. The youngest of the hunters saw her shivering, and covered her with a goatskin blanket. As she slept in the fetal position, he lay beside her, his elongated body crowded around her protectively, keeping her warm.

When morning came, they continued on their way. The hunters gave her the raggedy goatskin blanket to wear as a cloak against the still-chilly air, and she followed behind them as best she could.

The sloping ground grew more and more rocky, and Halima found it increasingly difficult to keep up with the long-limbed hunters. They ambled upward with the ease of mountain goats, and used the jutting rocks as stepping-stones. They untied her wrists, so that she could use her hands to climb, but after a few hours her fingers were blistered and running with blood from scrabbling on sharp stones. One of the hunters lifted her up and let her ride on his shoulders. Her bare thighs locked in a vise grip about his head and she held on for dear life.

The trees became sparse now, the ground drier. Halima marveled at the skill of the hunter who carried her as he maneuvered rapidly over the rocks without ever faltering. Eventually they came to a clearing, a saucer-shaped slab of granite that jutted out over the cliffs. The hunter put Halima back down on her feet, and the men stopped to rest. Halima could hear a thunderous rumble in the distance, and curious, wandered to investigate.

Halima walked gingerly onto the overhanging rock, and looked out. Her knees buckled at the view. They were high in the mountains now. Halima could see the treetops of the surrounding forest far below, looking like a carpet of tiny shrubs. She saw the plains stretching far into the distance, and her heart ached to see a hint of the ocean in the horizon.

Enormous billowing clouds wafted slowly, almost at eye level, so close Halima felt she could touch them. The sun seemed larger too, as if they were closer to the heavens now.

Giant gorges fanned out across the craggy face of the mountain. She could see them, one after another, going into the distance like the strands of a spider web.

The closest gorge was just ahead of them, a mile-deep crevasse hundreds of feet wide. Water rushed through its high, wet, moss-covered walls – fed by a tremendous, 400-

foot waterfall. It was magnificent and terrifying, full of power and majesty; the grandfather of all waterfalls.

A huge rainbow arched over the gorge, blindingly beautiful. Sweeping across the gorge was a long, intricate bridge made of thick rope and bamboo steps. Halima was astounded.

How could ordinary mortals have built this bridge, which spans from the high cliffs on either side? she thought. *Even the master builders of Kali would be hard-pressed to fashion such a bridge.*

One of the hunters rested a huge hand on her shoulder and pointed to the far side of the gorge. He said a word which sounded like "Abaka."

Halima repeated the word to herself. *That must be the name of the kingdom,* she thought, a thrill rushing through her. She repeated the word again, committing it to memory: "Abaka."

They crossed the bridge single file, taking slow, even steps on the slats, which were made of pieces of bamboo woven with strips of leather. The bridge swayed gently in the powerful winds that swept through the gorge.

How many centuries old is this bridge? Halima wondered as her hands groped along the frayed, yellow hemp railing.

Halima made the mistake once of looking down. Below them was a terrifying drop of thousands of feet. She felt herself growing dizzy, imagining the long plunge. She shook her head and concentrated on simply putting one foot after another.

As they neared the far side, the hunters began to sing, announcing their arrival. Halima couldn't understand the words, but their deep, rich voices were full of pride and joy. Halima glanced anxiously back over her shoulder. She felt as if in crossing this bridge, she were passing into another world – perhaps one from which she could never return.

Soon they reached the other side. Halima climbed off

the bridge, sighing in relief.

If I'm going to die here, at least let me die in one piece, she thought.

They were on a rocky bluff just above a plateau, crisscrossed with winding, sinuous paths. On the vast, flat plateau below, she saw young boys herding cattle that grazed on kikuyu grass. Women worked in the fields, harvesting crops of bananas, millet and yams. Some were carrying away straw baskets full of the produce on their heads. The women were singing. Their rich alto voices were beautiful, deeper and more powerful than the women of Halima's country.

The river that fed the waterfall ran straight from the white-capped upper reaches of the mountain down to the plateau. Halima could see women washing their clothes on the rocks while small children played in the water.

In the distance, built into the rocks, Halima could see a small city. Houses had been built on row after row of terraces ascending the mountain face.

It looks a thousand years old, Halima thought, *Like part of the mountain itself.*

The hunters made their way down the dusty road toward the city, with the game hanging from long poles. Halima, tethered once again, trailed behind them. The men sang loudly, braying and boasting of their success.

Although the women working the fields looked at them in approval, the men kept their eyes directly ahead, refusing to acknowledge the looks of praise.

The women towered above Halima. Some of them smiled at her as if she were a small, amusing child. They were the most beautiful women Halima had ever seen, walking with an erect, regal bearing, and in long, flowing skirts. She felt ashamed of the hole-pocked kidskin the hunters had given her.

Children ran along beside the hunters, staring at Halima with open curiosity, elbowing each other and pointing with their mouths agape. Even some who looked to be no more than eight or nine years old stood head and shoulders above her.

"I must look like a dwarf to them," she realized.

The doors of the city did not match the majestic gates to the city of Kali in size. But the workmanship and intricate carving, depicting scenes of an ancestral journey and ascent up the mountain in remote times, showed equal skill.

They passed through the city gate and now Halima got a closer look at the round houses that made up the city. They were made of clay, worked into rounded brick. The walls and doorways were neatly ornamented and the doors themselves were all carved in relief, each one having a different design.

Adolescent girls in tanned goatskins trimmed with brightly colored beads, and intricately beaded necklaces, walked swaying by with baskets on their heads, and watched the hunters pass with interest. When they saw Halima, they turned up their noses in disdain.

In most cities, Halima knew, the chief's compound lay in the very center. But here, the king's house was at the highest point of the terraced city. They mounted huge stone slab stairs to reach the house.

Surprisingly, the king's compound was a simple structure much like the others, surrounded by a wall of mud brick.

Well, Halima thought, *the proverb says, "A rich man can wear rags."*

One of the hunters blew a buffalo horn, and a few minutes later the doors were opened by a tall, broad-backed woman. She was the first ugly woman Halima had seen here.

She must be a servant, not a wife, she decided.

The bearded leader of the hunters exchanged some words with the stout servant, then she led the party into the compound.

Inside, there were about fifteen round buildings arranged in an oval ring, connected by a thick brick wall. As they passed by the open doors, Halima could see one was a granary, another a place where animals were housed. In one small building, women sat grinding millet. Through another doorway, she saw women working looms and sewing garments.

The largest of the buildings, Halima guessed, must be the king's quarters. And the second largest, which was adjacent to it, must belong to his first wife. It was into the second building the servant woman ushered the hunters' party. When they went inside, Halima felt convinced this was the house of the queen of the people of Abaka.

It was a large, spacious receiving room, with cushions to sit on and a small wooden table around which to eat. Through low doorways, Halima could see sleeping rooms, a nursery and a place for preparing food. The inside walls were smooth, polished as if they had been varnished, and a cool, delicious air circulated through the house. Beautifully crafted boxes and delicately carved statues were arranged on shelves along the wall.

The servant seated them among cushions and brought the hunters banana bread and millet beer.

After a while, the king's first wife swept into the room. Halima gasped audibly. She was the most gorgeous woman Halima had ever seen: tall and lean, with the bearing of a goddess. Her features were chiseled and strong to the point of being cruel; her brow high and intelligent. Her hair was crafted into a striking crown of ringlets and twisting braids and she wore long, silken robes dyed a deep purple, the color of royalty.

She looks well over thirty *years old*, Halima guessed.

The hunters hopped off the cushions and knelt as soon as she entered the room. They nudged Halima to kneel as well. It was strange for Halima, a princess in her own land, to kneel before another, but she obeyed.

Once I know her tongue, she'll learn I am a royal person too, she told herself. The first wife seated herself on an ivory stool in the middle of the room.

The bearded leader of the hunters stood and addressed the first wife. Halima focused and listened for her name. It sounded like "Rashida." In Halima's land such a name meant "righteous." Halima committed it to memory.

The hunter spoke at numbing length. From his tone, it was obvious that he was making a long, formal speech of praise. Then he gestured to Halima, proudly. Although Halima couldn't understand his words, she could guess what he was saying: "She is to be a gift to the king's household."

The hunter appeared to be expounding upon Halima's great beauty. When he made a gesture pointing to his tongue, it seemed as if he might be boasting of her pretty singing voice.

The first wife, Rashida, looked sternly down at Halima. The young girl trembled at the woman's naked glare. She was certain she'd never seen eyes so alive. They registered every emotion, like a lake shaken by gusts of wind. The first wife gave an order to the hunters; her voice had iron in it.

Obeying, the men scrambled forward and lifted Halima to her feet. She stood before the queen in her holey goatskin cloak, feeling like a filthy pauper.

The older woman considered Halima soberly, and addressed the hunters again. This time they stripped off Halima's cloak, so that she stood in the middle of the room, bare-skinned except for her dainty silk loincloth. Halima stood uncomfortably in the middle of the room.

Rashida rose regally from her ivory stool, so that she towered over Halima like a mother over her child. She was the tallest yet of all the women here, Halima noted. Circling Halima with the gait of a tigress, the first wife scrutinized the young girl from head to toe.

Finally, she faced Halima and stared directly into her eyes, as if finding no outer flaw, she hoped to see some flaw in her soul. Halima fought to meet the first wife's brooding stare.

Halima was sure that for a brief second, the first wife's face flushed with anger. For a moment, Halima was convinced the older woman was actually about to strike her. She braced herself for the blow.

The angry-eyed woman stood quivering for a moment, and then she called sharply for something. One of the hunters passed her a foot-long knife used for gutting game.

Halima's heart began to pound like a blacksmith's hammer. *This woman has a mad streak*, she said to herself nervously.

The queen took the glittering blade – and used it to slice away Halima's loincloth so that the maiden stood naked in the middle of the room. Then Rashida stood back, putting her hands on her hips triumphantly. Halima covered herself in dismay. No man had ever seen her unclothed before and now she was stark naked before the strangers, wearing nothing but the sea turtle amulet, the emblem of her clan. Hot tears began to roll down her face and she felt blood rush to her cheeks. She was overcome by shame.

"You mean old bitch," she cursed aloud angrily in her own tongue. "Old bitch!" She was fortunate no one could understand her – that insult might have cost her her head, she knew.

Rashida sniffed the air and her lip curled back as if she'd smelled something foul. She clapped her hands and the stout servant hurried forward. Rashida muttered something, and flicked her wrist toward Halima contemptuously, indicating she should be taken away. As Halima was led off, she heard Rashida beginning a long, obligatory speech of thanks to the hunters.

The stout servant took Halima to a little washroom in

the back, picked her up effortlessly, and put her to squat in a pot of chilly water. With the help of a long, skinny young servant girl Halima's age, the stout servant scrubbed the princess vigorously from head to toe.

Now Halima understood what the first wife had said: "Come bathe her – she stinks." She couldn't imagine what could make the other woman have such an instant dislike for her, but now the feeling was mutual. Perhaps once she could communicate, she could win the first wife's friendship. But she recalled the proverb, "There is no medicine for hatred."

After the women bathed Halima, they smeared her body with oils, so that her black skin glistened like a seal. They cut and braided her hair after the manner of the women of the city and dressed her in a long, colorful skirt. When they were done, Halima almost looked like one of the Abaka – except two feet shorter.

So it was that Halima, princess in the land of Kali, became a servant among the Abaka, the tall people of the mountain.

The stout servant indicated to Halima that her name was Tumpe. Using gesture, she showed Halima how to scrub pots and sweep the compound; wash clothes on the rocks; and how to watch over the flock of gangling children who roamed through the courtyard. Halima listened to the strange speech of the Abaka, trying to learn their language.

On her third night in the city, the warriors returned and there was a great celebration, because they were coming back from battle. All day the women prepared food, and Halima helped them carry huge jugs of honey wine to the hall where the celebration was to take place.

The feast took place in the Great Hall, a meeting place in the center of the city. It was a giant building made of bamboo, with a sloping thatched roof.

All the elders were sitting together, wise old men with sunken chests and hair as white as bone. They sat on one side of the hall and their wives, the old women of the town, sat on the other. The women looked sourly over the proceedings, Halima observed.

They look as if they believe in their day, everything was better: the women prettier, the music merrier, the meat had more salt.

Next to them the stools of the ancestors sat empty, so that their spirits could join in the celebration.

The nine wives of the warrior-king of the Abaka sat serenely on their cushions. Each was tall and beautiful. They looked like a row of sisters, separated from one another by two or three years. The eldest, the first wife Rashida, sat in the middle on the highest cushion. The youngest, who looked a year so older than Halima, sat furthest away.

Around them were the children of the king, beautiful boys and girls with well-shaped heads and long, strong limbs. The boys all sat as proud as lion cubs; even the youngest of them sat with their backs arrow-straight, with quiet dignity.

What manner of man must be he who fathered such a pride of young lions, the captive thought. She'd soon see, because the warriors were about to enter the hall.

Halima's task was simple that night. Tumpe showed her: She was to carry around a large jug, crafted in the shape of a standing crocodile, and keep the drinking cups of everyone in the hall full. In all the commotion no one thought to give her any water to drink, so she sipped diffidently from the jug of honey wine to quench her thirst.

An orchestra of a dozen musicians stood by the doorway, and now they began to play. Three men leaned into a trio of tremendous drums, while others began to shake rattles and calabashes filled with hard seeds. One musician held up a long, ivory horn on which a trail of elephants was carved and blew, signaling the warriors to enter.

The warriors burst one by one into the hall. Each had stripped to a loincloth and each wore the claws of a beast around his neck – one an eagle, the next a cheetah, the next a lion. Their chests were bare and rippled with muscles so powerful it looked as if an arrow couldn't pierce them. Each in turn did a heroic, acrobatic dance and when they leapt, their long, muscular legs carried them into the air like gazelles.

The crowd roared as the young men performed superhuman feats of agility, each trying to outdo the last. For each young man, the crowd shouted out his name and then added a new praise name that he had won in battle. Occasionally Halima heard names that sounded like words in her own language:

"Tree harvester!" the people chanted as one brawny young man back-flipped across the hall. At first the name seemed like nonsense – until Halima understood what was meant.

He must have felled many men in battle, like a forester cutting down trees, she shuddered. *Yes, the highest praise must go to the man who sheds the most blood.*

After the young men, the older warriors – the *ngitunga*, the strong ones – marched into the hall, high-stepping to the syncopated beat of the drum. All of them had old war wounds on their bare chests and shoulders that they wore like badges of honor. They thumped their spears to the ground and circled the room in an intricate winding line. Then they took their places, sitting in the hall.

Finally, the ivory horn blew again, announcing the warrior-king himself.

"Shomari! Shomari! Shomari!" the crowd roared.

Halima took a quick gulp of wine and turned to watch the king's entrance.

He was a giant among giants, nearly eight feet tall, but perfectly proportioned, with a barrel chest like a lion's and arms and thighs bulging with muscles on top of muscles.

He looked to Halima like a perfect bronze statue come to life. His brow was furrowed as if from profound thought; his nose broad and strong with savage flaring nostrils; his jaw powerful and his lips wide and sensual.

Over his shoulder he wore draped an ox-skin cloak decorated with cowrie shells and strips of iron. Down the back of it plumes of feathers ran. It was the uniform of the ncamba, the war leader, she knew. The only symbol of kingship was that in one hand he carried a knotted, intricately carved wooden staff that looked as if it had been wrought from the First Tree.

Shomari strode through the hall with the sure gait of a lion, and though Halima knew it was the thunder of the drum that made the earth shake, she imagined it was the footfalls of this giant man.

He waved to the cheering crowd with a small, modest gesture. Halima had never seen such love bestowed on a single person, even her father.

It does not seem the fawning behavior of subjects to their king, but genuine affection, she thought.

The king took his place among his wives. Immediately, all the smallest of his children leapt up and ran to him, hugging his massive legs.

Halima smiled and watched the giant warrior-king – who looked like he could crush any man she had ever seen with one blow – gently lift and hold the scrambling youngsters. Shomari sat beside his first wife, and she wrapped her arms securely around him like a rat trap slamming shut.

Just then, Tumpe elbowed Halima and made a gesture as if to pour, letting her know it was time to serve the honey wine.

Halima began diffidently passing down the line, first serving the elders and their wives. She realized the wine had made her somewhat woozy. She felt her feet wobbling under her, and had to concentrate each time she poured so as not to miss the goblet entirely. Now she regretted having sipped the wine. She recalled a proverb, "The drunken chicken does not see the hawk."

Now the unmarried adolescent girls of the city pranced into the hall, naked except for beaded loincloths. Lithe and graceful, they trotted forward like fawns in a straight line, and then formed a circle.

On their ankles the girls wore little bags which at every movement made a tinkle like a fistful of gravel being shaken. The tinkle seemed to say, "Come hither."

The drumbeat grew louder and the girls strutted around in a circle pumping their shoulders forward and back like hens, arching their backs and thrusting their breasts forward, singing loudly.

Halima had picked up enough of the language now that she knew they were singing about the warriors, praising them. They would trot up to a seated young man and just as the warrior leaned forward, the girls would skip coquettishly away, to the laughter of the entire crowd.

Halima felt the wine rushing to her head. She felt an impulse to run and join the girls, and take part in their joyful, rump-shaking dance.

Halima looked to Shomari, and saw that he was laughing. Although it was too noisy to hear it, she imagined it was rich and warm and deep. She wished she could dance with the wild abandon of the young girls of the Abaka, and earn the smile of their king.

The girls finished their dance, all throwing themselves

to the ground. There was more dancing, from the older women, who did little jerky steps and sang in strong, joyful voices. Even the children of the city danced, in concentric circles. The boys clapped their hands as they danced clockwise, while inside their ring, girls made a circle dancing counterclockwise.

Then an elder stood up, and all bowed their heads as he made a long prayer. As he fervently spoke, sometimes raising his gaze to the heavens, his words were often echoed by someone in the crowd.

Then he called the name "Shomari."

When King Shomari rose to speak, all mumbling ceased as the people listened to him enraptured, every face beaming. Halima could see the profound ardor the people had for their king. His deep voice was the timbre of logs tumbling together as they float down a river. Though Halima could not understand a word he said, she too knelt listening, entranced.

He seemed to be describing the battle, recounting what had occurred. His tremendous hands carved the air, depicting a movement of his troops, an attack by the enemy and then a hammer of his reinforcements slamming their opponents into disarray. His hands raked in toward his chest.

Livestock stolen from their enemies? wondered Halima.

Occasionally he would point to a warrior or mention one by name, and there would be murmurs of approval as Shomari described some act of bravery the man had performed.

Shomari's voice was full of warmth, and from time to time he would describe some comic error one of the *mbutu*, the quick young ones, had made. The young warrior would blush, and a wave of genuine laughter would cross the room, until the young warrior broke down and laughed at himself as well.

Finally, Shomari adopted a solemn tone as he mention-ed a few names and all heads hung in silence. Halima knew he must have said, "Now let us praise the dead."

For the first time, Halima felt these people were not strange or frightening. They had nobility to them and gentleness.

When Shomari finished, there was a roar of applause, and the music started up again. The servers began to bring around food, and Tumpe gestured to Halima that she must make busy keeping the goblets full.

Halima moved along, shakily. In a moment, she would be serving the king and it was frustrating that she couldn't speak his tongue. She felt like a toddler who hadn't yet learned to speak. She knew that he would hardly notice her.

How would Neema get his attention, she wondered. *I know, I'll lean before him as I pour his wine and catch his eye.*

Halima wanted to slap herself. *Not three days in captivity and I'm already thinking like a slave girl.* She pulled herself erect.

I will carry my captor's food and drink because I must – but I will do it with the dignity of a princess of Kali. Until I learn the language of the Abaka, and can petition for my release, I have no business with their king.

She refused to even look at Shomari as she approached the cushions of the king and his family. And yet when she knelt before the king to pour his wine, her slender arms trembled like those of a palsied old woman. She could not help but look up.

She glanced at Shomari's strong, handsome face, like a mask carved out of mahogany. He turned slowly, and his eyes – deep and dark as an ancient mountain lake – met hers.

He must have noticed her trembling because he smiled at her reassuringly. Halima smiled shyly in return. To her surprise, her heart began to pump furiously and a trickle of cool perspiration ran down between her breasts. She wanted that moment, that gaze, to last forever.

Then she noticed that the wine had overflowed the goblet, gushed over the table and poured into the king's lap. Halima covered her mouth in embarrassment, as the tiniest of the king's children giggled at their father's predicament.

Rashida leapt up and grabbed Halima by her long braids. Halima felt herself being wrenched up onto her tiptoes. Halima looked up at the older woman's angrily narrowing eyes, and this time she was sure a blow was coming. The back of the queen's hand streaked though the air toward Halima's face and she winced in anticipation of the sting.

But Rashida's hand stopped in mid-flight – Shomari had caught her wrist. How a man that huge could have risen so fast Halima could not imagine. Despite his giant frame he was as quick as a pouncing lion.

The king rotated his first wife to him. Her eyes were stormy. There was a moment of tension as all the other wives, and a few sharp-eyed onlookers, watched to see what the king would do. Suddenly, Shomari smiled and picked up the goblet, waved it in the air and with a flourish, splashed the dregs over his head.

The warriors nearby him roared with laughter, as did the rest of the onlookers. Even the first wife cracked a reluctant smile. The king turned to Halima and gave an easy, confident smile as if to tell her not to worry. Then Shomari picked his first wife off the ground and carried her out of the hall. There was much laughter and applause and the festivities continued.

Halima watched the giant striding away. And as her head swam from the wine, she remembered the words of her great-aunt and seer, Bimkubwa. What had the old woman said of her husband?

"He will be a lion among men. He will be wise, but for you he will throw wisdom to the winds. He will be strong, but to you he will surrender. He will be rich, but for you he will lose everything."

CHAPTER 5

A CAPTIVE

I n the weeks that followed, Halima began to learn the language of the Abaka, turning their odd, musical sounds into words like "goat" and "yam," "man" and "woman."

And as soon as she could string the words together, she told Tumpe, "I am a princess of Kali," and explained that she must be allowed an audience with King Shomari.

Tumpe scoffed, "Every captive says he was a prince in his own country. Here you're just a slave, like the rest of us."

Word of Halima's claim spread among the other servants, and her mocking nickname quickly became "The Princess" – as in "Princess, scrub this pot," or "Princess, go rub the feet of the third wife."

Halima was furious at first, but she bit back her anger. She told herself, "I must bide my time. I will have a chance to see the king eventually." And indeed, this turned out to be true – although it came about in a way she did not expect.

Along with the other women, Halima would go every day down to the river that flowed into the crashing waterfall. There they would wash the clothing of the first wife Rashida, and the eight lower wives, and all their children, holding the brightly colored robes over the smooth rocks, and letting the swiftly moving water cleanse them.

Sometimes the younger children came with their nursemaids to play, splashing each other in the shallow water. Some of the bigger boys would venture farther out and swim in the fast-moving water. But the smaller ones stuck prudently close to shore.

One, a nine-year-old named Kokayi – meaning "summon the people" – was the king's son by his fifth wife. He would always hang timidly to his mother's skirts. The others would call to him to join them, making clucking sounds like chicken, but he would refuse, sitting among the washerwomen, shamefacedly. Whenever Halima saw the boy, she would give him a smile as encouragement. She knew what it was like to feel like an outcast.

Halima knelt by the riverside, looking at the children play in the sparkling waters, and imagined she heard the gentle surf of the ocean near Kali, where she and her brothers and cousins played.

So many of those brave, happy boys were dead now, fallen as men in battle with the Zimbai. She felt tears beginning to well. Brushing them back, she began to sing a sad ballad of her native country:

"Death does not sound a trumpet.
Death does not sound a trumpet.
It comes silent like a snake
In the grass.
Death does not sound a trumpet.
Death does not sound a trumpet.
It comes like a coward, like a thief in the night.
Death does not sound a trumpet.
Death does not sound a trumpet.
It is not the crashing waves,

But the calm and silent waters
That drown a man."

First the children, then the serving women began to attend, and cluster around Halima as she knelt on the muddy bank, singing.

When the last note left her lips, there was a moment of silence and she looked about uncertainly at the wide eyes and purple-black faces. Then the serving women began to clap and smile. They hugged Halima and bade her sing more of the songs of her land.

Then they began to sing too, and tried to teach Halima the songs of the Abaka. They all laughed and sang together, down by the river, until almost sunset.

The next day, Tumpe told Halima that she had been summoned to the house of the king. Halima gulped. Her time had come indeed – but for what? She readied herself and headed for the tall building.

Tiptoeing catlike, Halima entered the inner chamber of the king's house. As much as the first wife's house was domestic and female, this place oozed masculinity, like a lion's den giving off the scent of its owner. The walls of the room were adorned with the hides of lions and boars, as well as weapons of war of all types: bows, spears, shields, and swords wrought from iron with fine, intricate designs carved into the hilt.

But to her surprise, she saw instruments of learning too: ancient, furled scrolls of papyrus and candles to read by; maps depicting the four corners of the earth, from the frigid land of the whites to the baking lands of gold in the south, from the land of silk and spices to the east, to the green forest across the western ocean.

Suddenly, a loud grunt like a boar's erupted from an inner room. Halima jumped, letting out a little girlish shriek. She cautiously approached the next chamber and peeped through the curtains.

To her horror, she saw that Shomari was locked in mortal combat with another giant. *An assassin!* Halima thought.

The two giants, dressed only in loincloths and dripping with sweat, were chest to chest, each with his arms braced behind the other's back with spine-snapping force. They barreled into one stone wall and then the next, as they staggered about on iron-thewed legs, each trying to toss the other off-balance.

At one point, the assassin wrapped a long-fingered hand securely around Shomari's throat. He grinned triumphantly.

I must help him! Halima thought, and she looked around for a weapon to throw to the king.

But at that moment, in a lightning-fast movement, Shomari snagged his opponent by the wrist, turned, and hurled him over his shoulder. The other giant crashed to the ground with an earthshaking thud, and the king planted his bare foot on the man's broad chest. The attacker lay panting, the wind knocked out of him.

Then, to Halima's surprise, Shomari grinned a gleaming white smile, reached down and helped the other man to his feet. Now she recognized the young warrior as the one given the praise name "Tree Harvester" at the feast.

"A good fight, Hasani," Shomari said. He tapped his temple with a laugh. "You are learning to use your head as well as your heart."

The young warrior, who looked about eighteen years

old to Halima, gripped the king's thick arm. "It will be a long time before I can best the lion that walks on two legs, Father," he said.

So this was the king's son, Halima realized, now feeling a little foolish. The king had been teaching him how to wrestle.

Halima smelled a whiff of musky perfume, and saw that two busty servant girls had drawn up silently beside her. The two were sisters and nearly identical.

Shomari turned to his son. "Come, join me in a massage. You've earned it today."

The young man bowed his head. "Thank you, Father, but Mother has asked me to build a fence in her fields today."

Shomari smiled. "Good boy. Though say no to your mother once in a while. You must learn to refuse the demands of women, or you'll make a henpecked husband someday."

"Yes, Father," the young man said. He turned to go. Hasani strode by Halima, stealing an appreciative glance at the girl. The king noticed Halima standing in the doorway for the first time and his warm, bemused smile returned.

"Is this the child they say sings so sweetly?"

"Yes, Sire," said one of the serving girls.

Halima was incensed. True, she was tiny, next to the two towering servants, but she didn't like being taken for a little girl – she was fifteen!

"I'm not a child," she spoke up. The king raised his eyebrows and Halima realized how petulant she sounded.

The two servant girls looked at each other in shock, and then one quickly said "Forgive her poor manners, Sire. She is an outlander, new to our country."

"Hunters brought her here as a gift," added the other girl.

"I see," Shomari said, smiling at Halima again. "You must make her welcome, then."

"Yes, Sire," the servant girls said in unison.

"Come," said Shomari. He spun around and strode toward a stone bench set against the wall, covered with velvet cushions. As the king walked off, he unfastened his loincloth and let it drop.

Halima stared with fascination at his bare, sweat-gleaming buttocks, as brawny as a young lion's. She quickly lowered her gaze to her own feet in maidenly shame – she didn't dare look at the front side of him. When she finally raised her head, the king had stretched out face down on the velvet cushions. One of the servant girls hovered over him and, tilting a flask, poured a glob of oil between his shoulder blades. Halima watched the river of oil run down his back, down the curve of his spine. The servant girls began to knead the oil into Shomari's sweaty back, which looked to Halima as broad as an elephant's.

The other servant girl lit a stick of incense, then took out a little finger-harp and knelt beside the king. Beginning to pluck it, she gestured to Halima to come forward.

"Come, Halima, it pleases the king that you should sing for him."

Halima cleared her throat and began to sing, haltingly at first and then in her finest sweet, clear voice:

"When love comes it is not like
Two worlds meeting
Or rain drops that fall
And merge in the sky.
When love comes it is not like
Two roads meeting.
It is a journey deep
Into undiscovered land.
When love comes it is not like
Two roads meeting,
But the taming of

Each wild heart by the other.
When love comes it is not like
Two roads meeting."

Shomari became attentive to the song and looked up, frowning curiously.

"Does she displease you, Sire?" one of the servant girls asked in alarm.

Shomari clapped his hands and pointed at the two servant girls. "Go!" he commanded.

The tall girls bowed humbly and scampered off.

He looked sternly at Halima. "Come," he said. Halima stepped quickly forward and knelt, head lowered.

She swayed, uncertainly. The aroma of the frank-incense which now clouded the room was almost dizzying. The king rested his chin on his fist and considered her soberly. And he smiled.

"No, you are not a child," he declared. "There is all the wisdom of the ages in you. I've never heard any song so strange and beautiful. I must have you sing for me again. It cures my melancholy."

"Yes, Sire," Halima replied.

"Sing again now, that your soothing voice may help me to sleep," he commanded, resting his head back down on the pillow. Halima commenced another ballad. But then she wondered if she should ask him now.

She summoned her courage and spoke. "Sire?" Shomari, drifting off, grunted.

"Sire, I have a favor to ask."

The king opened one eye and turned to her. Halima pointed to the sea turtle-shaped pendant that hung about her neck.

"Sire, I am a princess of the land of Kali. If you return me to my home, my father Babatunde the Good will pay you a handsome ransom. This I promise."

Shomari rolled onto his side, to take a good look at her. As the giant turned, Halima could glimpse his manhood, stretched out along the slab on which he lay. There was enough of it to put a bull elephant to shame!

She forced herself to concentrate instead on the king's scrutinizing gaze.

Shomari ran his hand over his jaw in mock contemplation. "Well Princess, before I send a ransom, I will need time to decide what you are worth – and whether I'm willing to give you up!"

So it was that Halima, as a captive of the Abaka, the giants of the Silver Mountain, became a singer for their ruler Shomari, whose name means "forceful."

Every day she was summoned to entertain him, to sing and regale him with stories from her land, from childhood tales of Anansi the spider to her people's history (drummed into her by the family griot Mwendapole).

He was fascinated by the great learning of the people of Kali and would ask her many questions about the world beyond his mountain kingdom. What Halima liked best was when the tale she told amused him, and he would let out a deep bellow, like a lion's roar.

About this time, Tumpe informed Halima she was to assist Kizza – a skinny, buck-toothed girl with a sullen disposition – in caring for Rashida's prized silk dresses. The two would find themselves carefully scrubbing the queen's garments down by the river, long after the other women had left, anxious to neither leave a single stain on the clothes or accidentally rip them.

This was in addition to her other duties, such as squatting on the ground cracking nuts brought in by the basketful by Shomari's sons and nephews. However, the added chores only made Halima's visits to the king sweeter. She would scrub until her fingers ached and were as wrinkled as prunes, all the time looking forward to her daily audience with Shomari.

One day, as Halima knelt beside the king, singing a song of her native land, Shomari stopped her and pointed to an errant tear rolling down her cheek.

"What is it, pretty Halima? Why do you weep?" Halima shook her head as if it were nothing.

The king knelt beside her. "Do you miss your homeland?" Halima nodded reluctantly.

"Do you wish me to return you to the land of your father?" asked the king.

Halima looked up in surprise and flicked away the tear. Shomari looked entirely serious.

"If that is what you want, I will order it, wise, beautiful, Halima," he rumbled gently. "You have given me so much joy in the past few weeks; I owe happiness to you as well. And there shall be no ransom demanded.

"But first, I have something to show you. Your land by the sea is not the only place of beauty that the Great One in the Sky created." He stood and took her by the hand, gently lifting her to her feet.

They walked out of the king's house and out of his compound, out among his proud, tall people who shouted greetings full of praise. Young children clustered around them and old men smiled broad, toothless smiles.

He took her into the holy grove where the royal ancestors were buried; each king buried in the base of a baobab tree. The grove looked out over the green, majestic mountainside.

Shomari told her about his race:

"Our people were the first men. It was our kind who stole fire from the heavens. It was we who first sailed to the Western Continent, and first understood the meaning of the stars."

Halima felt an urge to protest. In the legends told by her family griot Mwendapole, it was the ancestors of her own people who discovered those things. She held her tongue and listened politely.

"We, too, had our Golden Age," continued Shomari. "But as is the way of empires, folly and petty jealousy brought us down. Our people are now splintered – just as the mountain is splintered."

He pointed to far-off villages that peppered the mountainside, separated by enormous gorges.

"We are a dozen kingdoms on this mountain now. One year, one of those kingdoms is our ally, the next it may be our enemy."

Halima remembered the victory feast, which she knew had followed a battle. "So it is your own race you war against. You slaughter your own kind?" she asked.

Shomari looked at her in surprise. "When we make war, it is only to steal cattle and raid granaries, and sometimes to take captives for wives and servants. If we can do that without ever harming our enemies, then all the better."

"That seems a strange, peaceful way to make war," Halima said, shaking her head.

"It is the way we have known for 1,000 years. What other way is there?"

Halima lectured him: "When great kingdoms battle, it is to conquer the enemy and destroy them completely. That is the way civilized countries wage war."

Shomari looked at her for a moment and then laughed a deep, hearty guffaw that rang out over the mountain. Halima almost stamped her feet in dismay. *What have I said that is so funny? Sometimes he insists on treating me like a child,* she thought.

Shomari settled down, wiping tears of laughter from his eyes. He took her hand and looked at her seriously.

"I think you and I have much to teach each other, little one."

Halima smiled. Then she said boldly, "In our land we have great mathematicians and priests and astronomers. What do you have here that is as marvelous?"

Shomari turned around and, standing behind her, pointed out the very peak of the mountain.

"Up their lives Olushegun, our greatest seer, who has lived 200 years. He sees with the third eye, a vision unclouded by human folly and petty feeling. He can see deep into the past and far into the future."

"And you have met this wondrous man?" Halima asked, skeptically.

"Not yet – my father told me of him. Only for the greatest decisions does the king consult Olushegun. When even the great wisdom of the Council of Elders with which a king rules is not enough."

Halima stared at the mountain peak, which glittered like diamonds, trying to believe him. Sensing her doubt, Shomari explained, "Here in the mountains, more things are possible, Halima. This high the air is different. The mind is freer here, the soul more naked. Can't you feel it?"

Halima shut her eyes and leaned back against Shomari. She sucked in the pure, rarefied air. It tasted cool and fresh as spring water.

"Yes," she admitted. "This is a place where truth is clearer, and passion stronger. Where hate is great hate, and love is great love."

Shomari stood close behind her and put his hands at her waist.

"Halima. Wise, beautiful Halima, I do not want you to go," he murmured. He turned her head toward his and placed his lips over hers. Halima felt her moist lips melt into his, as he overwhelmed her with a deep, passionate kiss.

When she could breathe again, she moaned in protest, "In our country we do not touch our lips this way."

Shomari smiled. "Much to teach each other," he whispered.

The following day, Rashida appeared at the riverside, where Halima, Tumpe, Kizza and other women knelt to wash clothes on the rocks. The first wife's face was like a hurricane. Halima shivered as she recalled all the people who had witnessed her out walking with the king. What gossip had the first wife heard?

Rashida held up her most prized silk dress almost triumphantly. Halima saw that though it was bright and clean, it was ruined by an ugly tear that split it almost in half.

"Who is responsible for this?" Rashida demanded.

Kizza stood up hurriedly and pointed at Halima. "It was she – the one who calls herself Princess!"

"That's not true!" Halima protested vehemently, trying in confusion to recall the last time she'd seen the dress.

"Would you take the word of the outlander over a woman born of the Abaka?" insisted gangly, bucktoothed Kizza. She pointed accusingly at Halima. "I saw her rend it on purpose. She said because she's a princess, the garment was hers by right. She vowed that if she couldn't have it, no one would. I heard these words with my very own ears."

Big Tumpe lumbered to her feet and protested, "The ugly one lies out of jealousy, Your Highness. Like as not, she tore it herself by accident."

"You saw nothing!" Kizza spat. Tumpe fell into frustrated silence.

Rashida gave Halima a look that could have bored straight through lead. "I think it's time 'The Princess' learned her true station here," she said quietly.

In the queen's house, Halima was made to lay face forward over a stool, and to receive fifty strokes of the stick on her bare buttocks.

She wasn't terrified. No one had ever dared strike her before, even in play, so she could not truly anticipate the pain. Rashida stood behind her with Tumpe, who held a long, thin stick in her hand. "Begin," she ordered calmly.

Tumpe whispered, "Cry out, confess, Halima, and beg for forgiveness."

But Halima refused to cry out. She refused to give the first wife the satisfaction of watching her plead for mercy.

She heard the switch whistle in the air, and then it bit into her flesh like a barracuda. She winced at the pain. In her father's palace, she had once had a servant beaten for stealing; she had no idea it hurt this much.

Still, Halima would not cry out. Gritting her teeth, she forced herself to count the strokes. "One... Two... Three... Four... Five..."

By the tenth stroke, tears were rolling down her cheeks and her backside felt as if it had been stung by 1,000 fire ants. She was ready to grovel at the first wife's feet and beg for mercy – but she did not.

"Twelve... Thirteen... Fourteen," she counted to herself, clenching her teeth so tightly it felt like they might shatter.

Then, abruptly, Rashida commanded Tumpe to stop.

"Leave us," she ordered.

Tumpe gladly dropped the switch and, with a look of

concern for Halima, backed out of the room. Halima knelt, head bowed, sheltering her breasts with her arms. Her sweating body shuddered, still waiting for the next blow.

Rashida paced several times around her, then came to a stop directly in front of her.

"Look at me," the queen of the Abaka commanded. Halima tilted her head up and met Rashida's steely gaze defiantly. Rashida nodded to herself. "So you *are* a princess. You are too proud to cry out and show your pain."

Rashida bent down and put her hand against Halima's tear-soaked face. She considered her almost tenderly.

"You are indeed beautiful, Halima. I think I've never seen a face so perfect.

"Is that why he loves you? Because your skin is young and soft? Or is there more? What is it that he sees in you?" she demanded. "What in you?"

Halima knelt, looking up at her in silence. The queen's nostrils twitched like a leopard about to spring.

"You are a captive and a slave," Rashida said. "I could have you taken to the forest and thrown to the lions. I could have you thrown from the highest waterfall."

Halima continued to meet her eyes steadily. Rashida clenched and unclenched her fists again and again, and her eyes burned. *She is mad*, Halima told herself. *She is about to pound me to death with her bare hands.*

But Rashida shook her head vigorously, and stood, straightening up, taking on a queenly bearing again.

"But I am the queen of the Abaka," she said stiffly. "And you are an innocent."

She walked to the door, where she turned. "I will not beat you again, Halima. I will send a messenger to the King of Kali and tell him you're safe among us."

Later, Halima lay on her belly on a mat of woven rush later, in the room she shared with Tumpe. The older woman was rubbing hot, soothing palm oil into her beet-red backside, draining away the sting of her beating.

The servant woman's broad, coarse hands felt as big as a man's and Halima guiltily found herself imagining that it was Shomari comforting her.

Why am I thinking about him now? Halima asked herself. *Now that word is being sent to my father, I will be going home soon, never to see him again.* Up to this moment, she had dreamed every night of returning home. Now, though, the thought of leaving made her strangely melancholy – despite her terrible beating.

"Tumpe," she asked idly. "Do captive women ever marry into a family of the Abaka?"

"Of course," Tumpe replied, continuing to massage her, "with the permission of the man's other wives."

"Even an outlander?"

Tumpe told her, "First the outlander must be initiated into our clan. It is a complex ritual not often done." She lifted her hands. "Now tell me, child, who is it you want to marry?"

"No one," Halima answered hurriedly.

Tumpe snorted in disbelief. "I should give you a few more licks of the stick to cure you of lying."

Strangely, in the weeks and months that followed, no word came from the King of Kali, Babatunde the Good. Indeed, the two messengers who were dispatched by Rashida never returned – nor were they seen again in life. Halima might almost have doubted that the message was ever sent, but Tumpe told her she'd seen them leave at early dawn with her own eyes.

One night, Halima had a sad, troubling dream. She was on the seashore near Kali, skipping stones across the water, when she saw a black-cloaked figure treading along the surf. She called to the figure, but there was no reply; he continued to walk away. She approached the figure who, she now could see, was her father. She called to him, but he kept on trudging away. Halima ran toward him, but no matter how fast she ran, the sand held her in place. Babtunde turned to her and smiled sadly, then waved. Tears were running down his face – red tears of blood. He turned somberly, and marched into the dark, gloomy sea.

When Halima woke, she shared the unsettling dream with Tumpe.

"Perhaps it means your past life is dead. Your future is here with us," the servant woman told her, putting a fat, comforting arm around her.

The more time passed with no word from Kali, the more the idea of marriage to Shomari captivated the young maiden's imagination. He was, she felt with all her heart, "the lion among men" that her seer had prophesied would become her husband. He was brave, wise and kind – everything good a man could be. If the people of Kali needed an alliance through marriage with a warrior people, here was a warrior race unequaled. Certainly a much better choice than the People of the Snake and their pudgy, weak-armed leader, King Olugbodi.

With each passing day, she and Shomari became closer, and she was sure that any day the king would ask her to become his tenth wife.

One morning, she was ordered to come to the king's house. She'd never been summoned to see him so early in the day; something must be up, she thought. Tingling with excitement, she bathed thoroughly, perfumed her body with sweet scented leaves, and wrapped herself in her prettiest dress. Then, she hurried to the king's house.

She was told to wait in the outer chamber. Through the

silk curtains she could hear the voices of Rashida and Shomari. Halima knew it was wrong to eavesdrop on a private conversation between a husband and wife, but it was impossible not to overhear every word standing where she had been ordered.

Rashida said, "Husband, do you not think it is time for our eldest son, Hasani, to take a wife?"

"Yes," Shomari replied. "He's a warrior now, a tall, straight young man. He's passed all the tests of manhood."

"I think, husband, I have the perfect choice for him."

"Indeed?"

"She is a creature of perfect beauty, with a pleasing, gentle temperament and wise beyond her years."

"I thought I'd taken the last of those when I married you, Rashida."

Halima wondered which of the village girls had been chosen as Hasani's bride. The Tree Harvester was considered quite a catch. She would have a good piece of gossip to share with Tumpe and the others.

"Shall I summon her, husband?" Rashida asked.

Shomari must have nodded because there was a loud smack as Rashida clapped her hands.

"Halima!" she called sharply.

Halima stood frozen in utter disbelief like a gazelle startled by bright lights.

"HALIMA!" Rashida called again.

Halima passed through the curtains and into the inner chamber. Shomari and Rashida were seated side by side on stools. At his mother's foot their son Hasani knelt. The handsome young man's eyes lit up as Halima entered the room. He jumped up, rushed to her side and took her by the arm, leading her into the room.

Shomari's brow knitted as he saw Halima.

Rashida turned to him. "Do they not make a handsome couple, husband?"

For once, Shomari was speechless. He stared from

Halima to Hasani and then from Hasani to Halima.

When he did speak, his voice was hoarse. "Hasani, son, do you wish to take this woman as your bride?"

Hasani turned to Halima and looked at her, head to toe. He met her eyes and his face stirred with passion. *This boy looks like he wants to "take" me right on the floor*, Halima thought indignantly.

Hasani grinned with a smile uncannily like his father's.

"Father, she is the most beautiful woman I've ever seen," he said.

Shomari slumped slightly in his stool. For the first time, he looked old to Halima. He turned slowly to her.

"And you, Halima?"

Their eyes locked. *You know my answer*, Halima thought. She wanted to throw herself at his feet and declare her love.

Rashida interjected, "She is a captive, husband. We do not need to ask for permission. You can give her away to any man of your choice. You are as her father here."

Shomari frowned and he stroked his jaw thoughtfully. Softly, he said, "Hasani, Halima, leave us. We will tell you our decision."

His son grinned and bowed. "Thank you, Father." He took Halima's hand and led her out of the chamber. As soon as they were in the outer chamber, Halima pulled her hand angrily free from Hasani's. His bright smile faded as he saw her expression.

"Don't be frightened," he whispered. "I will never mistreat you." He ducked down awkwardly and gave her a shy peck on the cheek. Then he stepped back, bowed to her and smiled diffidently.

The moment he left, Halima fell to her knees by the doorway. Now she was eavesdropping brazenly – but how could she help it? This was her future they were deciding. She felt like a child listening in on her parents.

"What is the matter, husband?" Rashida asked. "Does

the maiden not meet with your approval? She is of noble birth, a princess in her own country."

"You know that I have feelings for this girl, Rashida," Shomari replied in a voice that sounded almost weary.

"For the bride of your son?!" Rashida exclaimed in a shocked tone.

Shomari's voice became stern. "This guile is beneath you, Rashida."

There was a moment of silence. Halima could glimpse through the gauzy curtain that both were standing, and that Shomari had put his hands on his wife's shoulders. Rashida cast her eyes down, refusing to look at him.

The king told her, "I wish to make Halima my wife. I wish to make her part of our family. I want you to give me your permission for this."

Rashida continued to look down. "Are we not happy as we are, husband?"

"Yes, dear one."

"Have I not chosen for you eight wives, each more beautiful than the last, and sent them to your bed? Have I for a moment shown jealousy toward them?"

Shomari shook his head.

Rashida continued, her voice rising in pitch. "Have I not given you strong sons? Have I not stood by your side through war and famine and illness, through the death of our parents and kin?"

Shomari nodded solemnly.

Rashida finally glared up at him. "Then what do you want from this outlander?"

Shomari took his hands from Rashida's shoulders and paced across the room, groping for words. Then he smiled to himself as if picturing Halima before him. "She... she is like a spring day," he said.

Rashida sighed in exasperation.

Shomari made a gesture with his hands as if beckoning for understanding. "Rashida, I am king of a country that has not grown for 1,000 years. One day is like the next. We live out our father's pasts, like ghosts, like the living dead, like ones asleep. And I am king, but I'm powerless to change anything. Sometimes I feel like the most asleep of all. But she is like a spark that ignites me. She brings me to life. When I am with her, I am a young man again, a king who could forge a Golden Age."

His rhapsody was wasted on Rashida, who cried out bitterly, "And what about me? What about Rashida, your first wife?"

Shomari smiled.

"You will always be the first wife."

Rashida shook her head, frowning.

Shomari stepped closer and hugged her reassuringly. "You will always be *my* first wife, Rashida. You were my first bride, and you will always be first in my heart."

"Do you swear?" Rashida said fiercely.

"I swear it," Shomari declared. She embraced him tightly. Halima watched Shomari kiss her as passionately as he had kissed Halima herself in the Sacred Grove. The two stood swaying, holding each other.

Rashida whispered, with obvious reluctance, "Husband, if it is your will, I shall put the question to the lesser wives. If they do not object, neither shall I."

"Thank you, dear one," Shomari said, kissing her throat.

"Now make love to your first wife, like you did on our wedding night."

Shomari grinned and drew her to him.

Halima slipped out of the king's house and rushed out of the compound.

She had always prided herself on her sober wisdom, but now her passions were running riot. She recalled the story Neema had told her of a doe-eyed woman in her village by the sea. This woman would lie with any man, even the husbands of other women. She was not wicked, but when passion seized her, she would be unthinking, like a lioness in heat. In time, the women of the village banded together and took their complaints to the village council, demanding punishment. The doe-eyed woman was taken deep into the forest and abandoned. Seasons later, hunters found her bones, gnawed by lions.

Halima felt like that wanton, doe-eyed woman now, like a fishing village trollop chasing another woman's husband. She sensed the great love between Rashida and Shomari and to break such a bond would be the greatest evil. She knew it would be fairer to withdraw and refuse the king's hand.

All my life, I have been fair and good, Halima thought. *I have been taught to be noble and to sacrifice my wishes for the welfare of the many. I agreed to marry fat King Olugbodi to save my people from the Zimbai. I surrendered myself to bondage to save the lives of my servants. But this time, Great One in the Sky, forgive me. I am too weak – I cannot sacrifice. I must be with him.*

She craved Shomari as a drunkard craved wine. She craved him in her heart and in her loins and in her spirit.

Weeping and confused, Halima wandered down to the river. She clambered onto a boulder and stared into the bright, chuckling waters. In the distance, she could hear the faint rumbling of the falls like distant thunder.

"I feel like throwing myself right off the cliffs," she said morosely. The women were washing now; she could hear them singing a few hundred feet away. The familiar sound soothed her soul.

She reached into the frigid water and splashed some on her face, trying to cool her passion. She fought to calm herself and prayed for guidance.

"It is out of my hands," she reminded herself. "The lesser wives will decide it."

Then she imagined Rashida putting the question to the group. "Our husband wants a new wife, a scheming outland vixen who's younger and more beautiful than any of us. How many vote for her?" Yes, somehow the evil witch would tilt the vote against her – while pretending to be neutral in the matter.

What's more, two of Rashida's co-wives were her younger sisters. Another was a cousin. No doubt she handpicked them to give herself greater strength in the king's compound.

I will never be allowed to marry my beloved Shomari! she thought in dismay.

Suddenly, Halima's deep reverie was shattered by a woman's scream, followed by a chorus of high-pitched shrieks. It was coming from upriver, where the cheerful singing had abruptly stopped. Halima hopped off the boulder. She'd lived her life by the water, and knew the sound only too well: Someone was drowning.

She hurried up the riverbank and rounded a curve, hopping as quickly as she could from one slippery stone to the next.

Ahead, Halima could see a cluster of women holding one another, screeching at such a volume that their words were unintelligible. Several others were wailing and pointing out into the river. Kizza and Tumpe and two other women were wrestling back the king's fifth wife, who was desperately trying to plunge into the river.

"My baby, my baby!" the fifth wife wailed.

Out in the middle of the river, a young boy thrashed and choked, one hand clinging to a slender branch, as the current spun him around and around. He was hollering for help at the top of his lungs.

Weeping, Tumpe told Halima, "It is Kokayi, son of Shomari. He wanted to prove his courage to the children. They said he was afraid to swim."

"He can't die!" the fifth wife screamed at the sky in absolute hysteria.

"It is the Great One's will," Kizza said, trying to

comfort her.

Halima took an anxious step toward the river. Where were the men to come rescue the boy? There were none in sight. She knew they would come – but too late. She hesitated, then unfastened her dress and sprang headfirst into the river.

In her days in the kingdom of Kali, the great port city by the sea, she had become a confident and expert swimmer. She plowed through the water toward the drowning lad with the speed of a porpoise.

Though the sky overhead gleamed with sunlight, the water was stabbing cold. Naked except for her loincloth, she felt like she was swimming through ice.

When she felt she must be near the boy, she pulled her head out of the water. She saw him nowhere. *No! Has he already slipped under?*

Then she heard again his frantic cries, and saw him many yards away. The powerful current was dragging him downriver.

Halima ducked her head back into the water, and took off after the boy, kicking furiously, driving forward with all the force her young legs could muster. She could hear the women wailing on the shore, crying out and beseeching the Great One in the Sky to be merciful.

Halima yanked her head out of the water. This time, the little boy was only a few yards away. Halima felt a rush of relief.

The relief was short-lived because suddenly she became aware of the thunderous roar of the falls, growing louder every moment. They had already drifted dangerously far downstream. Halima splashed toward the boy, flung out a hand, and grabbed hold of the tree branch that he clung to. She grabbed him so that his small, bare chest flattened her bosom. The little boy wrapped his arms tightly around her neck.

"Thank you!" Kokayi said through chattering teeth.

Embracing him, she began to kick with her long straight limbs toward shore. She could feel the strength of the current whipping her and the boy faster and faster down the river. No ocean waves could have prepared her for a force such as this. Out of the corner of her eyes she could see some of the women chasing them along the shore, their screams now drowned out by the roar of the falls.

Great One in the Sky, protect us! she thought. She kicked hard for the shore, fatigue starting to set in. She felt young Kokayi rising in her arms, trying to push her away.

Is he panicking now? she thought.

"Let go of me!" the king's young son spluttered. "Save yourself!"

That brave flourish made her hug him all the harder. They were only one hundred feet from the falls now and still nearly in the middle of the river. Halima continued to kick furiously with all her strength, but that was nothing against the raging might of the river.

The water was all white, angry foam now. All Halima could see in her mind's eye was the awful 400-foot drop ahead. *Everyone must die – but please, not like that!* a voice inside her head shrieked. It was impossible to swim now. Together, she and little Kokayi rushed through the water, clinging to each other as they hurtled toward the abyss.

The current raked them over submerged boulders in the shallow water near the waterfall. Halima felt a bone-snapping pain as her ankle bashed into one.

For an instant, they swirled around in a whirlpool as the currents toyed merrily with them. Desperately, Halima lunged for the jagged peak of the boulder that jutted above the water. Miraculously, she caught it and hugged the boulder with all her might, keeping the boy in front of her.

She praised the Great One in the Sky for the moment's reprieve. She could feel the power of the waterfall, yanking at her like an octopus. Her arms felt as though they were being ripped from their sockets.

The falls were deafening and the water tore along her body like ravenous teeth. Her loincloth was ripped clean away, all the jewelry shorn from her wrists, ankles and ears – all but the sea turtle pendant.

Halima's hands gripped the rock with white knuckles, her fingers losing some of their strength every second. She clung with all her will, knowing that to let go would mean being swept over the falls to die. Her grip was failing.

"Great One in the Sky, save us!" she screamed above the roar of the waterfall. Her hands were numb now. The left tore away from the rock, and then the right let loose, and she and the boy whooshed away from the boulder. *So this is how it ends,* Halima thought in horror.

Just then, Halima felt strong hands at her armpits. She felt herself being hoisted out of the water, so she hugged Kokayi as tight she could, bringing him with her. She was dragged into a canoe. Her rescuer was Hasani, the king's son. Another young man in the canoe was back-paddling furiously.

As she and the boy flopped to the bottom of the canoe like big, wet fish, Hasani began to paddle for shore. The two youths threw their backs into the strokes, moving their arms at breakneck speed. But it was too late. The current swept the canoe toward the waterfall. The little boat shot toward the precipice, riding on top of the foaming water.

The canoe rocked this way and that as it bumped over the rocks – then finally the bow shot over the waterfall. Halima looked down into the rocky, churning hell 400 feet below. She buried the little boy's face against her bosom, shielding him from the sight, and let out an animal howl of terror.

For an instant, the canoe paused in mid-flight, ready to dive headlong over the falls – and suddenly, fantastically, the boat was jerked back into the river.

Only now did Halima see that the canoe was tethered

to a long rope that stretched to the shore. There, knee-deep in the icy water, Shomari stood with the rope tied about his waist. The muscles of his arms rippled as, hand over hand, he pulled the canoe surely back from the brink. An ordinary man would have been hauled into the river himself, but Shomari stood his ground against the angry river, his legs planted as solidly as the pillars of a temple.

As soon as she saw him, Halima knew they were safe. For even if the strength of his arms were not enough, his unbending will would not let them perish. Slowly, he pulled them back to shore. Moments later, he was joined by three or four other men, who ran down to the river to assist. Together, they brought the canoe ashore.

The women of the city rushed to help Halima from the canoe and quickly wrapped her in a blanket, covering her nakedness. Her whole body shook and her teeth clicked together so hard it felt as if her jaw was about to drop off.

Still bawling, the fifth wife grabbed Kokayi out of the canoe. She embraced him – and then drew back and smacked him on the top of the head. "Who told you you could swim, eh?" she demanded. Then she embraced him again.

"I am sorry, Mother," the little boy said calmly.

Shomari proudly hugged Hasani and clapped the other canoeist on the back. Then he turned and strode toward Halima.

He seemed to take an eternity to reach her, as if he were wading through haze. Halima felt a weakness in her limbs, then a sudden dizziness. As he approached, smiling from ear to ear, his wives crowded around Halima, praising her for her bravery.

Just before Shomari reached her, the first wife stepped between them. Halima's knees suddenly gave way, but Rashida caught her. She looked into Halima's eyes gravely. She paused, then said, "You've saved the life of our son. My family owes you a life."

Rashida turned and told her eight co-wives, "Sisters, from this day forward Halima is no longer a slave of the Abaka. She is a free woman. Our husband and lord, Shomari, has asked for our consent to marry Halima and now we must give it. Now we must call her sister." She bent and kissed Halima gently on her cheek. Each of the other wives came up and did the same.

Surrounding them, the servant women cheered and clapped. Shomari pushed through the crowd, and hugged the soaking girl, then hugged his other wives to him, and then the two sons whose lives had nearly been lost.

He threw back his head and gave a shout of joy and praise to the Great One in the Sky.

So it was that Halima, Princess of Kali, the kingdom by the sea, came to be betrothed to Shomari, king of the giants of the mountain.

CHAPTER 6

INITIATION

Halima was prepared for initiation into the Abaka and marriage to the king. She was sent to kneel in the hall set aside for women of the city, where the old women instructed her in the ways and history of the Abaka, and told her how a wife was to behave. They spiced up their lessons with tales of wives who had been disloyal, disobedient, jealous of their co-wives, or had otherwise gone astray, and the terrible fates these erring women had encountered.

They told her of the origin of Woman and the secrets of the womb; of herbs that ensured her babies would be born strong and healthy. Halima recognized much of what they told her from her own initiation into womanhood in Kali, but many of the secrets they divulged were new to her.

In time, the old women told her she must learn how to pleasure her husband. Halima insisted, "I have already been taught how to please a man – I am no child!"

The eldest of the women smirked and pointed between Halima's legs. "Your little kitten would be split in two by one of our men, outlander. Listen, and maybe you'll live through your wedding night."

Halima's instruction in the laws and rituals of the

Abaka was the responsibility of the *oba panin*, the senior woman of the royal lineage. This was Shomari's grandmother, a stately, white-haired woman with a curiously unlined face.

Halima also learned of the system by which the Abaka were governed. The kingdom was divided into a dozen wards, each of which was occupied by members of a different lineage group, whose members shared a common ancestor. Each ward had its own shrine and *obot kepun*, a priest. The male head of each clan, the *abusa panin*, was responsible for the welfare of the group and for settling family disputes. He also held a stool in the Council of Elders.

This august body met regularly, to advise the king on important matters such as when to wage war and when to forge agreements with neighbors. Anyone in the kingdom who felt their own clan leader had treated them unfairly could ask for a hearing before the Council of Elders. It was the court of final appeal for all family disputes.

With a unanimous vote, it had the power to remove an unjust clan leader – or even a tyrannical king.

The Council of Elders was tremendously powerful. The only greater body still was a Council of Councils, made up of the leaders of each of the kingdoms spread out across the mountain. But this great body was convened only in times of tremendous crisis, perhaps twice in a century.

The training of Halima was complete after one month, and the day came for her initiation into the Abaka in an ancient ceremony that went back to the dawn of time, when men still feared thunder and dark.

The women took from Halima all her garments and possessions, all that she owned – even the sea turtle pendant she reluctantly surrendered to them.

When she was naked as the morning she was born, they shaved her long and delicate braids, till her head was shiny and smooth, and sheared away the kinky triangle of hair between her thighs.

Halima shivered; it was as though they were preparing her for burial. Ominously, the women coated her from head to foot with white clay, the color of death. They painted her body with strange, spiraling symbols, a circle around her navel and a red dot on her forehead, the symbol of the third eye.

She was carried to the Great Hall. The room was full of choking smoke from the roaring fire in the middle of the hall, amid the stools of the ancestors. Halima was made to squat before the fire and watch as, one by one, each of her possessions was tossed in and ravaged by the fire. A slow, mournful drum beat and voices sang out of the smoky darkness.

The chief *mugwe*, the blessing giver, pranced forward and stood above her, wearing a fearsome, skull-like mask from which vulture feathers sprang in all directions. He danced around her, swinging a sword over her head, taunting her to flinch. The sword swooped so close that Halima felt the cool breeze on her bare scalp, but she did not budge.

The priest touched the point of the blade against her breast, and then lunged forward as if to plunge the blade in – but still she did not flinch.

Finally the *mugwe* dropped the blade. He raised his arms aloft and shouted, "Who invites this woman onto our soil?"

"I do," a voice rang out from the swirling smoke.

"Come forward then," shouted the *mugwe*.

Rashida emerged from the smoke, dressed only in a crimson loincloth. In her hand, she carried a huge ceremonial goblet fashioned from a human skull. She knelt facing Halima and passed her the cup.

Halima brought the goblet to her lips. The frothing black liquid bubbled and churned, and foul, yellow fumes rose from it. If any liquid ever looked and smelled like poison, then this was it. She hesitated and looked into Rashida's steely eyes.

"Drink it," Rashida whispered gently. Halima grimaced, and took a gulp of the liquid. It raked down her throat like a spoonfull of nails. She gasped, tried to scream, and keeled over, as everything vanished in a cloudy purple haze.

For a few moments, nothing. Then Halima was racing through the air, seeing nothing but blue sky above her. Six strong men ran carrying her. A funeral dirge was playing and the women wailed.

"The Outlander is dead.
Let us all weep for her,
Taken before her time."

But I'm not dead! Halima thought, struggling to move. She found she was frozen stiff as a mummy. She tried to open her mouth and scream, but no sound came forth. *Am I dead in truth?* Halima thought in horror. Flower petals fluttered onto her bare body as children skipped along, throwing lilies on her.

Shomari, where are you? Rescue me! she thought. She saw her friends, Tumpe and the other serving women, swaying in grief and singing. And yes, there was Shomari, weeping with the others, and beating his chest dramatically as her body passed.

"No! No! No!" Halima tried to scream.

Halima felt herself being lowered. She saw the gray walls of a cave-like hole surround her as she descended. She made one last effort and she saw stone being rolled over the grave, extinguishing the sunlight. She heard herself cry, "I am alive!" But incredibly, no one paid any attention. The stone covered her, and she was in absolute darkness.

I must be dead. I must be dead and buried, Halima thought in terror. She lay still, feeling sweat gushing from her pores. Her heart pumped in terror, and she felt her bladder let loose.

Then she understood.

I am alive. I am alive, and this is my initiation. She lay in the pitch black, reason slowly overcoming her fear. *They gave me a drug that gives me all semblance of death, but I am alive!*

She lay in the dank hole, a strange calm coming over her. The silence and perfect blackness were somehow soothing. After an hour or so, Halima found herself able to blink, then felt a tingling in her fingers and toes as life returned to her body. She drew in a deep breath, and found that air was seeping into the hole from cracks around the edge of the cover stone.

They will come for me, Halima told herself. She waited patiently, lying on her back, staring up at nothing. Interminably the hours passed, with no sight and no sound.

Soon, in the black, her imagination began to play tricks. Strange images danced before her blind eyes. She saw the past: her mother, Neema, Madongo... She saw Shomari, laughing. She imagined him on top of her in a sweaty embrace, thrusting into her and telling her he loved her... She saw a rush of trees, as if she were flying high among the branches... She looked down on a giant ape woman, covered with hair, carrying a baby on her back, wading through a primordial lake... Now she herself was the giant woman and she was on her back, her belly before her, swollen with child... She was sweating, heaving, ready to give birth.

The boulder was pulled away, and a blinding white light poured into the hole. Outside, she heard the triumphant blare of horns and crash of cymbals. Strong arms reached in and hauled her out of the hole. They propped her up, and she stood on wobbly legs, as weak as a newborn's. Her eyes, burned by the light, were shut tight, but she heard the chanting of pride and joy, and the stamping of feet as hundreds of people danced around her.

They shouted, "We of the Abaka praise the spirit of the mountain for giving us this beautiful girl child!"

Halima felt jug after jug full of hot water pouring over, washing the stinking white muck from her. She blinked through the water, and saw the smiling faces of Rashida and the other wives of Shomari, and all the people of the city. Old Watende himself, head of the Council of Elders, grinned at her and gave her a welcoming hug, as did each of the crowd in turn.

So it was that Halima came to be initiated into the Abaka. It was the happiest day of her life; she had never felt such a rush of complete acceptance. More happiness awaited her, for now she could be married to Shomari, whom she loved deeply.

Halima's happiness, though, would be tainted with pain if she knew of events taking place miles away in her homeland, Kali.

Four months earlier, Halima's father, Babatunde the Good, had gone to join his ancestors. Some say that he died of old age; others whispered that an assassin had used poison to take his life. Before the ashes of his funeral pyre were cold, the ruler of the People of the Snake, King Olugbodi, and his troops marched into Kali.

For deceitful King Olugbodi had told the world that he had married Princess Halima, and that she had died in an attack by the Zimbai. He claimed that the throne of Kali was rightfully his by inheritance, and no one had the strength to challenge his claim. So now it was King Olugbodi who sat on the ancient throne of Kali. With the counsel of Masomakali, his cunning slave general, he was slowly but surely building an empire of unmatched greatness.

All this Halima would learn only much later; for now, she enjoyed the bliss of ignorance.

CHAPTER 7

MARRIAGE

As news of the impending marriage of King Shomari traveled by drum throughout the mountain country, guests from each of the smaller mountain kingdoms brought all manner of gifts: incense, spices, foods of all types and young, healthy rams.

A new house was built for Halima. As the tenth wife, hers was the smallest and farthest from the king's house, but when Halima saw it, she was overjoyed.

A special hut was also erected in the king's compound. This was the wedding night shack for Shomari and his new bride. It was a tiny bamboo shelter with a thatched roof and straw-covered floor. It was stocked with food and carved mahogany figures of full-bellied women and long-shafted men – powerful fertility symbols. The couple was to spend a solid week in the little hot house, never leaving it.

The morning she was to be married, serving women spent hours bathing Halima, scrubbing every nook and cranny of her body. They massaged sweet, dark oils into her black flesh; scented her skin with intoxicating perfumes that would drive any man insane with passion; and plied her with herbs and aphrodisiacs.

The hour for the ceremony finally arrived. Soft chanting filled the night air under the blue moonlight where

Halima knelt inside a ring of fire dressed in a long white robe, her head haloed by a garland of flowers.

Around her, a circle of young men strutted to the beat of the drum, thrusting their spears in the air and letting out manly bellows. Between their muscular legs, Halima could see an outer circle of women, dancing in the opposite direction. All the dancers wore masks, but Halima could recognize many people just from the shape of their bodies and their movements. She recognized Hasani, son of Shomari, among the male dancers, and saw all the king's wives dancing among the women.

The drumbeat quickened and Shomari approached the circle. His eyes were covered with a black cloth, and he wore only a headdress of bright feathers and a loincloth that contained his manhood like a sheathe. In his hand, he carried a ceremonial rattle which he shook as he staggered blindly forward.

The female dancers pranced around the blindfolded Shomari, beckoning him to stay and not press on to the center where Halima knelt. One at a time, each of them shimmied up and gyrated against him lasciviously.

The crowd whooped and barked in excitement – but Shomari was not swayed. He shook his rattle at each woman in turn, chasing them away.

The last of the masked women, the tallest and most beautiful, danced furiously about him, like a moth batting around a lantern. Halima recognized that this was Rashida. She stood nose to nose with him, grinding her pelvis against him, her hips whipping from side to side. It looked like he would never break away from her.

Halima frowned. *I know this is part of the ritual, but enough is enough!* she thought.

But again Shomari shook the rattle, and the masked dancer slunk away.

Shomari moved forward toward her, broad shoulders swaying confidently as if guided by an inner eye. Now it was the young warriors who blocked him by raising their spears in mock attack.

Though blindfolded, Shomari seemed to sense each lunge before it came. Each time he caught the spear and used it to lift the warrior up and hurl him out of the way. The last to block him was Hasani, who stood his ground the longest. But finally, Shomari uprooted him like a young sapling and flung him aside. When the last of the warriors was dispatched, a loud cry of approval went up from the crowd.

Only now did Shomari appear to be confused, staggering forward, arms outstretched, as if he had no idea where Halima knelt. Halima knew this was her cue to stand up. She cried, "Here I am. This is your love, Halima. This way, Shomari, King of the Abaka."

Voices chimed in from all around, imitating her with eerie precision. Halima continued to call out, but her tiny voice was lost in the cacophony of mimics. She stamped her foot impatiently, again feeling that enough was enough.

Something she could not explain seized her, a savage impulse. She began to dance in place, hips and shoulders shaking, as if that could somehow lure him to her. And indeed, as if sensing her now, Shomari turned in her direction and bounded forward, leaping over the flames and into the ring next to her. He ripped the mask from his eyes, and stood panting heavily, wearing a broad smile.

A cheer went up from the crowd, which died down as old Watende, head of the Council of Elders, stepped forward and addressed the couple. They stood, clutching hands in the circle of fire.

Said the chief elder to Shomari, "What is your name?"

Shomari cried over the crackling flames, "Shomari, son of Simba the Strong."

"And what is your pledge?"

Roared Shomari, "Before the people and my ancestors, before the Great God and the spirits of the mountain, I take this woman as my wife and pledge to protect her with my life."

Watende now turned to Halima. "What is your name?"

"Halima, daughter of Babatunde the Good."

"And what is your pledge?"

"I take this man as my husband, and swear to love him alone, to bear his children and to protect them as long as blood runs in my veins."

The crowd whooped and stamped their feet in approval. Halima and her husband, hand in hand, leaped over the fire. Sweeping her up in his arms and nestling her to his broad chest, Shomari raced through the crowd to their wedding hut.

Now they stood alone in the hut, a bamboo shell through which shafts of moonlight poked through. Outside, the chanting and the drumbeat continued. They stood facing each other, panting.

Shomari grinned. Halima giggled nervously. "You were so sure," she marveled. "I was shaking in front of all those people."

"After nine marriages it becomes easier," Shomari joked. Halima laughed uneasily. She wished she could calm down. Her heart thumped louder than the drum.

"You are more beautiful than ever tonight, Halima," murmured Shomari. His nostrils suddenly flared wide, as if taking in her fragrant flesh.

He moved forward. Halima found herself beginning to tremble and stopped him with a palm on his sweaty chest. Shomari looked at her with concern. She felt so embarrassed, but she could not help herself – her knees were literally beginning to knock together.

"Forgive me," she said.

"Forgive what?"

"I'm so frightened," she admitted.

"Of me?" Shomari asked gently. His voice was so tender, he made the thought of being afraid of him sound ridiculous. But it was true; she was afraid.

Stammering, she tried to explain. "My lord, I am a good girl. I want to please you so much, but… I'm afraid that I am not passionate enough to satisfy you." She bowed her head in shame. Almost in tears, she felt like running home, back to her room in the servants' quarters.

Shomari tilted her chin up with a finger. She was surprised to see he still wore his easy smile. He took her hand and kissed it.

"Wife," he said in a deep, rich, bass voice that seemed to say I will protect you, I will defend you, I will cherish you forever.

Her fear drained away.

Shomari stepped backward and unfastened his loincloth, and let it slip away, so that he stood naked before her. She gave a little gasp at the sight of his purple-black *foto,* which was already beginning to rear.

Shomari's big hands settled on her shoulders and pulled off her white robe, then he gently unlaced her loincloth so that it scuttled to her ankles. They faced each other stark naked. The drum pounded away in the distance, a slow, sensuous rhythm.

Halima shivered and began to feel sweat trickling down her spine. The eyes of Shomari swept over Halima's bare body. They glistened like a cat's in the dark, and he flashed a toothy smile full of a lion's savage hunger. He took her full breasts in each hand, as if weighing two melons at the market. He began to stroke her nipples with his thumbs until they tingled deliciously and stood up, erect and hard as pebbles.

Halima threw back her head, and her hips began to sway from side to side, as if they had a will of their own.

Outside, the drums beat louder.

Shomari drew Halima to him and embraced her, her pillowy breasts crushing up against his iron-hard chest. His broad hands roamed over her bare back and then gripped her buttocks, kneading them apart. He kissed her, just as he had on the mountaintop, deeply and passionately, his tongue snaking down her throat. She could feel blood rushing to her loins, leaving her dizzy. Her own hands slid around his waist and raked into his back.

Soon she felt his fingers creep between her legs, invading her womanly part. "Oooh!" she cried out, and flashed him a look like a startled hare. Shomari grinned and continued to touch her there until she was sopping wet.

Now he rolled down slowly on his back, took her by her narrow waist and gently drew her over him. Halima held her breath in anticipation – as the king lowered her slowly down on his upright member.

Halima threw back her head and let out a scream that split the night, so shrill and loud it nearly shattered her own eardrums. There was such a pain!

Yet with that pain there was a scintilla of pleasure. As she slowly sank down, the pleasure grew stronger and stronger, overwhelming the pain. Soon he was crowded into her, filling her up completely.

Shomari held her waist and looked up at her with a confident smile. Then, to the rhythm of the drum, he began to arch upward and gently stroke her from below.

She heard herself letting out a stream of vile curses she had never before uttered – followed by sighs of delight. Her husband rose up into her to the relentless beat of the drum, thrusting deep into her with sure, steady strokes. Halima had never imagined there could be such intense pleasure.

"Yes, Shomari," she gasped.

She shut her eyes and rode the giant, rolling her hips around and around to the drumbeat. Buckets of sweat were pouring off her and she was hot as an oven all over.

Halima rocked on the black pillar wantonly, moving her hips up and down, impaling herself on it, her fingernails ripping into his chest every time his manhood drove into her. She felt drool running down her lips and wiped it away with the back of her hand.

Shomari reached up and affectionately touched her cheek – then he began to quicken his pace. Halima's jaw fell open wide and pleasure suddenly shook her body with the ferocity of an earthquake.

Her husband's brow furrowed as if he were in deep concentration, and rivers of sweat ran down his forehead. Grunting and mumbling incoherently, he plunged into her again and again, each stroke sending a new quiver through her.

The king somehow scrambled to his feet and carrying her easily, he continued to plow into her. She wrapped her arms around his neck, her legs around his waist, and she held on for dear life.

Halima found herself kissing his neck, biting at him, weeping. "Shomari, Shomari, Shomari," she moaned. He stomped around the hut, carried her in a bear hug, as she clawed at his back, flaying him with her nails and sinking her teeth into his massive shoulders.

The drumbeat grew faster and more furious. Halima was all uncontrolled heat now, an unreasoning animal.

She leaned in and whispered in his ear, "Take me from behind now, as the lion of the jungle takes his mate!"

She climbed down off him onto her hands and knees and arched her back in invitation. Shomari eagerly knelt behind her, his throbbing member whacking impatiently against her upraised bottom.

Halima reached hungrily back and grabbed hold of him – though she could barely wrap her hand even halfway around his manhood – then guided him into her.

This time he slid into her straight to the hilt, so that the hair of their loins meshed together like fishing nets entangling. Halima groaned in pleasure and backed onto him, rotating her buttocks in a slow, eager wind. The drums were wildly chaotic now, louder and insistent

Shomari's strong hands gripped her shoulders and he

burst into a series of jack-rabbity strokes, his seed sack smacking against her with each thrust. Ecstasy rocked Halima's entire body in tidal wave after tidal wave. She became dizzy – and everything dissolved into a stormy sea of pleasure.

Shomari worked her shuddering body for a solid hour, insatiably. Finally, she heard him let out a roar of delight. His whole body stiffened spasmodically and she felt his seed fill her.

Gasping, whimpering, she called out his name just once more… and then passed out!

Halima awoke on Shomari's chest, smelling his manly sweat. The scent was that of a predator's den. He gave a slow, powerful lion yawn and smiled lazily at her. Memories of the night before brought blood rushing to her cheeks.

"Good morning, wife," Shomari said.

"Good morning, husband," she said.

"Did I please you, Halima?"

"Oh yes, my husband and my king. Forgive me for being so timid."

Shomari chuckled. "I was more timid than you, little one."

"You, Shomari?"

"I wanted so much to make my young wife happy." He kissed her tenderly on the neck. Halima felt a rush of new passion.

She suggested shyly, "Again?"

Shomari raised his eyebrows. "You must want to make yourself a widow," he laughed heartily.

The scent of him, the memories of the night before were exciting her beyond all measure. She smiled and groped between his legs for that which had given her so much pleasure. It began to uncoil in her hand like a hungry boa constrictor.

But at that moment there came a high, urgent horn. Faster than eyes could see or words describe, Shomari was on his feet.

"What is that, husband?" Halima asked.

"It is the alarm," Shomari told her. "Stay here."

He drew on his loincloth and darted from the hut. Halima threw on her robe and hurried after him. *Wait here indeed!*

In the middle of the compound, a small crowd clustered around a wounded man who lay dying, his head in Tumpe's lap. A hole gaped in his chest and a steady river of blood poured from it.

The people of the mountain city surrounded him. Hasani knelt beside the man, his ear to his bloodstained lips. He listened to the man's choking whispers and interpreted them for his father Shomari, and the gathering crowd of servants and warriors.

"He is of the people of the lower mountain. He says his village was destroyed, burned to the ground… Many men killed, many women taken," Hasani said.

The crowd mumbled in dismay.

"How many in the attacking force?" Shomari demanded. The dying messenger whispered into Hasani's ear.

Grimly, the boy repeated what the runner had said: "About 800, father." There was a collective gasp from the crowd.

Shomari bit his lip. "Are they advancing up the mountain?"

"No, Father. He says the raiders are in retreat, returning from whence they came."

"What army?"

Hasani listened to the runner's answer, then told his father, "He says there were three flags on one standard. There was the eagle, the symbol of the Zimbai. Above that the python, the symbol of the People of the Snake. And yet above that was the sea turtle, the symbol the ruling clan of Kali."

At the mention of Kali, some eyes turned to Halima, who stood listening to all this with dismay. Shomari stepped over, blocking her from view.

One citizen cried out, "Is it possible, King Shomari? All three, so long enemies, aligned against us? We will surely be vanquished."

There were fearful mumblings of agreement in the crowd. Shomari silenced them with one raised hand. His calm voice quieted their terror, like water dousing flames.

"None of them know the secret pass to the upper reaches of the mountain. We are safe here – but we must protect our sister kingdoms and avenge the blood already spilled."

He fired off orders, left and right: "Abasi, send word by drum to all chieftains of the mountain, and warn them of the danger. And to those too far to speak with by drums, send our youngest, fastest runners. Tell them each must send a war leader here. We must hold a Council of Councils."

The warrior he spoke to was gone in a flash.

"And you, Hasani, climb to the lower peak and look out to the low hills, and find where this enemy is."

Hasani nodded and turned, and Shomari caught him by the shoulder with a firm hand. "And Hasani, do not try to take on the whole of the enemy by yourself – save some glory for the rest of us."

The crowd laughed nervously. The king's young son

nodded sheepishly, and raced off, quick as a gazelle.

Shomari turned to the remaining warriors. "Men of the Abaka, make peace with your ancestors and say gentle partings with your wives. Prepare your arms, for this very day we will go into battle and overtake this raiding party and destroy them.

"I swear to you we will avenge the blood of the Abaka. We cannot let this atrocity go unpunished. Sound the horn of war!"

Men scattered in all directions.

Shomari turned and saw Halima behind him. He caught her in his arms. She thought he'd forgotten all about her. Grimly, he told her. "My beautiful young wife, I'm sorry. Your honeymoon will not be long or bright."

Around them, warriors collected swords and shields, and ran back and forth like frenzied insects.

Halima felt tears welling in her eyes, but held them bravely back. She threw her arms around Shomari.

"Please, my husband, be careful," she pleaded. He flashed that confident, kingly smile and stroked her still-bare scalp.

"It will take more than an earthly army to keep me from returning to your side," he declared.

Before the sun reached its zenith that day, the army of Shomari marched through the city gates, shaking their spears and chanting a song of anger:

"We are the sons of the mountain.
When you tread on the feet of
Our mother we will kick back.
We are the sons of the mountain
When you spill the blood
Of our cousins, we will avenge."

CHAPTER 8

WAR

After scouts reported with absolute certainty that the attacking army had long since retreated down the mountain, Rashida announced that she would take a party with food and medicine down to give succor to the survivors. Halima, anxious to help, volunteered to accompany her.

Together they crossed the great rope bridge and headed down toward the village. They were followed by a dozen donkeys loaded with provisions, led by boys too young for war.

They passed through the hidden pass, a maze of narrow, twisting passages betwixt granite boulders. Halima had been blindfolded when the hunters had brought her this way before. Now she could see why it was kept secret. To those who did not know the way, it presented an impenetrable barrier to the upper reaches of the mountain.

Descending the mountain was far quicker than climbing it. Soon they reached the outskirts of the village, which was hidden among a cluster of giant trees.

Long before they arrived in the village, they saw vultures circling about it. They heard the wailing of women, singing of anger and grief. The smell came next: the unmistakable stench of blood.

They rode solemnly into the village, Halima's donkey a few paces behind the queen's. Her eyes widened as she saw the desolation. Houses had been toppled, roofs burned, nothing intact.

All the young men had been butchered, all the young women in the village taken captive and the cattle stolen. The only ones left were the elders and a few squalling children. Somehow the survivors had managed to drag the bodies of the slain men and lay them in one neat line. Fifty or sixty of them lay side by side, like sleeping brothers. Halima heard an evil squawk above her and saw a vulture descend to peck at a corpse. One of the old, bent men shuffled forward and shooed it angrily away.

Rashida whispered to Halima, "Wait here. I must find the head woman of the village." Halima nodded and remained on her donkey, which shifted restlessly from foot to foot.

The old giantesses knelt in a circle beside the corpses, swaying together like mournful elephants. They wailed:

"We will never see our daughters again,
"The children that we carried in our wombs.
"We will never see our husbands again.
"We will die alone."

Halima shivered, sharing their pain. *Soon I might be a widow,* she thought grimly. She climbed off her donkey, went over to one of the bearer boys, and collected a basket full of fresh melons. She walked down the line, giving nourishment to any of the women who would take it.

One wailing giantess, who was about Halima's height even while kneeling, turned. Her red, teary eyes bugged out of her head, giving her a look of madness. The bug-eyed woman grabbed Halima by the wrist.

"I know who you are. You are the wife of King Shomari. I was at your wedding feast."

Halima nodded uncertainly, not relishing the touch of the woman's talons.

The woman called to the others, "Look who is here! The princess from Kali – here to mock us!" She knocked the basket of fruit from Halima's hand and the melons rolled in all directions. The bug-eyed woman stood up and loomed over Halima menacingly.

"Do you know it is your people who have murdered our men and stolen our children? Look at their corpses, already rotting."

Other women stood up and picked up the cry. "Go back to your pretty palace in Kali! "

"Be gone, strumpet!"

Halima looked down at the kneeling women help-lessly.

"Have you nothing to say?" the bug-eyed woman demanded. Halima stared at the woman's froglike eyes, unable to muster a reply.

"I am sorry – truly," she said finally.

The bug-eyed woman gave a choked laugh. "Sorry she is! The Kalian should die!"

Pieces of half-eaten melon sailed through the air and splattered across Halima's robe. Halima tore herself out of the bug-eyed woman's grip and stood back in anger.

"Bitch!" an anguished voice cried. Halima saw a rock the size of a fist hurtling toward her eyes. She jerked her head out of the way, but the stone grazed her cheek. She felt blood running like teardrops from the wound. The women began scrambling on the ground, looking for more stones.

They cursed her: "Outlander!" "Devil!"

Halima turned to run, crouching low and shielding her breasts. She sprinted a few yards, then smashed into a towering form. The vengeful harpies instantly ceased their cries for blood.

Halima looked up to see Rashida facing the women down. Taller than any of them, she stood with her hands on her hips, nostrils flaring. Halima hugged her co-wife tightly, burying her face into her bosom.

The first wife raised her cloak, shielding the girl from view. With the other hand, she pointed an accusatory finger.

Hotly, Rashida called to the women, "What is this madness? Are you women of the mountain or are you beasts of the jungle? Is this how you honor your dead – with shameful violence? If your grief is so great, then cast yourself in a funeral pyre and burn with your husbands. But do not seek to sacrifice a child who never harmed you."

Shamefacedly, the women dropped the stones.

Rashida smiled coldly. Then, with iron in her voice, she commanded, "Now kneel before the wives of King Shomari."

The proud women stood facing her sourly.

Rashida's voice grew more strident. "Kneel, I say! We are on an errand of mercy – but if you defy us, I swear to you that our husband's army will return and finish the havoc the enemy has wrought here!"

One by one, the women, shoulders slumping, sank to their knees, until even the bug-eyed woman knelt before them, head bowed in submission.

Said Rashida, "Go then, and bury your dead, and answer your hurt with prayer, as is the way of the Abaka."

On the ride back to the city, they rode together on Rashida's horse, Halima clinging to her, unable to unclench her fingers from her cloak. In her ears still rang the cruel names the hill people called her. She still stung from their blows, and worse, their searing hatred. Rashida rode proudly erect, as if completely unaware of the shivering girl who sat in front of her, nestled in her bosom.

When they were safely inside the compound, in the

first wife's house, Halima took the other woman's hands and knelt before her.

Rashida protested, "You don't need to kneel before me – you are a free woman."

"I kneel out of respect for you. You are as brave as any warrior. You saved my life."

Rashida shrugged uncomfortably. "You saved the life of our son. I owed you a life. Consider it a debt paid."

Halima bowed her head. "My mother is gone. May I call you Mother now, as the other wives do?"

Rashida looked down at the kneeling girl, her sternness melting. She reached out, hesitantly, and touched Halima's bald head. She was about to speak when Kizza ran in.

"The men are returning," the bucktoothed servant announced with excitement.

Like a tidal wave, an army of warriors of the Abaka marched toward the city gates, waving their spears above their heads and singing of their victory. Women converged on them, each looking for her son or her husband.

Shomari led the march, with his eldest son Hasani by his side. His robes were drenched in the blood of the enemy, but he walked unscathed.

Hasani puffed up his bare chest and waved his still-dripping sword through the air. "How many men did I strike down, Father? Was it twenty – or more than that?"

Shomari looked at him sternly. "Do not count fallen men as if they were sheep we have slaughtered."

Hasani bowed his head in shame.

"This is a game you will quickly grow tired of, my son," Shomari told him.

The king saw his wives waiting for him at the city gate. Before he greeted his first wife or any of the others, he embraced Halima.

"I am not accustomed to this kind of war," he told her. "We always battled for a few head of cattle and we tried to harm as few people as possible. Not this... carnage!"

"Yes, you told me," Halima said. He seemed almost to be weeping. Had they not *won* the battle? All the other men were cheering and singing, like any other army she'd ever seen return in victory. Then it dawned on her that something was missing.

"Where are your prisoners?" she asked.

Shomari shook his head. "We took no prisoners; we let none escape. They were testing our strength. We must let the enemy think the party they sent disappeared from the face of the earth."

Shomari reached into his pouch, and pulled out a sea turtle medallion, the symbol of the royal clan of Kali. It was identical to the one she once wore. He handed it to her solemnly.

"I'm sorry. I know this man must have been your kin."

Halima grasped the medallion numbly. *Men and their horrible wars*, she thought bitterly. Then she had a flash of insight.

"Shomari, let me go to Kali, the land of my father. This bloodshed – it is mad. Our people are not warlike folk. It must all be a mistake, a misunderstanding."

Shomari shook his head. "It is no misunderstanding, little one. When we engaged the enemy on the battlefield, their war leader, who wore that symbol, told me the King of Kali himself had sent them. And that our people, the Abaka, must submit to his rule – or else taste destruction."

Halima shook her head in confusion. She could not imagine her gentle father sending such a cruel message.

"And how did you answer him, husband?"

Shomari pointed to the blood on his robes. "By shedding his blood and all with him."

Halima bowed her head. "Is it over then, husband?"

"No. We have only now touched spears with the enemy. Now the war begins in earnest."

CHAPTER 9

TRIAL AND PUNISHMENT

o it was that the war began between the people of
Abaka, the giants of the mountain, and the
kingdom of Kali.

The Council of Councils resolved that Shomari would
act as the great *ncamba*, the war leader of all the mountain
people. He would be their King of Kings. They knew that
only with his great strength and wisdom could they hope to
prevail against the armies of Kali, the Zimbai and the
People of the Snake united.

Each day, the king rose from the marriage bed and
armored himself. Each day, he went into battle and led the
charge. Each night, he returned to Halima. Bloody
sometimes, wounded sometimes – but always he returned.

Once, three days passed in which the mountain sky
burned with lightning. It rained and thundered furiously,
and ravens cried out omens of death. Still he returned to
take his young bride in his arms.

He quieted her tears with smiling words: "Do you
think anything would stop me from returning to such
beauty? Each time in battle I am surrounded by death, I see

your face, I hear your voice, I smell your flesh, and a lust for life seizes me and gives me strength.

"I will always come for you, Halima. Even from death I will come for you."

Every night when he returned, he made fierce love to her, as if for the last time. Halima reminded him of his duties to his other wives, especially the first, but he was deaf to her words. If this night might be his last on earth, he would spend it with his true heart, Halima.

A few months into the war, Halima was in the compound's grinding house, singing a song of loneliness. She sat with the other wives and serving women, grinding millet. With all the men gone, there was always work to be done. The women now had to tend to the men's fields as well as their own.

Now that she was married, Halima had been given her own field by the king on which to raise yams, banana trees and oil palm. The properties were hers until death and would someday be inherited by her sons.

Because she had no sons of her own to help her tend the field, however, some of the other wives "lent" their boys to help her – those who were too young to go into battle, such as Kokayi, whom she had saved from the river.

She and the other women were laboring side by side when a horn blew, announcing the return of the warriors. Halima ran out with all the women, and looked out over the wall of the compound.

She saw the line of men crossing the bridge, now a

familiar sight. But this time they were singing in low, somber voices, with their heads bowed. Overhead, they carried a white flag – the color of death. Royal blood had been spilled.

With all the wives of Shomari, Halima bounded toward the city gates. Some of them were beginning to wail already and pull out their hair. As they reached the city gates, they could see the grim, stony faces of the approaching warriors.

The young swift warriors who had galloped off with such an eager gait now shuffled, heads bowed and many weeping like girls.

Halima dropped to her knees. "No. My king, my lover, my husband, cannot be dead," she cried.

She saw a corpse being carried, dripping blood, with his strong, familiar features. She stood up, feeling faint, and stumbled toward it.

She saw that it was Shomari, brow furrowed, pain etched in his face, who carried Hasani, the brave Tree Harvester in his arms. He held the boy tenderly, as one might carry an infant. The youth's perfect, sculpted body was marred only by a small crimson badge at his heart where a spear had pierced it.

Shomari's eyes were full of tears as he trudged along blindly, listing to one side as if he were barely able to carry the load. He looked like an old, old man. When he saw Halima, he stopped and met her eyes.

Helplessly, he stood there swaying, and whispered hoarsely, "He was all that was best in me."

Halima started to comfort her husband, when from behind her she heard a high-pitched squawk, like the scream of an eagle struck by an arrow in mid-flight. Rashida, mother to Hasani, elbowed through the crowd and flung herself into the dust.

Shomari knelt down to rest the body of the slain Hasani on the ground before her.

"Don't you let him touch the ground!" Rashida hissed angrily.

Shomari knelt, his son's corpse still in his arms. Halima knelt behind him, and placed her hand on his shoulder. His head drooped on her hand. Halima could feel his tears dripping on her fingers.

Rashida exclaimed, "Old man, you take your son to be butchered and then pleasure yourself with your outlander concubine – who you stole from him!"

Shomari reached for her to quiet her rage. Rashida snapped, "Let your Kalian whore comfort you!"

Shomari sighed, and gently rested the remains of Hasani on the ground before him. He stood up, shaking off his grief like dust, and pulled himself erect.

He commanded Rashida, "Woman, see that the body of my son is bathed and prepared for burial."

He turned to the crowd of gaping onlookers and roared so that all could hear, "My people, grieve for three days – then we return to battle."

After the death of Hasani, Shomari fell into a deep melancholy. Only the sweet songs of Halima could bring a smile to his face. When not battling the enemy he refused to be anywhere but at her side.

One day, as Shomari lay resting in her house and Halima sat beside him singing gently, the head of the Council of Elders visited. Watende was a stooped old man with a beard the color of cotton. Shomari bid him to sit down, and Halima rushed to bring him some food and drink.

After exchanging greetings and eating some millet cakes Halima brought him, Watende told the King the reason for his visit. Halima sat listening quietly, as she had been taught a wife must when her husband discusses matters of importance with an elder.

"Shomari, a case has been brought against you in the Council," Watende said.

"By whom, venerable Watende?"

"By your first wife, Rashida."

"What?!"

"She says you have neglected her. That you have brought gifts as spoils of war only for your youngest and least wife, Halima, and none for them. And that you have refused them your company at night."

Shomari gave a sharp laugh. "Venerable friend of my father, we are in the thick of war. Does the Council have time for this womanish nonsense?"

"It is her right by law, great lion. There has been talk in the Council as well."

"About what, old one?" Shomari laughed bitterly. "Which of his wives the king chooses to sleep with?"

"There are those in the Council who say it is not fitting our king should make love to the daughter of the king of Kali, while Kalians and their allies murder our sons."

Shomari's voice became angry. "Did you not welcome this woman into our kingdom with your own hands? Or is your memory failing you so much that you forget?!"

"It is not I who says these things, son of Simba. But others say the king acts like a lovesick boy, thinking of nothing but this woman while our kingdom faces destruction. There are those who say we will lose this war."

Shomari leapt to his feet, looming over the old man. With a bitter rage Halima had never seen in him before, he growled, "Yes, we will lose this war, I swear it – if our elders spend their hours gossiping like old hags at the marketplace instead of telling us how to defeat the enemy. We will be destroyed like every kingdom – from within."

He clutched the old man by the shoulders in a grip so savage, it looked to Halima as if he were going to break him in half. He glowered into Watende's eyes. Then, he embraced the old man.

"By the name of the Great One, they call us giants – but we are truly small and pitiable as ordinary men."

The trial took place in the Great Hall, which was packed with curious spectators until it reeked of sweat. Rashida's kin, all long-boned and stern folk, sat on one side of the room, ready to give support to her cause. The strong-jawed kin of Shomari sat on the other, glaring at their in-laws icily. Between the two camps were crowded most of the adults in the city.

The elders of the Council sat on stools in a semicircle, with Shomari and Rashida seated facing them.

Halima sat behind the king and queen, along with the other of Shomari's wives. To her dismay, she had learned she would not be allowed to say anything at the proceedings. She would have to remain in frustrated silence while Shomari and Rashida waged verbal warfare.

Watende, as chief elder, first called upon Rashida to speak.

Rashida stood up. She was attired regally in her finest silk dress and she paced as she spoke confidently:

"Venerable Watende, respected members of the Council. Forgive me. I know that our country is at war, and you can little spare time to hear the troubles of one woman and her family. But there is a proverb: 'The ruin of the nation begins in the homes of the people.'

"It is our families, it is our traditions we are warring to protect. We are only our laws – without them we are nothing. We are as air.

"And our traditions say a husband is to love and protect each of his wives, holding none in higher regard than the other – save only his first wife, whom he must hold above the others, that she may guide the others and be a mother to all his family."

An enthusiastic relative from the back interjected, "Yes, speak the truth, sister!"

Halima had to admit that Rashida was riveting to watch as she paced back and forth, tigress-like. Now her voice became more strident:

"But the king, Shomari, who should set an example to all, has given his least and youngest wife a place of special favor. He brings her back gifts, booty from the enemy. Such as this, which was found in her house."

Triumphantly, she held up the sea turtle medallion which Shomari had given Halima. As she displayed the symbol of the enemy for the crowd to see, there was a collective gasp from the people. The point made, she tossed the pendant contemptuously into Halima's lap.

Rashida went on. "In this time of crisis he has not sought our counsel nor our succor, nor has he comforted us in our fears. And in these three months of war, he has not lain with me as a husband, nor with any of his wives, except the Kalian, Halima."

At that there was an explosive outburst of mumbling from the spectators, which Watende quickly silenced.

The queen went on, "I cannot say if my husband has committed these wrongs willfully, or if the outsider has used *uchwari*, witchcraft, to bend him to her. But I have been wronged. That is my complaint." Having spoken,

Rashida sat down.

Halima's heart began to pound as the crowd turned and looked at her fearfully.

"That is why we are failing in this battle when arms have never failed us before," she heard a spectator whisper. "The King of Kali has his daughter working witchcraft to destroy us from within."

Agreed another, "Who knows the secret meaning of the muttering she makes in her alien tongue. She may be cursing our sons to die!"

Watende hushed the wagging tongues and soberly called on Shomari. "Shomari, King of the Abaka, what say you in your defense?"

Shomari rose slowly. He was silent for a moment, then the words, spoken in his rich, mellifluous voice, came pouring out:

"It is true that I love Halima. I love all my wives, as a husband should. Halima I love in a different way, a way that is new to me."

As he spoke, his deep, black eyes met Halima's, and he smiled.

"There is something in her, a wisdom, a goodness, a childish innocence and a freshness of spirit that gives me courage and hope. Without her I could not live or rule."

He turned sternly to Rashida.

"Queen Rashida asks you to protect our traditions. But she herself attacks tradition. She attacks tradition when she calls Halima 'Kalian,' and would make you hate her for it. Yet you all know that through the ancient rites of our grandfathers, Halima has become one of us, an Abaka.

"And she again attacks tradition when she shows jealousy for her co-wife, whom she should love as a daughter. If breaking traditions is the crime, then it is she who is guilty!"

The people mumbled again after hearing Shomari's eloquent words, some in agreement, many others unmoved.

Watende bade Shomari and his wives leave, along with the spectators, while the Council of Elders pondered its decision.

Outside, Shomari, Halima and Rashida stood in a triangle, with the other wives in an awkward huddle nearby. They stood silently under the intense, flooding light of the noon day sun.

Finally, Shomari broke the silence. He stepped forward and clutched Rashida's shoulders.

"Rashida, we have aired our naked feelings before the people. Can we end this shameful spectacle now and go home?"

When Rashida spoke, her voice trembled with emotion. "If once, only once, you looked at me the way you look at her," she said. She stared into the king's eyes beseechingly.

Shomari returned her gaze helplessly, and whispered, "Rashida, I'm sorry, I cannot."

The eyes of the queen narrowed and her features became cold as ice. She turned her back on them, and holding her shoulders with stiff dignity, she marched back toward the hall.

A moment later they were all called back in.

Watende rose and spoke for all the Council. "Shomari, whom men called lion, King of Kings of all the Abaka, son of Simba the Strong, we cannot say your love for young Halima is wrong. There are many tales from our people about this kind of love; love stronger than the normal love a man has for a wife or even his own mother.

"Yes, and in an ordinary man and in an ordinary time this type of love is no evil. But in a king, in a time of crisis, such an all-consuming passion is a dangerous thing.

"The people surrender themselves to your rule because they trust your wisdom, and the lucid vision of your third eye. If we let you rule by impulse and hot blood, forgetting law and tradition, you become not a king but a tyrant.

Shomari, the Council rules against you. You have wronged your first wife."

There were murmurs of approval from the packed hall, especially from Rashida's kinfolk.

The old man turned to Rashida. "Now the question arises, 'What is to be done?' This Council can order many things, but it cannot order your husband to love you, Rashida." He quoted a proverb: "To love someone who does not love you is like shaking a leaf to make the dewdrops fall."

Rashida bowed her head.

"So the Council puts it in your hands, Rashida. You decide what is to be done."

Again the crowd murmured in general agreement with the Solomon-like decision. The elders of the Council exchanged glances of self-congratulation.

But Halima felt only bitterness. This way, the elders managed to restore harmony to the community while ducking all responsibility for what became of her – and putting the entire burden on Rashida. She knew without a doubt, as they did, that the first wife would demand banishment.

Then Rashida stood up, her whole body trembling.

"Say again that the choice is mine," Rashida demanded.

"Indeed, the choice is yours," replied Watende.

Rashida flung out her hand, pointing at Halima.

"Then I choose that with his own hands, King Shomari cut out the heart of Halima, and that he is to throw her body over the great falls."

Halima almost fell out of her seat.

Instantly, there was complete pandemonium in the great hall, as people traded astonished reactions with their neighbors. She overheard snatches of arguments and commentary:

"Yes, when a vine encircles your house, it's time to cut

it down!" one old crone said to another.

The elders looked at each other in dismay.

Shomari was on his feet, objecting. "Watende, by the spirit of my father, who called you friend, stop this!" he roared above the crowd.

Again, Watende silenced the crowd. He called to the queen, "Rashida, daughter of the Abaka. I've known you since you were a child. You are not so cruel as to command the murder of an innocent, I know you are not. I ask you as High Elder of the Council to think again about what you have said, and ask whether it will truly bring you joy."

"You have promised me what you have promised me," Rashida intoned stubbornly. The old man sighed.

Shomari cried, "This is madness!"

Watende turned to Shomari.

Sternly he told him, "Shomari, we of the Council have ruled in favor of your first wife. Even a king must obey the law, and you have heard what the law demands. Before the sun rises tomorrow, you must do as Rashida said – or you are our king no longer."

Watende turned back to Rashida, who sat stiffly, facing forward, flushed with emotion. He shook his head, and said "I pity you."

Shomari and Halima were in the sacred grove where his ancestors were buried, looking out over the majestic mountainside. Overhead, thick, gray clouds pregnant with rain crawled. Shomari stood brooding, while Halima knelt beside him quietly.

"Without me as their king, our people would be crushed like grass beneath an elephant's heel. I cannot step down," he said grimly. "Reason and law are both against you. All that weighs for you is my love."

"I trust you to do what is right, husband," she replied.

Shomari lifted her to her feet, and looked her in the eyes. "Your soft words cut me like a knife," he said.

Halima pushed away. Angrily, nostrils twitching, she told him, "I am a princess of Kali, Shomari. I will not beg for mercy. And you are my husband, sworn to protect me forever. I will not plead with you to spare my life!"

Shomari winced at her flash of anger. She realized she had never been angry with him before.

He bowed his head and thought for a moment, then he looked up and pointed to the mountain peak. "I will go to the mountaintop and speak to the great seer, Olushegun. I shall return before nightfall."

He bent and kissed her on the cheek, tenderly. He turned and went off.

No ordinary man today could scale that terrible mountain face of ancient, jagged, crumbling stone. But Shomari, whose limbs were strong as iron, crept up the nooks and crevices of the mountain as easily as Anansi the spider might race up a wall.

Halima waited in her little house, feeling awfully helpless.

I could run away, she thought, *and return to my people – but even if I escape, how would I make it through the forest? And could I truly bear to live without Shomari? No, better to stay and face him. For if he truly loves me, he cannot harm me.*

The storm clouds broke and heavy raindrops began to pound on the roof of Halima's house.

A clap of thunder and a flash of forked lightning

announced Shomari's return. His garments were drenched; water poured down his face.

Halima helped him off with his soaking clothes, and they sat together on her bed. She saw that his face was drawn and weary.

He told her, "I sat with the great seer, Olushegun, he who sees into the far reaches of the past and the future. I sat with him by the fire, in his cave, and he spoke these words. He said: 'This woman from the sea loves you more than life or truth or family or honor. If she lives, the day will come when, for love of you, she will betray the Abaka and bring destruction upon your people. If she lives, the Abaka will die. If she dies, the Abaka will live.'"

Halima saw that her husband's eyes were full of tears. He embraced her.

That night, Shomari and Halima made violent, furious love. They never slept, but all through the night were locked in a sweaty and animal embrace, clawing each other. His manhood never lost its steel, penetrating again and again, rummaging inside her.

She howled, thrashing under him as wave after wave of drowning passion swept over her. He burrowed deep down inside her and filled her with all that was in him, crying out her name, weeping.

At dawn, Shomari and Halima left her house. The morning birds were just beginning to sing, and a soft orange light conferred a gentle radiance on the city.

Halima decided she had never seen a more beautiful

day. She walked along in the white, pleated dress she had worn at her wedding. She felt strangely serene – although she knew she was being taken into the woods to die.

Shomari marched three paces ahead of her, carrying a long, deadly spear over his shoulder. Its jagged iron tip was nicked from battle, sticking up like the leering head of a viper.

Halima realized that her serenity came from her deep feeling that Shomari could not hurt her. In the belly of her soul, she did not believe he would harm her.

When they were quite deep into the forest, in a little clearing, Shomari turned to her. His face was as gray as a dead man's.

"Turn from me, wife, and kneel," he ordered gently. Halima did as she was told, slowly kneeling in the soft, dewy grass.

"Wife, give me your gown."

Halima obeyed her husband, unfastening her robe and passing it to Shomari. She knelt on the jungle floor, in her loincloth, shielding her bosom. The morning air chilled her naked skin and she began to tremble. She threw back her head and looked up through the trees to the sunshine penetrating the leaves.

Halima thought about how much she loved life. She saw herself playing with her brothers and sisters in the bright, shallow waters of Kali. She remembered Neema, her friend; the first time she met Shomari's eyes. Her eyes began to water.

He could not, she reminded herself. He could not, he would not, harm her. She would believe that, no matter what – even if it was to be her dying thought.

"I know you will not harm me," she said defiantly, proudly holding up her head, as tears began to roll down her cheeks.

He stood behind her grimly now, casting a giant shadow on the forest floor. Halima bowed her head. She saw his shadow bring up the spear above his head for one swift thrust.

Shomari's voice was choked with pain. "Great One in the Sky, spirits of these mountains, forgive me!"

Halima saw the shadow of the spear hurtling down and closed her eyes.

An hour later, Shomari went to the house of his first wife. She was waiting on her bed, looking more beautiful than ever, with her long, black braids painstakingly twisted by her servants. She looked at him diffidently.

Without saying a word, the king flung at her the bloodstained wedding dress of Halima, turned, and stalked out of the room with absolute finality.

At the same time, Halima ran through the woods, the cooling dew of the rain forest cleansing her naked skin. She cast her mind back to the events of that morning,

When Halima had opened her eyes still in this world, she heaved a sigh of relief. Then, hearing a grunt of pain behind her, she whirled to see Shomari standing, holding his thigh in pain. He had sliced open a gash in his own flesh with his spear. Now he quickly wrapped her gown around the wound, allowing the blood to soak freely into it, turning it bright red.

Halima gasped and reached to help, but he held her back. He grinned weakly. Halima stood up and faced him.

"I could not, Halima," Shomari said. "No, even though duty and the will of the Great One demanded it."

Halima smiled. "No complaints here, my lord."

At that moment there was a noise in the bush. Halima turned in alarm – and saw emerge Kokayi, the king's son, whom she had saved from drowning. The boy, who carried a satchel and a bow and quiver, stood panting. He stuck out his skinny bare chest proudly and said, "No one saw me come, Father."

Shomari limped forward and took Halima by the shoulders, and put her cousin's sea turtle pendant about her neck.

"Beautiful Halima, I am returning you to the land of your father. I cannot protect you here. Kokayi will guide you."

Halima grabbed his broad hands. "Come with me, husband!"

He shook his head. "My place is here, defending the kingdom."

Halima looked at him earnestly. "Then...?"

"You must forget these mountains, Halima, and all your life here."

Halima turned away bitterly. "And will you forget me, Shomari, King of the Abaka?"

He stood behind her and gripped her tightly. "I will forget you the day I breathe my last," he whispered.

He tore himself away from her and turned his attention to his son, who had grown a trifle in the past few months and was about as tall as Halima.

"Kokayi, never forget the river. This woman saved your life, and now you must guard hers, even with your own."

The boy – who, Halima knew, up till then had never had a duty more important than tending his father's goats – nodded solemnly.

Shomari said, "This is a man's job, I know, Kokayi. But you alone can I trust in this. Sometimes, in times of war, a boy must fast become a man.

"Travel quickly, through the thickest forest of the mountain, and avoid any people you see. Take Halima to the Winding River. The caravan of the famed merchant Kamau will pass there in three days, and with them she can travel safely to Kali."

He handed the boy his spear. The youngster took it as if it were magical.

"This is the spear of your grandfather Simba, the great warrior-king. Do not dishonor it," Shomari said.

"Yes, Father," the boy replied. The king bent down and kissed him. "Be careful, beloved son."

Shomari turned to Halima. Their eyes met, both full of emotion. He took her in his arms. Halima, fighting tears, whispered, "I will never love another, Shomari."

Hoarsely, he said in her ear, "Someday, I swear I will come for you." He pressed his lips against hers.

Now Halima and Kokayi, both in loincloths, ran through the rainforest on the start of their journey. Lithe and quick, the boy moved through the woods like a small forest goat. But he would never get too far before looking back in concern and waiting for Halima to catch up.

"Hurry, Little Mother, hurry," he would shout. "We must run faster."

Halima followed him. But first, she paused to look over her shoulder at the silver-peaked mountain. With defiance, she declared, "I will return to this place!"

So it was that Halima, wife of Shomari, the King of all the Abaka, was banished from his kingdom and set forth on a journey back to her homeland Kali. She knew not that on the throne now sat a usurper, King Olugbodi, who had at his disposal the great wealth of Kali, the ferocious might of the Zimbai, and the endless cunning of the People of the Snake.

PART TWO

CHAPTER 10

ᛒANIᛋHEᛏ

They ran together through the mountain forest,
Halima and Kokayi, he leading the way and she
a few yards behind.

Running was awkward at first for Halima. Huge, leafy
branches slapped her face, coming from nowhere. Bounding through the steaming jungle until she dripped with
clean sweat felt good, though, for it cleansed her of worries
and regrets. When she ran, she felt like an animal thinking
only of the next meal, the next time to drink, the next
chance to rest.

Still, her legs always tired long before the boy's. She
would see his brown body vanishing out of sight in the
forest up ahead and, out of breath, she would be ready to
scream for him to stop. He would always seem to know
he'd left her behind, and would dart back and very
apologetically guide her to a smooth boulder on which she
could sit.

Kokayi was only ten – five years younger than Halima.
His broad chest was small, but lean and muscular.
Although his gait and bearing were proud, his manner was
shy. He never met Halima's eyes directly, and he always
addressed her, respectfully, as "Little Mother."

At one of their rest stops, Halima sat on a stone,

stretching out her weary legs while the youngster squatted beside her, preparing his small bow and arrows.

"I saw the droppings of a hare. I will try to catch it, so that you have something to eat tonight, Little Mother," the boy informed her. Head bowed, he concentrated as he struggled to fit the notch at the back end of the arrow into the string. He fumbled for a moment, hands shaking, and wiped a dribble of perspiration from his forehead. Halima realized he was quite nervous.

"Kokayi," she called to him. The boy looked up at her, startled into looking her in the eyes. Halima smiled reassuringly.

"Kokayi, you are doing well," she told him. Kokayi looked at her and blushed. He nodded appreciatively and strung the arrow.

That night, full of rabbit stew, they lay under the stars, their loincloth-clad bodies covered by a goatskin blanket. The little boy amused her for a while, playing a sweet tune on his *bumpa*, a small instrument like a clarinet made from millet stalk. After a while, he tired and bid her good night. Halima had time to think.

She lay on her back, gazing up into the star-rich sky, entertained now only by the incessant concert of insects. In the past, the night sky always seemed like a warm, protective blanket. Now, it seemed cold, vast and empty.

Halima felt an unfamiliar loneliness. Shomari had

bored a hole in her, and now he had left her – but the hole still remained. She ached for him. She'd heard of people who had suffered, through battle or accident, the loss of a limb, and yet still they would feel pain in their missing hand or foot long afterward. They would reach for the aching limb again and again and each time be surprised by its absence. This is how much she ached for Shomari.

She knew she would never see him again. But in her mind, so wise and yet in so many ways a child's still, she imagined bright fantasies in which he returned to her: a party of the Abaka appearing at the fire, Shomari in their lead, him telling her that she was welcome among them again. Or Shomari, spear in hand, telling her he had forsaken his throne and was hers forever. She felt Shomari holding her, embracing her, telling her he loved her.

She saw these images with such clarity that as each mirage vanished in turn, yielding to darkness, she wept with loneliness.

"Little Mother," whispered Kokayi. "Are you awake?"

Halima sat up. To her surprise, she saw the small boy was sitting up, also staring at the stars. She thought he had been sleeping, but now she realized he was as restless as she was.

"What is it, Kokayi?"

"Is it true that you know many stories?"

"I know a few."

The lad looked down, and said diffidently, "When I was small, if I was afraid, my mother would tell me stories to put me to sleep." Then he added hastily, "Not that I'm afraid now, but I thought it would help to pass the time."

Halima smiled. Happy to escape her troubled thoughts, she agreed, and ran through all the many fables her family griot had told her, trying to find one that would suit the tastes of the young boy.

"Would you like me to tell you about the master of the caravan we are going to meet?" she asked.

Kokayi nodded eagerly, scooting closer to her.

"Well," Halima began. "Kamau, whose name means 'quiet warrior,' is sung of in many legends. He is a merchant whose caravan has traveled from the deepest lands of the south, and across the deserts of the north. No one knows where he was born. Some say he was the son of a great king, others that he was the bastard child of desert thieves. But the stories all say that he is the bravest of the brave, and the cleverest of men. And on his journeys many times, he has helped people in danger, and he defends the unfortunate."

Kokayi nodded reverently. Halima could see he was enthralled already.

So Halima told him the story of Kamau and the great Jenn:

"The caravan of the great merchant Kamau was crossing the desert, and after a sandstorm, they became lost. They came to a city they had never visited before.

"Kamau told the other merchants of the party, 'Let us enter this city, and see what goods we can trade with the men who dwell there.'

"But the great merchant Kamau did not know that this was the city of the Jenn, the city of magicians and only those versed in sorcery were permitted to enter.

"As they wandered through the marketplace, they saw many strange things for sale: a magic device that told north from south and east from west; a glass through which sand fell, counting off the passing of hours; a metal pipe through which far things seemed near.

"One of the merchants marveled at the strange devices and said, 'What are these wondrous things?'

"The people of the city knew immediately that the men were outsiders, and dragged all the merchants away.

"They were taken before the Great Jenn, the ruler of the city, who told them, 'Do you not know that you are in the city of the Jenn, and no mortal man may enter here, on pain of death? Now you must die and we must eat your souls.'

"Kamau and the other merchants dropped to their knees and pleaded for their lives.

"But the Great Jenn said, 'You must all perish. Ordinary men may not steal the wisdom of the Jenn.'

"That is when wily Kamau stood up and laughed heartily.

"The Great Jenn looked in surprise at the merchant, wondering if he were mad.

" 'What are you laughing at, mortal?' demanded the wife of the Great Jenn, who sat by him on the dais.

" 'Why, laughing at all of you,' said Kamau, pointing at the court of the Great Jenn. 'You Jenn are no wiser than mortal men.'

"The Great Jenn turned purple in rage.

" 'I will prove that what I say is true,' said Kamau. 'Let me tell you a riddle. You in turn tell me one. If you answer correctly, and I answer wrong, you win, and you may eat our souls. But if you answer wrong and I am right, you will give me the greatest treasure of your city.'

"In front of all his court, the Great Jenn could not admit he doubted his own tremendous wisdom, and so he agreed to the challenge.

" 'Very well, first state your riddle,' he roared.

"And Kamau said, 'I can vanquish entire villages without pity, but the humblest woman can master me in her house. I can spread myself from one end of the forest to the other, yet one man can carry me. I breathe and feed, live and die, yet I am not a man, and I am not an animal. Who am I?'

"The Great Jenn heard the riddle and stroked his jaw uncertainly. He said, 'I must have until tomorrow to answer your riddle. Now let me tell you mine: I bear four legs, four arms, four eyes and four ears, and two hearts beat within me. Tomorrow I will roar in pain, yet it will be my happiest day.'

"Kamau thought and thought, but he did not know the answer. And he told the Jenn, 'Tomorrow I will give you my answer.' And so the men were held prisoner overnight in the city.

"All night long, Kamau puzzled over the riddle of the Jenn, but the solution eluded him. So he crept into the bedchamber of the Great Jenn, where the ruler slept with his wife. And in the darkness, the great merchant, who could imitate any voice having heard it but once, spoke in the woman's soft tones. He whispered, 'Husband, I cannot sleep. Please tell me, what is the answer to the riddle you asked the mortal?'

"And eager to sleep, the king of the Jenn replied, 'Foolish wife, do you not know? If I have four legs, four arms, and two hearts beat within me, then I am a pregnant woman. And I will scream tomorrow when I give birth, but it will be my happiest day for I will have a new child.'

" 'Thank you, husband, for now I can rest in peace,' whispered Kamau in a tiny voice.

"Triumphantly, he appeared before the Great Jenn the next day.

"And he told the Great Jenn, 'I know the answer to your riddle. Any fool would know it: a woman full with child.'

"The Great Jenn frowned in anger.

"Kamau told him, 'And you know the answer to mine, King of the Jenn?'

"The Great Jenn, reddening with shame, admitted that he did not know.

"Kamau laughed. 'Why, the answer is simple: fire.'

"Now, having been bested in the battle of wits, the Great Jenn was forced to give Kamau the greatest of his people's treasures. Kamau and his party were taken to the sacred grove of the city, where a great tree grew.

"And from that tree there hung a single fruit.

"Said the Great Jenn, 'This is the Tree of Wisdom. And every thousand years, from it grows one fruit, and in this fruit lies a single seed – the Seed of Hope. And where the seed is planted, a Golden Age will spring up.'

"Kamau took the fruit. And where he planted the seed or if he still carries it no one knows."

When Halima finished her story she looked over at Kokayi and saw that the boy was fast asleep, his head on her shoulder.

Halima sighed. "Perhaps I am not alone after all," she said to herself. "Now I have a little brother." She snuggled up next to the lad and went to sleep.

By the next day, the pair had climbed down through the secret mountain pass and out through the maze of prickly nyika bushes and tall bamboo stalks that concealed its entrance. In a few more hours they were well on their way to the knoll where Shomari had told the boy to wait for the caravan.

They waded through the tall grass of the plain, the white sun beating down on their naked shoulders like a scorching brand. Clouds of flies hung around them. The grass was so hot it smelled like burning straw.

It was the dry season now. It had not rained in many months on the veldt. All that stretched ahead were thin, stunted trees, their branches contorted into grotesque, twisted shapes, and short scruffy bushes with needle-sharp leaves. The landscape was scorched, all vegetation shriveled, the only color a ubiquitous burnt yellow-brown.

Halima trudged, staring down at her toes, as one foot then another trod on the dry soil. She was perspiring so heavily that her whole body was as wet as if she'd been swimming in the ocean. She sniffed her underarm and was appalled by the stink.

Far overhead, a flock of cranes sailed with their long legs outstretched, one after another letting out hoarse bleats. They sounded as thirsty as Halima felt.

Soon her gait slowed into a shuffling stumble and she felt suddenly faint. Her knees buckled and she began to fall. But before she slammed to the ground, she felt Kokayi's strong arms loop around her waist. He lifted her up and pointed ahead to a gnarled old baobab tree.

"There's a water hole, Little Mother," he said. They ambled together toward the centuries-old tree. Then, seeing a waterhole beside it, they ran eagerly to the murky pond beside it.

Halima threw herself to her belly and buried her head in the water. The muddy water was as cool and sweet as banana wine. She lapped up the water into her scorched throat like a jungle cat.

When she was finally satiated, she leaned back against the sloping, muddy bank of the waterhole and sighed with satisfaction. She saw to her alarm that Kokayi was neck deep in the middle of the waterhole. She bolted to her feet, the horrible experience in the river rushing back to mind – the pair swirling toward the waterfall in the raging mountain stream.

"Kokayi!" she screamed.

Kokayi laughed, and bobbed up and down happily in the water.

"Do not fear, Little Mother," he called. "Father taught me how to swim. Look!"

At that, he glided back and forth effortlessly, looking as at ease in the water as a seal. Then he took a deep breath, grabbed his nose, and dove head first, his small bare backside flashing in the air before his legs and feet followed the rest of him underwater.

He disappeared for moment, and Halima found herself holding her breath as she waited for him to resurface.

At last Kokayi came up for air, and spit out a tall geyser of water. He breast-stroked over to the muddy bank. Halima clapped rowdily. "Well done, Kokayi," she called to him. The young boy beamed from ear to ear. He turned and splashed back into the water.

Halima relaxed and sank back against the muddy bank, which felt as soft as her mother's arms. Big, yellow-striped butterflies fluttered gaily about her. For the first time in so long she felt at ease. It was so peaceful now; it was as if she and her make-believe brother were the only people in the world. To the gentle sounds of the boy's paddling about in the water, she closed her eyes and a sweet, dreamless sleep fell over her.

A lion's roar jolted Halima awake. She realized that she was already running, her heart pounding like a sledgehammer. Kokayi was pulling her along by the wrist and they were flying over the ground to the baobab tree. She smelled the hot fetid lion's breath as it bounded behind them.

She smacked into the baobab tree and scrambled frantically for handhold. She felt Kokayi grab her wrist, then he hoisted her up into the lowest branches. She caught one low branch and then another and was soon up in the tree. As the lion roared again, Kokayi scampered like a monkey up the tree after her.

Panting, her lungs burning, Halima looked down to see a tremendous lion hurl itself against the tree, its mouth yawning wide and its jagged teeth gleaming.

Halima shrieked and almost toppled from the tree. Kokayi, his eyes wide with fear, caught her shoulders just in time.

The lion reared up on its hind legs and dug its monstrous claws into the tree. It craned its neck and leered hungrily at them. Halima shrieked again and broke free from the boy. She struggled to her feet and stood tottering on the branch.

"It can climb, it can climb!" she screamed, reaching for a higher branch. The boy pulled her gently down and pointed. "He must be sick or injured. See, he cannot reach us," he said.

Halima squatted back down on the branch, tentatively. Below them, the lion dropped to all fours and snarled in fury.

Halima tried to fight back her fear. She felt the momentary panic retreat, and after about five minutes, her heart settled down and she could breathe again. The boy squatted next to her, shielding his hairless, still uncircumcised *foto* from view. He was still soaking wet and shivering either from cold, or fear – or both.

Below them, the lion paced impatiently around the tree. He indeed limped badly, just as Kokayi had suggested, as if his hind legs had been trampled upon by an elephant.

"Where is your spear?" Halima whispered conspiratorially, as if the beast could understand them.

Kokayi pointed grimly to the waterhole twenty long yards away. Squinting into the bright sun, Halima could see the spear, the bow and arrows neatly laid out on the banks of the waterhole, along with the boy's loincloth. When she turned back to Kokayi, his eyes were full of tears.

"I ran like a coward!" he wept. "I betrayed the name of my father."

Halima sternly took the boy by his narrow shoulders.

"You saved my life, Kokayi. You protected me. That is what your father told you to do."

The boy straightened up a little and wiped away a dribble of snot with the back of his hand. He nodded. Halima peered down through the branches at the giant beast.

"Maybe he'll go away?" she suggested hopefully.

Kokayi shook his head. "Not with an empty belly."

The sky grew dark and the lion lay down, nestled against the base of the tree like a faithful dog. Halima and the boy crouched down together in the baobab. Against the cold night breeze that whistled through the branches, they embraced each other, trembling.

They were crouched in the nook of the big old tree, and fairly safe from tumbling out. But every few minutes Halima would wake with a start, heart pounding, convinced she was falling, and she would clutch the branch above her with a death grip.

The boy would at times cry out and clutch her closer, and she knew he too was in the throes of man's most ancient of nightmares – the falling dream we inherited from our tree-dwelling ancestors.

A cock crowed, announcing the coming of morning. Halima opened her eyes and realized Kokayi was shaking her arm with excitement.

"I don't see him," the little boy whispered.

Halima, aching from a night sleeping in an awkward position, unfurled her twisted limbs. She blinked at the rising orange sun, then leaned over and surveyed the ground. Indeed, the lion was nowhere in sight.

"You see," whispered Kokayi.

Halima scanned the nearby countryside, which was clear and open except for a few scraggly bushes.

"But you said he would not leave," she said warily.

"He must have smelled bigger game," the boy replied.

They agreed that Kokayi would very cautiously climb down and retrieve his weapons.

"Be careful," Halima whispered as he disentangled himself from her.

The boy clambered out of the branches and skidded down the tree trunk. He dropped to the ground and took a few stealthy steps on tiptoe away from the tree. Then, growing more confident, he stuck out his chest and strode toward the waterhole where his weapons lay.

Halima watched him like a mother hen looking out for a chick on its maiden flight. His narrow, bare backside got farther and farther away as he approached the waterhole.

Halima began to breathe easier. It was over at last.

Then, on the right, in the periphery of her vision, a shadow moved. Halima screamed so loud her lungs nearly split apart. The boy turned around and from behind one of the scraggly bushes, the lion leaped. He charged the boy with terrifying bounds.

"Run, Kokayi, run!" Halima shrieked.

Kokayi spun about and raced back toward the tree. The lion veered toward the tree to intercept him.

"Run!" Halima screamed in terror. "Faster, he's catching up."

The boy glanced over his shoulder, only to see the lion just a few feet behind. He stumbled, kicking up dust, then sprinted ahead.

With the lion at his heels, Kokayi sprang for the low branch. He fell a foot short. But Halima caught his hand and hauled him into the tree. Below, the lion leapt, claws bared and outstretched, letting out a terrifying roar. It crashed to earth a few yards away.

"No more of that," Halima scolded, trembling. "We will stay in the tree until he goes away."

They sat on the tree branch until the sun was high in the sky.

The crippled lion lay silently, midway between the tree and the waterhole, sleeping. Occasionally, he lifted his head, craning to look at them on their perch, then relaxed back to sleep – or feign sleep. Twice more the lion pretended to go away, vanishing into the tall grass.

Each time, when they failed to take the bait, the lion trotted back and returned to its place.

Halima's body was boiling hot, sweat streaming off her. Having gone without liquid for a solid day now, she and the boy watched enviously as the lion knelt from time to time beside the waterhole and leisurely lapped up water.

She ran her tongue over her parched lips, recalling how good that water tasted. Beside her, Kokayi eyed the waterhole. He looked as if, maddened by thirst, he might at any moment fling himself down toward it.

And which would be worse indeed, to be swiftly disemboweled by the lion or to die slowly of thirst in this tree and be picked apart by vultures? Above them the winged scavengers were already making slow circles in the sky, patiently awaiting the outcome of the contest.

She looked at the lion and remembered an old fable about the chief's son and a lion. The youth had been set upon by a lion out in the woods. The chief's son had escaped home to his village. But somehow the lion, over miles of hills and rivers, trailed him to his village. House to house, the lion searched for the youth, whose blood it had tasted. And the villagers, who loved the boy, offered the lion the meat of slaughtered goats and rams, and finally their own young children. But the lion only wanted that particular young man. And though every warrior in the village plunged his spear into the lion, it would not die until at last it ate the unfortunate young man.

The story had seemed so grim and melancholy to her, but the royal griot explained it to her and she understood. There is such a thing as fate; one cannot escape one's destiny.

She looked at the boy beside her. He looked as if he might keel out of the tree from dehydration at any moment

I do not accept that it is our destiny to die here, she thought, sticking out her lower lip defiantly.

She took Kokayi by the arm, and though by now her throat was so parched it was painful for her to speak, she called to him.

"Kokayi, the proverb says that for every cage there is a key. We must find that key."

The two stranded travelers thought and schemed and

strategized, and together they came up with a plan: Halima would climb around the back of the tree, take a broken branch and shake it in the lion's face, harassing it, until the lion was fully distracted. In the meantime, Kokayi would climb gingerly down from the tree. Fast as his stiff legs would carry him, he would run and retrieve his weapons, then shoot the lion dead with his bow.

That was the plan.

Kokayi, newly energized now that they had a goal, climbed up into the baobab and found the perfect branch – straight and strong, dry but not brittle. Using all his weight, he managed to snap it off cleanly. Halima watched him skid quickly down to her, like a sailor descending from a crow's nest.

The boy sheared away some of the jutting twigs, fashioning the branch into a small club. He put it in Halima's hands and demonstrated to her just how she must poke the lion's face and taunt the beast, as if this were a task he engaged in every day. Halima smiled to herself, a smile he caught when he looked up. For an instant, self-doubt flitted across his unlined face.

Halima took the boy's narrow shoulders. "Who was your grandfather?" she demanded.

"Simba the Strong," Kokayi said.

"And who is your father?"

"Shomari, whom men call lion," he shouted almost boastfully.

Halima smiled, and the boy returned a fearless grin like his father's.

Halima lay face forward on the huge branch, thighs tightly wrapped around the tree and her ankles locked. She inched forward on the branch, the rough bark scraping her inner thighs.

Below, the lion trotted up to her with interest. Halima swung the stick down.

"Hey! Hey, ugly one! Here, up here!" she shouted in

her now husky, dry voice. "Do you not want to eat me? Are you not hungry?" The lion reared up, snarling, and swiped at the branch, its sharp talons ripping the air with a whooshing sound.

Halima, though out of reach, trembled at nature's raw fury.

Kokayi must now be down from the tree and tiptoeing toward his weapons, she knew. It was even more crucial now that she kept the beast's full attention. She poked at the lion again, aiming the stick at its eyes.

Whoosh!

With one angry swipe, the lion clawed the branch out of Halima's hand. She watched in dismay as the branch twirled through the air like a baton and landed out of sight.

The lion snarled up at Halima, then dropped to all fours. Knowing he couldn't reach her, he gave a roar of frustration and turned away. She knew Kokayi was on the ground somewhere and exposed. As unhesitatingly as if he were her own flesh and blood child, she swung down, grasping the tree branch. She dangled above the lion, now an easier target, and kicked at the beast, continuing to divert its attention.

The lion growled, and rearing up at her, swiped again like a kitten at a ball of yarn.

Halima screamed, twisting her bare legs left and right, out of the way of the curving, dagger-like claws that raked at them through the air. She felt her hands beginning to lose their strength. She could not hold onto the branch much longer.

Then she heard the twang of a bow releasing and the swooping sound of an arrow racing through the air – and then the thump of it striking home. She looked down and saw the lion lurch out of the way, an arrow in its shoulder.

She could hang on no longer. Halima dropped through the air and slammed down hard on her rear end. She sat up, dazed, in swirling red dust. The lion turned toward her, snarling angrily, the stem of the arrow protruding from his shoulder.

She scooted backward in the dirt as the lion bit away the arrow with contempt, then slunk toward her.

Now she saw just how huge the animal really was. Its head looked the size of an elephant's. Halima froze, too terrified to scuttle back another inch. She stared directly into the animal's large hazel eyes as its jaws yawned cavernously open. In a second, she would become a mass of bloody meat.

"Here, you stinking beast!" she heard Kokayi shout. He fired another arrow, striking the lion in the haunch.

The giant beast spun about, snapping at the arrow in fury like a dog bitten by a flea. It spotted Kokayi, and growling in rage, bounded toward the boy, who stood a few yards away, his feet planted wide. The ten-year-old hurriedly strung another arrow. His hands were shaking as if there were an earthquake beneath him. *He'll never make it*, Halima thought.

She covered her mouth and screamed as she saw the lion leap and sail through the air toward the young boy.

Kokayi let loose a third arrow and the lion crashed down, shot between the eyes. The animal moaned and dragged itself along in a semicircle, leaving a bright crimson smear on the ground.

Kokayi snatched up the spear of his grandfather. He rushed over and buried the weapon deep into the lion's back, right between its powerful shoulders. He sank his small, bare foot into the animal's thick tawny fur and wrenched out the gory weapon. Then he hurled the spear again into the writhing beast. He did this three more times, until the predator's death throes began. Then he backed away.

Halima knelt watching. She could not see the boy's face as he backed toward her, but his shoulders were heaving. He stopped and stood stock still, looking on as the lion choked, shuddered, and then died.

Finally, Kokayi turned toward the kneeling young woman and grinned, looking in the bright noon sun everything like his father.

In a hoarse voice that sounded like a man's, he told her, "Little Mother, the waterhole is ours!"

CHAPTER 11

THE
⟨ARAVAN

It was two days later, and Halima and Kokayi crouched on a hill in the tall grass, watching the caravan of the merchant Kamau pass.

The caravan stretched back far into the veldt: great lumbering elephants carrying carriages covered with silk tents, shaggy camels with bright rings in their noses, laden with giant crates, donkeys burdened with calabashes full of water. On horseback, turbaned warriors rode proud black stallions.

The boy's eyes widened with wonder; he had never seen such a grand procession.

Halima whispered to him, "Come, Kokayi, let us go down and speak with them."

He shook his head. "No, Little Mother. My father said I must stand apart and watch with my bow until you wave to me that you are safe. I am not to let the men of the caravan see me lest they take me hostage."

Halima understood. "And here we must part."

She leaned forward and took his shoulders. "If ever I bear a son, I hope he is like you, Kokayi."

The boy bowed, then looked up at her and said,

"Thank you, Little Mother."

Halima smiled and kissed him gently on the lips. It was like biting into a clean, fresh mango. She recalled her husband Shomari weeping bitterly over the death of his eldest son Hasani and proclaiming "He was all that is best in me."

Now she told Kokayi, "When you return to your father, tell him I say, 'All that is best in you still lives.'"

Then she turned and headed down the hill toward the great caravan of the legendary merchant Kamau. Behind her Kokayi crouched in the grass, invisible, pulling an arrow from his quiver.

Halima approached one of the horsemen, who was turbaned, wore long striped robes, and had a fuzzy black beard.

"Sir!" Halima called to him. "Sir!"

The bearded horseman glanced at her and slowed down, but did not entirely stop, forcing Halima to trot alongside of him.

"Sir, I wish to speak to the master of the caravan."

The bearded man frowned down at the loincloth-clad girl, whose bare skin was covered with dust. She was without a single piece of jewelry except for the turtle-shell pendant bearing the symbol of her clan. She knew she looked like the most pitiful peasant.

"What business have you with our captain?" he replied gruffly.

"I am Halima, Princess of Kali. I wish passage with your caravan to my home country," she told him breathlessly, still running to keep up with him.

The horseman raised his eyebrows skeptically. Halima thought for moment he was going to spur his mount and gallop away. But instead, without a further word, he reached down, looped his arm around her waist and scooped her up onto the horse in front of him, all in one fluid gesture.

"Those who lie to Kamau the Cunning are known to have their tongues cut out," he warned her.

The horseman whipped his speckled gray mare to a gallop and raced ahead to the front of the caravan, kicking up dust. She resented the man's surliness, but to keep from falling off, she had to tightly clutch his broad forearm.

They came alongside a turbaned man on a sleek black stallion, and the two horses stood still, as the river of trudging elephants poured past them.

Said the surly horseman, "Master, this dusty wench claims she is a princess of Kali and needs passage there."

The caravan master was gaunt and lean with a somber frown and deep set, calculating eyes. A long scar ran from just under his right eyelid down to his lip. Around his neck he wore a string from which dangled a tiny pouch. Halima imagined it must be a piece of his native soil, which many traveling men carried with them. He wore his sword strapped to his back like a desert bandit.

Surely this cannot be the legendary hero, Kamau the great merchant, Halima thought. She realized that he was appraising her, taking in her long neck and full breasts. Halima felt like a plump chicken being considered for purchase at the market.

"What do you offer in return for passage?" he asked in a low, husky voice. His accent was from a far distant land she didn't know.

"Much gold," Halima told him.

"I see none," the merchant said coolly.

Somehow Halima had not expected this kind of wrangling from the great Kamau!

"I promise you one hundred miktals of gold dust if you deliver me safely to the palace of the King of Kali."

The caravan master gave a crooked smile, as if such a paltry sum was beneath his ability to reckon. His narrow, squinting eyes openly sized up the swell of her breasts.

"For 200 miktals there are pleasure dens in the eastern

world that would gladly purchase a woman of your beauty as a slave," he said.

Halima shivered, realizing how vulnerable she was. Then she remembered Kokayi, crouched in the bushes, ready with his sure aim to put an arrow in the heart of the first man to molest her.

She tilted up her chin and regarded Kamau contemptuously.

"Are women cattle that you talk of buying and selling?" she rebuked him.

The merchant yawned and squinted at the sun. Then he looked back at her.

"What proof do you offer that I will get my payment?" he demanded.

Halima told him proudly, "I promise you in the name of my father, the King of Kali."

Kamau spat lazily on the ground, then replied, "It is said the King of Kali is a lying coward and a usurper, and that his word is not worth the dung of a pig."

The blazing sun robbed Halima of all her patience. Without another word, she reached over and smacked the merchant across his leathery face. The scarred, stubbly skin scraped the palm of her hand like sandpaper.

The surly horseman caught her wrist and wrenched it far behind her back. In a split second, he had a curved dagger at her throat.

"Forgive me, master. I did not mean to invite a leopardess into your tent," he apologized.

Bitterly, tears rolling down her cheeks, Halima shouted at the merchant, "My father, Babatunde the Good, is revered from here to the great sea. His honesty is known even by his enemies! How dare you, you jackal, how dare you?!"

She glared at the wiry merchant, ready for him to either return the blow or order her throat cut. To her surprise, Kamau nodded to the surly horseman somberly, and the other slowly lowered his blade.

"How long have you been away from Kali?" he asked gently.

"Almost a year," she replied, wiping her tears away with one dusty hand.

"So you do not know, child, that your father is dead. And that Olugbodi, King of the People of the Snake, now rules Kali."

Halima covered her eyes and bowed her head and gently began to cry anew. The tears came slowly at first, like the softly falling rain, and soon became a river.

For the first time, the merchant's narrow eyes reflected a glint of kindness. "You are truly Princess Halima then."

She nodded, still weeping.

"You do not remember me, because you were only a child when I last visited your father, but I knew him. Many kings never earn the praise names, but he was good indeed."

Halima looked up at him, proudly stifling her tears.

"Thank you, Kamau."

The merchant nodded to the surly horseman. "See that the princess is fed and given a berth in the caravan."

He bowed to Halima and galloped off, back to the head of the train. She turned and waved goodbye to the place where she knew brave Kokayi lay.

Halima was put in a *tipoye*, or carriage, borne by a huge white elephant. It carried four women of one of the southern kingdoms, all bound to the palace of the King of Kali, to serve as dancers and royal bathers.

The four women had the most womanly figures Halima had ever seen, all pillowy, curving bedroom flesh. Each was adorned in a king's ransom in gold; ankle bracelets, rings in their ears and noses, all the gifts of male admirers.

Halima had some difficulty understanding the women's thick accents, but she took comfort in the women's bawdy, cheerful banter, which gave her a momentary break from worry and grief.

"I hear King Olugbodi is a master of the art of lovemaking. He's traveled to the pleasure domes of the east, and learned every secret trick to please a woman," said the youngest girl, Folashade, who sat next to Halima, playing with one of her earrings thoughtfully.

An older woman, in her mid-twenties, snorted, "Ha! You silly girls believe everything you hear. What man have you ever known who doesn't roll on his back and start to snore after he climbs off you?"

A pouty-lipped, lazy-eyed woman shook her head and said with a broad smile, "You must have never been with a Zimbai. A warrior of the Zimbai once rode me for two solid days."

The youngest girl turned to Halima, "What men do you think are the best?"

Shyly, she told her, "I have only been with my husband. That was wonderful beyond words. But I do not think we will meet again. I suppose I will live the life of a widow from now on."

The older woman grinned. "The lot of a widow isn't so bad. My husband was drowned by a hippopotamus three weeks after we were married, and I've been a widow ever since."

"I'm sorry," Halima said.

The older woman snorted. "Pah! He was good for nothing. The widow's life isn't so bad. You see, when I lived in our village, it was the duty of the widows to introduce youths to the delights of woman. They are so eager to prove their manhood, and to learn the ways of women. And I taught them well, believe me!"

The other women laughed raucously.

That night, they all sat around the campfire beneath the stars, dining on a meal of ostrich eggs and dried water buffalo tongue.

One of the men of the caravan was playing a *kora*, an instrument like a harp, and singing tales of faraway lands. Some of the women danced to the music, while others knelt with Halima and Kamau, eating with their hands from a common bowl.

The merchant told her, "It may not be wise, Princess, for you to return to Kali. King Olugbodi has already proclaimed you dead. He might find a resurrection now untimely."

He paused, running a finger thoughtfully over his scar. "Your father's clansmen are the ironsmiths of the hills, aren't they?"

Halima nodded.

"Perhaps you would be wiser to take refuge with them."

"I must go back to my people. That is my duty," Halima said firmly. She looked at his hard, gaunt face.

"If there is peril, will you stand by me?" she asked.

Kamau hesitated, then gave a crooked smile.

"I stand by myself. For no one do I put my head on the chopping block."

Halima shook her head in disbelief.

"All those wonderful tales about your bravery, your adventures, how you help others... all lies?"

Kamau stood, wiping his mouth. "Don't believe every fairytale you hear, girl," he snorted. He strode off to his tent.

Halima stamped her foot in anger, putting her fists on her hips. She didn't realize the widow had sidled up beside her.

Said the widow, knowingly, "He is not an easy man. I should know – I've been trying to lie with him our entire journey!"

That night, Halima lay in a tent among the dancing women, thinking solemnly about the death of her father, and wondering what trials awaited her in her homeland.

She prayed, "Father, who now walks among the shadows, watch over your beloved daughter, and protect her from harm."

CHAPTER 12

RETURN TO KALI

In three days time, the caravan of the merchant Kamau reached the walls of the city of Kali, the great port city of ancient days.

Earlier that day, Kamau had dispatched the surly horseman to the city to let them know of the caravan's impending arrival. The caravan was stopped at the city gates, where a tax master of the king assessed the goods they carried. Halima peered through the curtains as Kamau spoke with the guards in the watchtower making arrangements.

The widow told the others, "Best be prepared to wait here awhile. This will take a long time. The king will not be denied his share of any wealth brought into the city."

Halima closed the curtain and leaned back. The carriage swayed as the elephant that bore it shifted restlessly from giant foot to foot.

Soon she would be face to face with King Olugbodi and she would learn how he came to sit on her father's throne. Perhaps she would learn the reason for his war against the Abaka, the people of the mountain, and she could convince him to bring the bloody conflict to an end.

They sat there for a good hour until they were all sweating like pigs. Flies buzzed against the silk curtains of the carriage, eager to drink their perspiration.

"How long will they keep us here?" demanded Folashade.

Halima opened the curtains again and saw three soldiers on horseback trotting along the line, inspecting each carriage of the caravan. Further off she could see at least seventy other soldiers atop the city wall. Halima pulled the curtain shut. She suddenly felt trapped and unable to breathe in the close quarters of the carriage – but there was nowhere to run.

A moment later, the curtains were ripped open and one of the soldiers stuck in his flat, ugly face. His features were dotted with the tribal scores of the People of the Snake. The dancing women cowered, some giggling, covering their faces.

The soldier demanded, "Which of you claims to be Princess Halima, daughter of King Babatunde?"

The widow spoke for them all. "Stupid man, do you see any kind of princess here? We are dancers coming to entertain the court of King Olugbodi, ruler of Kali and all the People of the Snake."

The guard hesitated, scrutinizing the slew of females.

"Well, get in or get out!" the widow demanded. The other women cackled and the ugly soldier shrank back with embarrassment.

Outside the carriage Halima heard another voice grunt, "Make the rascal earn his gold. He's the one who says he saw her."

Suddenly, the surly horseman's head appeared beside that of the ugly soldier. The traitor pointed at Halima and declared emphatically, "She is the one."

The ugly soldier told Halima sternly, "Princess, you must come with me."

Halima saw that she had no choice. As the dancing

women looked on helplessly, Halima clambered over them and crawled into the arms of the ugly soldier, who swung her by the waist to the ground.

"What do you want with her?" the widow demanded.

"Yes, leave her alone," cried Folashade.

"You sluts shut up and forget what you've seen," the guard told them.

The women cursed the soldiers, who ignored them as they escorted Halima off.

They rode to the front of the caravan, which stood waiting at the gates of the city. The long line of elephants, horses and donkeys were still, as if frozen in time. Troops stood waiting upon the wall, the officers pacing nervously. Stillness and a sense of impending violence filled the air. It looked as if had one person said, "Boo!" arrows would let fly from all directions.

Halima was marched into the guard tower. It was strangely cool inside the dank, narrow stone chamber, and Halima felt a shiver as the soldiers guided her in and closed the door behind her.

The chamber was dark – illuminated only by the light that poured in from two small windows. One was at eye level, the other twenty feet high at the top of a stone staircase that spiraled up into the tower.

Halima saw Kamau in the middle of the chamber, and took a step toward him in relief. Then out of the shadows stepped a second man.

It was Masomakali, the crafty advisor of King Olugbodi, he who had arranged her marriage to the ruler and fled with him when the party was attacked by the Zimbai.

The slave general turned toward her, flashing his crocodile smile, and raising his deformed, three-fingered right hand in greeting. Halima instinctively recoiled from him as if he were a childhood bogeyman returned.

"Welcome home, Princess Halima," he said with a

bow. His familiar, hissing voice made Halima want to hop back as if from a slithering cobra.

Masomakali turned toward the merchant.

"In the name of King Olugbodi the Trustworthy, I thank you, honorable Kamau, for returning this daughter of the realm to her homeland. We apologize for delaying you here. You may be on your way now. In keeping with the promise the princess made to you, gold dust has been loaded into your caravan. As a token of our gratitude, it will be twice the sum you asked for delivering her safely home. You are free to take your caravan into the city."

Kamau's untrusting eyes moved slowly from Masomakali to Halima and back.

Somewhat sharply, Masomakali told him, "I am sure it would be in your best interest to leave at once – and to speak to no one of this matter."

There was a deathly silence. Kamau's eyes wandered about the room, following the spiral staircase up to the high window where a stream of dust particles hovered in the sunlight.

Then he shrugged lazily. "As I told you, I am a simple merchant. What happens here is not my concern." He turned to Halima. "May I give the princess a parting gift?"

Masomakali nodded.

Kamau drew from around his neck the tiny pouch he wore. He took Halima's hand and pressed it into her palm.

"Please keep this as a memento. Goodbye, sweet princess."

Halima could not believe he was abandoning her in this uncertain predicament. After all, he had dozens of armed men with him in his caravan. He turned and strode out of the room. Halima anxiously clutched the little pouch in her hand.

Masomakali, slave general and chief advisor to King Olugbodi, turned to Halima and considered her through his cold, reptilian eyes.

"You have grown even more beautiful than when we first met, Princess, much more," he whispered.

"Where is King Olugbodi?" she said, ignoring him. "Does he not wish to see me?"

Masomakali did not answer, and Halima fought from trembling visibly. "Has he been told I am here?" she demanded.

The three-fingered man began to pace back and forth before the narrow slit of a window. Through it, Halima could see the wrinkled gray hides of elephants now lumbering by as the caravan passed into the city.

Kamau, how can you have abandoned me, she thought in anguish. *I felt sure you were my friend!*

Masomakali drew from a sheath strapped to his calf a short, jagged-edged dagger and held it up to the light of the window. It glittered, savage-looking as a shark's tooth.

"A wicked little blade, for wicked little deeds," he hissed. Halima moved toward the doorway, and fast as a lightning bolt, the three-fingered man was there, blocking her path.

Halima put her fists on her hips and mustered a defiant stare. "You know that I am betrothed to your lord, King Olugbodi."

"Yes Princess," Masomakali hissed, stepping closer. "And do you know there was much mourning in Kali when King Olugbodi announced that you were killed by the Zimbai *after* your marriage to him?"

Halima shook her head furiously. "We were never married. There was no ceremony, no oaths taken."

The three-fingered man continued as if she had not spoken. "And it is through that holy bond of matrimony the King Olugbodi inherited your lands and the crown of Kali. It is because of that marriage that he now rules two kingdoms: Kali, and our own homeland. The Zimbai are our allies by treaty, and the mountain country of the Abaka will be ours through conquest."

Masomakali stepped toward Halima again and she backed against the wall until her shoulders crushed against the stone.

"So you see the dilemma," he whispered. "Here you are alive," he stood so close to her, she could smell his sour breath, "when you should be dead." He put the fine point of the dagger under her chin and tilted up her face so that she stared into his saurian eyes, her throat exposed. Halima proudly tried not to let her eyes betray her terror, though she was shaking like a virgin about to be taken.

Her hand squeezed the tiny pouch so firmly that its contents cut into her hand.

"Please, let me pray," she pleaded.

Masomakali scowled contemptuously.

"Please, I beg you," she said. "It is our custom for those about to die to pray for our ancestors to welcome us among them."

Masomakali stroked his jaw with his deformed hand and then nodded. Halima dropped to her knees and began to mutter to herself fervently.

Masomakali paced back and forth uncomfortably.

Halima rattled off every prayer she knew, thanking the Great One in the Sky for every good fortune, and begging forgiveness for every transgression; appealing to every departed member of her family of the past six generations.

Finally, Masomakali clapped his hand over her mouth. "Enough!" he hissed impatiently. "It is time to die."

He put the razor-sharp blade against her naked throat, preparing to slit her jugular with one savage swipe. "It will be quick, princess," he promised. And now she saw a dark passion in his eyes, and Halima recognized at last what it was that gave this strange man joy. She felt the dagger begin to cut into her throat.

Then she heard a long, low whistle.

Masomakali released her and she tumbled forward onto her hands. He staggered back, wearing a mask of fury like a crocodile from which a piece of meat had been abruptly stolen.

He pointed in anger at the top of the spiral staircase – where Kamau sat casually on the window ledge, wearing a bemused smile. Halima's heart leapt. She knew her friend would not so easily abandon her! He must have scaled the outside of the tower. The guards outside the door saw him leave, but he was here to defend her.

"You!" hissed the slave general.

"Is this the royal treatment in Kali or can every visitor expect such special attention?" Kamau said mockingly.

The slave general strode toward the foot of the staircase brandishing his dagger. "You will pay for putting your snout where it doesn't belong, hyena," he growled.

Kamau seemed entirely unfazed by the threat. He began to stroll cockily down the stairs, reaching behind him and pulling out the long sword that hung on his back. He twisted the sword in the streaming sunlight, as if examining it for the first time.

"It seems mine is bigger than yours, snake man," he noted.

The slave general slid his dagger back into its sheath. Then he turned to the wall, where an array of spears, shields and other armaments hung. He pulled a huge, curving scimitar off the wall.

"I will gut you from your chin to your seed sack," he bellowed.

Kamau smirked, resting his blade on his shoulder. "I thought you only fought women," he retorted.

At that, Masomakali charged up the stairs, raising his blade in anger. But just as he drew near, the wily merchant vaulted off the stairway and landed with catlike grace on the floor. He pulled Halima to her feet, crying, "Run, Princess!"

Halima hesitated for a moment, reluctant to abandon her friend, and then she scrambled to the iron door. With some effort, she cracked it open. To her dismay, she saw that a pair of guards stood there. The men turned in surprise.

The young woman shoved the door shut and slid fast the iron bolt. She whirled to see Masomakali and Kamau hacking at each other furiously, the blades filling the air with clatter and sending up a shower of sparks. Their artful lunges and darting retreats were so quick her eyes could barely follow them. She stood watching, riveted in place.

Masomakali was a fierce, formidable warrior, she realized. He soon had Kamau in retreat.

"Please do not let this one die for me," she prayed. But in a moment's time the slave general had driven the merchant to the base of the stairs. He took a mighty swing at Kamau's head.

Whoosh! Kamau ducked just in time and the blade clipped one or two uneven hairs from the top of his head. The caravan master began to back up the stairs.

"You handle that blade well for a man with three fingers," he taunted his rival. "Let's see how you fare with one arm!"

He brought down his sword on Masomakali's wrist, but with the speed of a lizard, the slave general pulled his hand out of the way before the blade hit home.

Masomakali swung at Kamau's legs and Halima gasped – she expected to see the merchant's limbs come tumbling down the stone steps. Wily Kamau hopped in the air in time, barely clearing the blade, which struck the wall of the tower with a horrible clang.

With savage strength, Masomakali thrust again and again, while Halima's defender desperately parried the scimitar. Finally, about halfway up the stairs, the merchant fell against the steps. Continuing to parry, he inched up the stone steps on his backside.

"Great One in the Sky, protect him," Halima pleaded, wringing her hands.

But her prayers went unheeded. The three-fingered general battered the sword out of Kamau's hand. The weapon twirled through the air, hit the floor and skated across it.

The three-fingered general gave a crocodile grin and brought the blade down with all his might toward Kamau's head. The merchant rolled desperately to the right, and then to the left as the scimitar slammed into the stone step, nearly amputating first one ear and then the other.

Halima, meanwhile, crawled across the stone floor and grabbed Kamau's sword, which was still spinning on the ground. She was ready to throw it to him, but when she looked up, she saw she was too late. Masomakali stood over him on the staircase, one foot planted on his chest. The merchant could not squirm out of the way of the scimitar this time.

Masomakali screamed in triumph, and brought the blade down.

But Kamau had not given up yet. He reached for the sheath strapped to the slave general's calf, whipped out the other man's dagger – and quick as a flash, plunged it into Masomakali's thigh.

Masomakali howled in agony. Taking advantage of the moment's reprieve, Kamau grabbed the other man's foot with both hands and uprooted him. The three-fingered man went tumbling down the steps.

The wily merchant climbed to his feet and ran up to the top of the spiral stairway. *Now I must a*ct, Halima told herself. She ran forward and, using all her strength, launched the sword up to him. It flew close enough to the merchant that he was able to snag it out of the air by the hilt.

By this time, Masomakali had righted himself. He tore the dagger out of his thigh and, with the glare of intense rage, marched up the stairs toward the warrior merchant. Masomakali held the scimitar in one hand and the bloody dagger in the other.

"Your time is up, peddler," the slave general said with determination.

Kamau gazed soberly down at the approaching menace. Then he looked out the window and grinned. "No, *your* time, brother!"

At that moment a great cheer went up outside and Masomakali froze in his tracks. Halima looked out the lower window. Through the narrow slit she could see a crowd of more than 600 men, women and children pouring out of the city gates and converging on the guard tower.

Her subjects! Kamau must have sent word of her arrival into the city with his caravan. She looked at the merchant, her heart filled with gratitude, and also shame that she had ever doubted him.

Kamau caught the look and gave a crooked grin. He bowed to her and said wistfully, "I wish this were another time and another place."

Then he sat in the window ledge, spun and leapt from the tower.

Masomakali groaned and began to limp down the staircase.

"My cruelty is too imperfect," he sighed. "I should not have delayed." He lowered his dagger and slipped it back into its sheath. "Your merchant friend Kamau is indeed cunning. He ate just enough time for your people to save you."

Halima looked in her hand and saw the tiny pouch, and emptied the contents into her palm. There fell a single object, a perfect raindrop-sized seed as black as coal. It took a moment for the meaning to dawn on her, and when it did, it shook her like an earthquake.

"The Seed of Hope," she whispered in awe. So at least one of the legends of the merchant Kamau was true.

The hubbub of the crowd grew louder as the citizens of Kali approached the tower.

Masomakali sneered. "The merchant will not leave the city alive. That I promise!"

Halima gripped the seed, and then returned it to the pouch, which she looped around her neck. She threw back her head haughtily.

"A man like you could never best a man like him."

Masomakali stepped menacingly toward her. At that moment, however, the crowd reached the iron door and began to furiously beat on it.

"We have guests, general," Halima said with a smile.

Masomakali threw down his sword and allowed his frown to wax into a sickly grimace of a smile. Gently, he took Halima by the arm and guided her to the door and out into the blinding sunlight.

The people – old, snaggle-toothed men, fat middle-aged women, scampering children – swarmed around Halima, their faces bright and tears of joy running down their faces. They raised Halima onto their shoulders and swept her away. Laughing and weeping, people sang:

"Halima, the wise, beautiful daughter of our
Beloved ruler has been restored to us.
Praise the Great One in the Sky!"

They carried her through the tall gates of the city and into the wide streets of Kali. The crowd grew as word spread of Halima's arrival. Children ran alongside, and women showered the princess with strings of beads and gold finery and draped their finest cloths about her.

Halima, accustomed now to the simple ways of the mountain, found herself gaping like a country bumpkin at the magnificence of the city, as though seeing it for the first time. The crowd swept her past street after street of beautiful, multi-storied houses built of coral and mortar, with intricately carved wooden doorways chiseled from massive ebony timber.

When they reached the center of the city, the people ran up the great stone steps to the palace carrying their prize. The palace guards parted in confusion, having never before seen such a torrent of faces.

The crowd hurried Halima past giant stone statues that guarded the receiving hall of the king – huge simple figures of a man and a woman at either side of the entrance.

They pushed by the crowd of vassals seeking an audience with the king, and past the gauntlet of 100 soldiers who stood at attention. They brought her to the throne of Kali, the golden stool wrought by smiths in ancient times.

Twenty generations of Halima's ancestors sat upon that throne: all brave, wise, good kings. But now, as Halima was rested reverently on the floor before that throne, she saw that the plump body of King Olugbodi filled the seat.

He had fattened up considerably, from pleasantly plump to grossly obese, and his rump cheeks spilled over the stool like jelly rolling off the edge of the table. He was covered with thick hides of lion and leopard and oxen. Rings of opal, emerald and ruby glittered on his fingers. A pair of buxom serving girls knelt massaging his feet, while behind him, broad-shouldered menservants fanned him with great palm leaves, chasing away flies.

Dozens of pages stood armed with spears and shields of solid gold, lining the path to the throne. Knights on white horses stood beside the king and young aristocrats from the land of the People of the Snake knelt in attendance.

The people rested Halima down and she strode up to the throne, the throng of people waiting, mumbling behind her.

King Olugbodi smiled broadly at her and stood, his potbelly jiggling. He beckoned Halima to the dais on which his throne sat, and a pair of thick-muscled palace guards escorted her to the side. He threw his chubby arms around her, then turned to the crowd that filled the room.

"People of Kali," he said. "Welcome your daughter home!"

Heralds in bright tunics repeated his words loudly so that all could hear. The people cheered, and outside the chamber a huge chorus of voices rang.

"By what miracle she has been returned to us, alive and well and out of the hands of our enemies, whom we believed had put her to death, we do not know – and it does not matter. All we know or care is that our beloved Halima is home!"

To her amazement, Halima saw that big, fat tears were rolling down the young king's face.

"People of Kali, go. Spread the word. Halima lives!" he bellowed.

Halima turned to the crowd that was pouring from the hall, full of joy, shouting boisterously.

"I would speak to them," she said.

"You must rest from your journey now, my love," King Olugbodi replied, cutting her off. He shouted to the crowd, "Go! Let songs of thanksgiving fill the streets of our city!"

He threw up his arms, and as if on cue, some people burst into song. Others quickly picked up the song of thanksgiving, and as they chanted, soldiers began to herd them from the hall.

King Olugbodi turned to Halima, still smiling.

"That was very clever, Olugbodi," Halima told him.

"You and I will speak later. Now you must rest yourself," he said gently, taking her palm with his pudgy hand. He snapped his fingers and two guards stepped forward. "Escort my queen to her chambers."

Moments later, Halima found herself in her childhood bedroom. It was unrecognizable now, filled with opulent cushions and saturated with some saccharine scent from the land of the People of the Snake. She threw herself on her bedding, pulling on her braided hair and burying her face in silk sheets, screaming a muffled plea.

"Great One in the Sky, let this be a nightmare from which I will awaken. Can this pig really have taken my father's throne unopposed?"

She called a servant and asked for each of her father's old advisors: the *Togo Nabla* (the prime minister); his minister of finance; the mayor of the palace; the *Rassam Naba* (chief of slaves of the crown and high executioner); the *Kidiranga Naba* (head of the cavalry).

Each, she'd learned in turn, had been executed for treason against the new king. Every advisor, every soothsayer and diviner, every physician who specialized in every part of the body from eyes to feet, every slave and every servant who had been in the palace was gone – save one.

She did learn that Mwendapole, her father's griot, was alive. If there were one man remaining in the court whom she could trust it might be he, The old man had enthralled her as a tot with tales of Anansi the spider and educated her in the history of her people and her family, all the way back to the Dawn Time. Nevertheless, she would have to find out why he had been allowed to remain alive and free. The proverb said, "When a tyrant rules, all the good men can be found in prison."

She told her new servants that her first duty was to take libations to the shrine of her deceased father and ask for his blessing. She had the servant summon the old man to meet her by the ancient burial grounds, which stood on a cliff overlooking the sea.

Together, she and Mwendapole said prayers by the shrine of her father, sharing with his spirit a simple offering of palm wine and bread.

"Father, do not travel yet into the land across the river.

I need your spirit here beside me. Lend me your strength now," Halima said.

She and the old man strolled along the rocky shore nearby. They were accompanied by guards, but Halima made sure they were far enough away that their whispering voices were drowned out by the crash of waves.

The slight old man bowed his head as he walked beside her in his long cotton robe, which fluttered in the sea breeze.

"Your father was a great man, Halima," he said. "He's greatly mourned among the people. I shall miss him much."

"Worthy Mwendapole, tell me what has happened here?" she demanded.

"Word came from Olugbodi's country that you had been married – and then killed in a raid by the Zimbai. There was no other heir of age. The snake people said that by right, the crown fell to your husband."

"No one disputed the claim?" Halima said in disbelief. "What of all my cousins?"

"Some disputed it. But by then the armies of Olugbodi had already marched into the city. We are simple merchants, no match for such a force, as you well know. Now all the royal princes of Kali are guests – hostages, really – in the land of the People of the Snake."

"And did not a messenger come from the mountains, from the land of the Abaka, demanding a ransom for me?"

Mwendapole shook his head, puzzled. "No, Your Highness. No such party came."

"And what of Madongo, my bodyguard, and my maidservant, Neema?"

"They never returned – unless they took refuge among her people, the fishermen of the southern shore."

Halima hoped this was true. For it was certain that the messengers Queen Rashida sent here, with word that Halima was alive among the Abaka, had been put to death as soon as they delivered the message to King Olugbodi.

"What became of my father's counselors?" she asked.

Mwendapole bowed his head gravely. "They were executed for treason, Halima. It was said they insulted the old king, your father, after his death, and stole from his treasury."

Halima spat in the sand contemptuously. "You believe this?"

Mwendapole said nothing.

"Who spoke for them?" Halima demanded, putting her hands on her hips. The old man looked as if he wished the sand could swallow him up.

"Halima, Princess, a man like King Olugbodi... I am alive only because he thought I was an old fool, good only for amusing women and children of his household with songs and fairytales."

Halima raised her hand to silence him. It was a gesture of her father's, she realized, which he used to stop underlings from prattling on.

"You are not a warrior, Mwendapole," Halima said. "No one demands that you be brave. But I must know where you stand."

The old man looked at her. "I have served your family all my life. I, and my father before me, and his father, and his. My family has always served the King of Kali."

"But there is a new king in the land," Halima reminded him sternly. "To whom do you owe your loyalty – to him or to me?"

Old Mwendapole stuck out his sunken chest and stared directly into her eyes. "To you, my princess, and those that share your blood."

"Kneel and swear," Halima demanded, stonily. The old man struggled to his knees before Halima. She put a hand on his balding, gray-haired head. He swore a solemn oath of loyalty.

Halima helped him to his feet. She embraced the gentle old man, and whispered, "Great One in the Sky, master of the seas and builder of mountains, protect the land of my ancestors."

When Halima returned to her chamber, the servants, all foreigners, sharply told her that she was to prepare herself for a private audience with King Olugbodi.

Halima was bathed by the women, and her body perfumed, then she was given a soothing massage.

Folashade, the long-eyelashed young girl from the Kamau's caravan, had joined the palace as a servant woman, and it was she who now gently kneaded the princess's flesh.

Halima lay on her belly on velvet cushions, sipping a goblet full of cool, sweet palm wine, while the serving girl massaged hot oils into her back. She was trying to think what she would say to Olugbodi when they were alone, face to face. She imagined herself haughty and full of disdain. He would not dare harm her now, she thought. A princess could not be quietly done away with like her father's counselors; the people would cry out. She rehearsed in her mind a speech in which she called King Olugbodi a villain and a usurper, and demanded that he give up the throne and return to his own godforsaken land.

Occasionally, the prattle of the servant girl intruded on her private thoughts.

"You are so fortunate, Your Highness," Folashade was saying. She was a slender, slant-eyed creature with long fingers and a honey-smooth, singsong voice. "Many women in my country would give their firstborn to be the wife of Olugbodi."

Halima felt a trickle of warm oil run down the hollow

of her back, tickling her spine. The servant's soft hands kneaded her neck and shoulders. Her delicate fingers were surprisingly strong, like those of a baker accustomed to kneading bread.

Halima took another sip from the silver chalice full of dark, cool wine. It was an unfamiliar taste, a peculiar concoction of the People of the Snake.

"Yes, I am lucky indeed," she said dryly.

"He is the richest king of the coast, and the most powerful ruler from here to the western sea," the servant girl continued.

Halima took in another mouthful of the sweet wine. It was early yet, but she was feeling sleepy. The soft hands on her shoulders and neck relaxed her more. She felt herself sinking into a dreamy haze of contentment. She was unafraid of facing Olugbodi. *I can handle that rogue*, she thought, and ceased planning her speech.

Folashade worked her way down Halima's back, drumming her flesh with the edges of her hand. Halima closed her eyes, enjoying the sensation of soft hands kneading the soothing oils into her flesh.

Continued the serving girl, "Olugbodi is said to be a lover of exceeding prowess. They all say he makes the pleasing of women an art."

Halima's head was swimming now and her tongue felt the bitter aftertaste of the wine.

"You are almost ready for the marriage bed," Folashade told her.

Halima groggily rolled over, and forced herself to sit up. She picked up a silver goblet and shook it angrily.

"What is this?" she demanded.

The servant girl smiled. "It contains an herb to relax you, and help you give yourself over to passion. I was told to prepare you for –"

Halima tossed the contents of the goblet into the serving girl's face. "Get out!" she cried. Young Folashade spluttered and gasped for air.

"Get out!" Halima repeated. Bowing several times, the young servant backed out of the room.

Other servants came and dressed Halima to meet the king. She stood solemnly as they put her into a beaded loincloth and a long gown of fine, diaphanous silk. They adorned her wrists and ankles with thick bracelets and anklets of gold.

Like shackles, Halima thought grimly.

The servants then ushered her toward the private chamber of Olugbodi – once her father's bedchamber.

Halima walked uncertainly on tiptoes as a servant guided her. The aphrodisiac with which she had been plied made her lightheaded; her thoughts were becoming muddy. She was angry about having been tricked into taking the drink. But now she could barely remember why.

Her loins felt warm as if she were squatting over hot coals and her nipples tingled so much it was difficult to keep from stroking them. She dumbly obeyed the servant's direction to the door. For a moment everything went black.

Suddenly, Halima realized that the servant had left her inside a darkened room, which was thick with sweet, flowery incense. Only a single, flickering torch gave light to the cave-like chamber. Somewhere a *muet*, a type of lute, was playing a gentle love ballad.

Halima felt no fear; the potion she'd been given dampened such sensations. If anything, she felt a giddy courage.

Olugbodi appeared out of the clouds of swirling incense. He held the stringed instrument in his hand, and Halima realized that it was he who had been singing; it had been his high, sweet, boyish voice.

He was dressed regally in a long, purple robe that fell to his ankles, and he wore a shy smile. Halima realized just how young he was – he was a boy, really, only a few years older than she.

"Halima," he said softly. "Your name means 'gentle,' doesn't it, in your language?"

Halima said nothing. Her tongue felt thick and heavy in her mouth. All she could muster was a frown of disapproval.

"You are a noble girl, Halima," Olugbodi said. "You believe in all the fine things, I know – duty, mercy, love, courage. You think I'm wicked, and perhaps you are right."

He gestured at his slender arms and pear-shaped body.

"I am not a great warrior, Halima. If I must use cunning, it is because it is the only way I can survive – not because I'm a bad man. I know you are angry with me and you have good reason. I'm ashamed, myself, of what has passed. I apologize for any hurt I caused you."

He stared into Halima's eyes with grave sincerity. She nodded grudgingly, accepting his apology.

Olugbodi stepped closer to her. "I want you to be my queen, Halima, my first wife, and rule by my side all the lands I conquer. All of Kali, the lands of the Zimbai and of the Abaka, of the People of the Snake – all this will be yours as well as mine."

Halima's sleepy eyes fought to meet his penetrating gaze.

Olugbodi stepped closer. "You are so beautiful, Halima – more beautiful than I remember. Do you think any man under the sun would not want you as his bride? Turn to the light, so that I might see you better."

He put a finger on Halima's jaw, and gently turned her face, presenting her delicate profile to the torchlight. Halima looked at his bejeweled hand and was finally able to cut through the haze of the potion and answer him.

"You think I am another jewel for your plump fingers," she scolded in a voice that sounded strangely languorous to her own ears.

"You are a jewel I will possess."

He put his hands on her waist and drew her close to

him so that his big belly squashed against hers, and her hard nipples grazed his chest. He bent and whispered in her ear:

"I will take you to places you've never been, Halima. Places in you dark and secret. I have visited the pleasure palaces of the east, and the hidden temples of the south. I have lain with buxom women of the fertile valley and mated with prisoners from the caves of the icy north. And from each I have learned mysteries that I will teach you."

He slid a practiced hand between her legs, and she could feel the aphrodisiac rushing through her veins now, ordering her to surrender all she had. She tried to remember how much she loved her husband Shomari and detested this wretch, but her thoughts were cloudy as a muddy lake and she could not even picture her husband's face.

Still, summoning all her will, she pulled away, and laughed at the king contemptuously. Her hands were back at her hips.

"Olugbodi, save your honey talk for silly servant girls. I have a husband among the Abaka and you are like a worm at his feet. I will never be yours."

She threw back her head and stared at him haughtily.

Olugbodi made a grimace of a smile, as if trying not to seem wounded by her remark.

"Have your loins been so cruelly used by the Abaka that it would take a giant to satisfy you now, Halima?" he whispered.

Halima laughed harshly. "It would take a man, at least," she spat.

Olugbodi's hand lashed out of nowhere and she felt a nasty sting as he slapped her face. Halima threw up her own hand in response, but Olugbodi caught her wrist. He squeezed her slim wrist, his pudgy face flushed with rage like a fat boy who has been teased once too often by his playmates.

"So you want to fight, is that it, sweet Halima? Good."

He shoved her back, so that she tumbled onto the stone floor.

"Your father Babatunde promised you to me and I will have you," Olugbodi said. "It is my right to have you as my wife!"

He pulled off his robe, and loomed naked before her, his huge belly swaying like an elephant's – and then he pounced upon her.

Halima fought him like an angry cat, scratching and clawing. They wrestled on the floor, toppling porcelain vases and snapping finely carved wooden stools around the chamber.

As the young king huffed and panted from exhaustion, Halima was able to pin him facedown on the stone floor, his girlishly slender arm twisted behind his back.

"Guards!" Olugbodi gasped weakly, like a boy yelling for his mother.

"Yes," Halima taunted. "Call a man to help you." At that insult, the fat king roared like a boar in fury, and bucked, throwing her off.

Olugbodi caught Halima around the waist and with a sudden burst of strength hoisted her up and tossed her onto her father's bed. He belly-flopped on top of her. On her back, Halima kicked furiously at him, clipping him a few times on the jaw and chest with her heels. But at last he caught hold of her legs.

"Am I man enough for you now, proud woman?" he growled.

Halima squirmed, but she could not wrest free. The fat king wrapped one arm around her violently kicking legs, holding them still. With one hand, he clawed down and ripped away her pretty gown. Halima screeched in fury at the rending sound.

Just as easily, Olugbodi grabbed hold of her beaded loincloth and wrenched it way. He pitched it into the dark. Halima lay before him naked, trying to shield her small triangle with her hands.

"I am going to teach you humility, daughter of Babatunde," Olugbodi hissed. "In your own father's bed. I will enjoy teaching you – and you will enjoy learning."

Halima felt tears of shame rolling down her cheeks. *Why am I so weak*, she thought. *I must fight him. Oh Shomari, why did you send me so far away from you? Why are you not here to rescue me from this shame?*

Olugbodi grabbed her ankles and forced them back so they hovered behind her ears. Dripping hoggish sweat all over her, he rasped, "I shall plant my seed in you. You will bear me a son, and we will begin our dynasty that will rule all the lands that the eye can see, from the ocean to the top of the Silver Mountain. Now prepare for the drilling of your life, Kalian."

Olugbodi's words hit her like a splash of ice water. Halima planted her hand on his fleshy chest, holding him off. The usurper looked down at her in surprise.

Halima glared up at him defiantly, feeling her head beginning to clear. Through clenched teeth, she declared, "You had a chance to make me your woman when the Zimbai attacked their caravan. And you failed. We saw you. Running like a frightened girl."

With all her strength she pushed him off her.

"Away! Away, you foul pig. Or by my father's ghost I swear I will tell the entire world what a coward you are!"

Olugbodi rolled slowly off her. He sat slumped, his belly sagging.

Halima drew up her knees protectively.

"If you ever touch me again, I will tell every servant, every visitor, every guard, every man and woman and child what happened. And then none will follow you, either from Kali or the Zimbai, or the People of the Snake. For all people value courage – and hate the coward."

Olugbodi drew back, regarding her like a disappointed little boy, his manhood wilting.

Halima promised, "Leave me alone and I will hold my tongue, and sit by your throne, and call you husband – in name."

Olugbodi continued to sulk. "I told the people that tonight we would finally consummate our marriage. And it is our ancient custom to display the stained sheets on which the bride has surrendered her virgin blood. If the sheet is not displayed tomorrow, I will be a laughingstock."

Halima folded her arms. "My marriage is already consummated, Olugbodi."

She let him stew a moment, then suggested, "In the villages in the hills of the ironsmiths, where my father's kin reside, there is a similar custom. And there, when a man's bride is not a virgin, he sometimes cuts himself and spills his own blood on the sheet."

Olugbodi frowned dubiously. Halima could tell he was not enchanted with the idea.

He climbed abruptly to his feet and clapped his hands. A lithe youth in servant's robes appeared at the doorway, a good-looking boy about the same age as Halima. She covered her nakedness modestly, although the youth wore a mask of indifference as impenetrable as any ceremonial mask.

"Lend me your sword, boy," Olugbodi demanded. The servant obeyed, drawing from his belt a short, sharp blade.

"Now, put out your hand."

Slowly and unable to disguise his dismay, the boy stretched out his hand.

The king held the youth's wrist and quickly drew a thin red line across the palm. The youth closed his eyes and grimaced in pain and bewilderment. He looked like a frightened animal, stunned and unable to conceive of the reason for his torment. Olugbodi forced the lad to lean over the bed so that his bright scarlet blood dripped onto the sheet.

Halima looked down in disgust as the boy's blood

poured freely onto the sheet. And she recalled how her real husband, Shomari, bravely shed his blood for her on the day he faked her execution. What a swinish mockery of a man this was by comparison. She wanted to crawl into a bath and wash his sweet, evil stink off her.

Finally, after inspecting the widening circle of scarlet on the bed and finding it satisfactory, Olugbodi released his youthful victim. The boy stood up, holding his hand and wincing in pain.

"You can go," Olugbodi told him simply, turning away as if the boy had only brought in a cup of palm wine.

The youth bowed weakly, regaining his composure. Before he scurried out, he tarried for one second too long, and glanced at the tableau before him: Halima, crouched on the marriage bed, apparently unsatisfied; her "husband" Olugbodi standing sullenly, his flaccid manhood lying dormant in the shade of his big belly.

A bitter smile flitted across the wounded boy's lips as he turned to go.

But the king glimpsed the glint of contempt in the youth's eyes, that belittling look that said, "I may be your slave, but I am more of a man than you." Olugbodi allowed the youth to turn completely, and then buried the sword in his back. The youth shrieked, then toppled over, groaning.

"Guards!" Olugbodi cried.

Halima began screaming at the top of her lungs, as the handsome youth writhed on the floor like a crushed insect, coughing up blood. Four burly guards rushed into the king's bedchamber, spears in hand.

"This traitor tried to kill us," Olugbodi told them. "Search the palace for accomplices – then tell me how an assassin came so close to my beloved queen."

"Yes, Ruler of Rulers," they responded. The guards bowed and barreled out, two of them hustling the still-twitching corpse away.

Olugbodi turned to Halima, who kneeled in the bed,

weeping, aghast at the king's wanton butchery. He faced her with a mild smile, as if he were quite pleased with his sanguine behavior.

"I am not good, I am not brave, but I am unyielding, Halima – and I will prevail. I will eat the heart of your tall mountain king, and I will make you beg for me to be your master. This I swear."

He turned and stalked out of the chamber.

CHAPTER 13

THE
ASSASSINS

In the weeks that followed, each honored their pledge. Olugbodi made no further attempts to bed Halima, and she outwardly played the role of the dutiful wife.

Each day she appeared seated beside him at his throne as he held court and met ambassadors from foreign lands. Most of these obsequiously covered their heads with dust, a sign of respect, before seeing him. Each day she sat beside him as he handed down edicts and settled disputes between the subjects.

But each night she plotted against him.

She vowed to herself she would do everything in her power to save her native country from his rule. Through the griot Mwendapole, she sent word to her father's ancestral clan, the ironsmiths of the hills, asking for their help in overthrowing the tyrant. For it is said, "One lineage is one blood."

Meanwhile, the war raged on against the Abaka, the people of the mountain. Though it was three peoples now united – the People of the Snake, the warriors of the Zimbai and the armies of Kali – the giants of the mountain would not be subdued.

For in the low hills where the fighting took place, the giants would strike like angry bolts of lightning from the mountaintop. Then they would escape back to their mountain lair, where, as if swallowed by the rock face, they would vanish like ghosts.

Some anxious soldiers of the People of the Snake whispered that the war magic of these tall, mystic warriors made them invincible, or that they had the gift of the third eye.

The generals of King Olugbodi, however, insisted that if only they knew the location of the secret pass to the upper reaches of the mountain, they could crush the giants. They asked Halima if she knew of such a pass, and she lied by saying she knew it not. Fortunately, they seemed to believe her – all except Masomakali, Olugbodi's crocodile-eyed slave general, who watched with undisguised skepticism as she spoke.

In these days and weeks, Halima was consumed by loneliness. Though she was home in her native country, she felt utterly helpless, a stranger in a strange land. All men seemed smaller now – petty, cowardly, fainthearted – compared to the giants of the mountain.

She longed for the cool air of the Silver Mountain, the place of magic and mystery. She could see the rugged form from her palace window, tall and majestic. Each time she looked at its glittering peak, memories of her life there rushed back anew.

In these times, Halima felt girlish tears beginning to well in her eyes, and then she would force herself to turn to the task at hand. For she knew that Olugbodi must be destroyed if freedom were to come to her people. If he were slain and the heads of the iron-working tribes in the hills had the courage to rise up against him, then the dominion of the People of the Snake over her countrymen would not stand.

The man was a pig – no worse, a snake. Yet Halima could not imagine killing him or anyone. In her life, she had never deliberately harmed another.

"And yet it must be done," she told herself. "I must steel myself against pity."

For counsel, Halima went to her great aunt Bimkubwa, the midwife who had delivered her from her mother's womb, a healer and a worker of herbs, as well as a keeper of ancient lore.

The bent old woman seemed grayer and frailer than when Halima saw her last, and her withered dugs seemed to dangle lower than ever at her waist. *Have I been away so long*, Halima asked herself as they met in the woman's cramped round stone house a short distance from the palace.

A guard accompanied them and stood outside as they embraced.

"You are ill?" old Bimkubwa asked in her raspy voice.

"Only a little bellyache," Halima replied. The truth was she had been puking every morning.

"You don't eat enough," Bimkubwa scolded. "I've told you no man wants a skinny wife."

Halima laughed and pointed to her gently rounded belly. "Oh yes?" she laughed. "Look at this!"

The old woman's falcon eyes narrowed.

"Come, Halima," she said, pointing to a mat of woven rush. "Lie down."

Halima protested again that she wasn't ill, but the old

woman ushered her forcefully to the bed. To humor the hunched old crone, Halima grudgingly lay on her back and tried not to wince as Bimkubwa probed and prodded her belly, nodding and grunting to herself.

When she was done, she allowed Halima to sit up.

"You are with child, daughter of Babatunde – a boy child."

Halima's eyes began to water.

"This is happy news, my child?" Bimkubwa asked.

Halima flicked away a tear and smiled. "This is happy news, old mother. What does the proverb say? 'Children are the reward of life.'"

"This is the king's?"

Halima shook her head emphatically, and she told her old kinswoman who the father was. As she spoke, all her love for the mountain king rushed back to her like the rising tide. Shomari was with her still within her, alive!

And the child would be the heir to the throne of Kali. She imagined her boy child seated on the golden stool of her father. But then she bowed her head in sorrow – for he would not live to rule if this foul tyrant Olugbodi learned of his existence.

The old woman rose, bones creaking, and turned to her shelves, which were chock full of herbs and medicine.

"From this day on you must eat no fat or beer or wine, or the meat of animals killed by poison arrows," she instructed. "You must remove all iron from your bedchamber and refrain from lovemaking and carrying fire. You must keep a bowl of water beside your bed, which the Great One in the Sky will use to mold the baby as you sleep. And you must visit the shrine of our family's fertility spirit, our *ase*, and make an offering to safeguard your child."

Halima nodded, making sure she forgot nothing on the list.

Continued Bimkubwa, "I will prepare medicine for

you, to help your child grow healthy and strong. It is made from the potent soil of an ant hill." Only now did Halima remember her mission. She stood up quickly beside her great aunt.

"There's something I need more, old mother."

Bimkubwa turned slowly, her eyes narrowing, spreading a spider web of wrinkles across her leathery face.

Halima told her, "I need a poison."

"For yourself or for another?"

"For another. The king, Olugbodi. A strong and subtle poison."

Bimkubwa sighed. She looked about her cluttered house, then her sad old eyes turned back to Halima.

"The Great One in the Sky gave you a gift, Halima, a gift she does not give to all. You are a bearer of life, child. It is not your nature to destroy life."

Halima heard the words of the woman whose hands had delivered her into this world and was the first to hold her, and saw the earnest tears in the aged woman's eyes.

"I must do what I must do," Halima said.

The old woman nodded gravely. "You have heard of the sorcerer, Maguso?"

Halima shuddered at the infamous name, often used to frighten children when she was small. She had seen him only once, striding through the marketplace – a black-bearded man with a wizened, skull-like face.

"Yes," she answered.

"This sorcerer can prepare a poison that cannot be tasted, that cannot be smelled. It will not touch the food tasters of the king nor his cooks nor his pet monkeys. But to the king, it will bring a quick and certain death. It will drive the very breath from his body."

She fixed Halima with a severe, damning stare.

"There is no undoing of this, Halima."

"How long will it take? Halima whispered.

"A week's time."

Halima met her eyes. "Then let it be done," she said with finality.

A week later, Olugbodi was still very much alive. They sat on velvet cushions in his dining hall: Halima, Olugbodi and his fourteen other wives. A dozen musicians played, two beating drums, three shaking resonant calabashes filled with hard seeds, four more men on horns and three others piping away on flutes. Olugbodi popped ripe berries in his mouth and told jokes to his giggling women. He was in a festive mood tonight, for some reason.

Halima watched uneasily as servants paraded before the king bringing food on gold plates. Each new dish sailed into his greedy mouth. Thick slabs of hippopotamus meat, fat from oxen hump, loaves of *manioc* (sweet fried caterpillars), yams soaked in honey, all washed down with goblets of *pombe*, a fermented drink of millet and bananas – and all with no apparent effect, not even indigestion.

Which contains the poison? she wondered. *Was it none of these, but instead some evil powder sprinkled on the floor of his bedchamber, to attack him through the soles of his feet?*

However it was to be done, this was surely Olugbodi's last day on earth – that much was certain.

Through her bath servant Folashade, she had sent messages to her father's kinsmen, telling them to be ready to attack when news of Olugbodi's death reached them. She felt now that she could trust the serving girl, who no longer spoke so glowingly of Olugbodi's skill as a lover. Folashade had been subjected to his attentions firsthand and now spoke of the monarch with hatred.

Olugbodi glanced at Halima. The unsmiling princess was the only one of his wives who was not rolling with laughter at his jests. He grinned and clapped his hands.

"My beautiful wife Halima requires more lively entertainment. Bring on the dancer!" he roared.

Now the music quickened. The ram horns squealed higher, the beat of the drum became low and steady. From the shadows emerged a female dancer. It was no one that Halima recognized. Olugbodi tired of dancers quickly and there was a never-ending flow of female flesh in the palace. Most of them performed the *sloth dindiki*, a solo dance in which a skimpily clad woman pranced about imitating a mare in heat.

But this was different.

This dancer's head was clean-shaven and her black-as-coal body dripped with animal fat. She strutted into the open and Halima saw that she carried an enormous python draped casually over her shoulder. It was thick as a man's body, and hung onto the floor. If it was one foot long, it was sixteen feet long!

The dancer's muscular legs strained under its massive weight.

Halima recoiled at the sight of the squirming reptile. Even though there wasn't a bowl, a shield or a spoon of these invaders that didn't bear the figure of the snake, their national totem still made her shudder.

To the throbbing beat of the drum, the dancer swayed, hips swinging left and right. Olugbodi grinned appreciatively and bit into a dripping hunk of hippopotamus meat. Halima held her breath and eyed him carefully, hoping to see him keel over – but he did not.

"This is the Python Dance, a traditional dance of our people," Olugbodi told her matter-of-factly.

The dancer allowed the scaly creature to roam freely over her body. Halima watched in a mix of repulsion and fascination as the snake encircled the woman's arms, becoming a bracelet, then slid like dripping molasses over her firm belly.

Halima stole another glance at Olugbodi, who gazed back at her with glittering, mischievous eyes.

The snake slithered about the woman's legs, now encircling them completely. For the first time now, Halima realized the peril the dancer was in. Like a creeping vine, the reptile hooped around her narrow, muscular abdomen, pinning her arms against her torso.

The dancer writhed silently in the snake's grip. The horns now screamed plaintively, imitating a woman's love cry.

It was impossible to know whether she was genuinely trying to escape. Her eyes were closed and she wore a mask of ecstasy. The horns screamed and wheezed, and she thrashed about in the grip of the python. Its tail stuck out, lashing violently left and right.

The awful beast was choking the life out of the dancer – and no one was stopping it! Halima looked around her in disbelief. The fourteen wives of King Olugbodi watched the scene, mesmerized, swaying rhythmically to the music. Several let out soft moans of passion. The whites of the dancer's eyes were showing now.

Halima bolted to her feet.

Olugbodi clapped his hands and the musicians ceased playing. As if some spell were broken, the snake loosened its grip and the dancer sank to the floor.

"Does the dance offend you, wife?" Olugbodi asked her, sweetly.

"It does not amuse me," Halima said through gritted teeth.

Olugbodi smiled and waved his hand. The dancer jumped to her feet, none the worse for wear, tossed the beast over one strong shoulder and sauntered off into the darkness.

Halima knelt back on the cushions beside the king. Only one pot of food remained covered. The big-bellied monarch had devoured all the rest, seemingly with no ill effects.

She must keep him from leaving the table before he consumed the contents of that final pot.

"Forgive me, Lord," she said. "I did not understand the dance."

He explained, "It is an ancient ritual that tells the story of our people. You know that we are called People of the Snake. Our legends say that the serpent of the Garden mated with a mortal girl and she gave birth to our people.

"Here, let me sing the tale to you." He signaled with his hand and a servant passed Olugbodi the stringed *muet*. All his wives and servants clustered around him. They all look upon him with fawning adoration, but his gaze was directed at Halima.

In his sweet, clear, boyish voice, he sang:

"In the Dawn Time, the time before, when man walked unafraid, two people lived. The Man and the Woman. He was simple and good, and she was tall-necked and vain, and lived to gaze at her reflection in the dark forest lakes. One day, as she bathed in the lake, the hissing snake, who had been spying on her, sang to her –!"

At that moment, as Olugbodi plucked the strings, it seemed that one somehow cut him. The plump king put his finger to his lips. His long tongue flickered and kissed away a tiny spot of blood. He smiled at Halima and continued to play.

Halima felt her blood run cold. For in a flash, she understood that the king had just been poisoned – and no food taster could have saved him.

King Olugbodi was oblivious, however. His eyes still met Halima's warmly, as he sang on: "Said the snake to the beautiful woman, 'Lie with me, pretty one, and to you I will teach the knowledge of good and evil …'"

Halima's face was taut and an awful trembling overtook her. It was as if he knew she was his murderer, he was staring at her with such intensity.

Suddenly, in the middle of the verse, the fat king faltered. Olugbodi's face froze in an awful grimace and he began to turn a purplish hue. His hands clutched his throat and, gurgling, he tumbled backward from his cushion. A gasp went up from the court, and servants and guards rushed forward in a great wave to surround their fallen king.

Masomakali stood at the front of the crowd, staring down in disbelief at the king's body. Olugbodi looked like a great whale, dead and washed up on the beach.

Halima sat on the cushion, unable to move. The enormity of what she had wrought struck her slowly. Wave after wave of remorse flooded over her. *What have I done*, she asked herself. She closed her eyes tight, shutting out the horrible image of Olugbodi's bloated corpse, and rocked on the cushion like a little girl.

"At last it is over," she whispered to herself.

She heard the sound of laughter and opened her eyes again. Who would dare laugh now, she wondered in astonishment.

Olugbodi stood before her, his hands on his wide hips, chortling.

The crowd of servants drew back silently from him like a receding wave. He faced Halima wearing a broad grin, enjoying his jest immensely. She stared in stunned disbelief as the king clapped his palms twice together. A servant placed before Halima the one pot that had not yet been opened.

"Let me tell you the end of the story," said Olugbodi in a soft voice. "Our legends say that we are the offspring of the serpent and we have his own venom in our veins."

He held up his finger, the one pricked by the poison.

"But the truth is this: From the cradle, each prince of our land is plied with poisons, each day with poisons of greater potency. Until the day when he is king, and not even the vilest poison can harm him."

He stared at Halima triumphantly. "So you see, you cannot best the King of Serpents at treachery."

Halima knelt before him, expressionless, her defeat slowly sinking in. Olugbodi clapped his hands again and the servant yanked the lid of the pot away.

There sat the gory head of Maguso the sorcerer, his mouth open and an apple stuck in it, his yellow teeth sunk into the fruit.

A gasp of terror went up among the servants. Halima shut her eyes and slumped down.

"Your servant Folashade told us everything. But do not be angry with her. She did not betray you willingly. She condemned you only squirming on a hill of ants, before they stung her to death. Do you deny your part in this?"

Halima slowly shook her head.

Masomakali stood beside his king, his yellow eyes glittering.

"Others must have been involved in this treason," he said. "Let me take the queen and use my implements of torture to exact the names of all the conspirators who dared betray you. Her body will soon surrender all its secrets."

The king smiled. "No, old friend. I am not ready yet to give up that exquisite body. But from this day forward, the queen will speak to no one. And she will never leave her chambers without my ordering it, upon pain of death."

CHAPTER 14

THE AMBASSADORS OF THE ABAKA

So it was that Halima of Kali became a prisoner in her own kingdom. The servants who attended her now spoke only in the hissing whispers of the People of the Snake. She was again overtaken with a searing loneliness. She missed Shomari and her stepson Kokayi, she missed her friends, the servant Neema and loyal Madongo, the bodyguard.

She had little to do but look out from the window of the stone tower, out across the placid sea. She dreamed that her husband Shomari, lord of the Abaka, the great ones of the mountain, would come for her; that his triumphant armies would march through the broad streets of Kali and he would slay the beast Olugbodi and free her.

In reality, the war had reached a standstill. The forces of Olugbodi and his allies had blazed their way to the very foot of the Silver Mountain, but they still could not discover, even with all their scouts and spies and intrigue, the secret pass through the rambling fields of bamboo, and the maze of narrow crevices that led up the mountain. Again and again, Masomakali and Olugbodi's other generals questioned Halima for that secret – but she swore to them that she had been blindfolded going up and down the mountain.

In truth, of course, when she and Kokayi climbed down the mountain they came straight through the secret pass. But nothing could ever make her reveal that.

Halima lay in bed, feeling the gentle curve of her belly which now subtly grew with every passing week. As she lay half-asleep on the blanket of soft lion fur, a servant appeared over her and sharply told her to dress.

"I will not be bullied," Halima retorted, rolling onto her belly with a frown.

The servant woman told her, "A party has arrived from the Abaka, ambassadors suing for peace. The king would have you at his side to greet them."

Halima hurriedly dressed in a long linen skirt and a guard escorted her to King Olugbodi's receiving hall. He sat on her father's golden throne, fully decked out in his kingly regalia, holding the royal scepter in his hand. Halima took her place silently at his side. It had been weeks since they spoke last.

He glanced at her hips, widening now, and at her bust, which was swelling up like a water-filled gourd.

"Our cook's dishes agree with you, Halima," he said with a sly smile. "I'm glad you're not wasting away in sorrow."

An ivory horn blew now, trumpeting the arrival of the visitors from the Silver Mountain, the land of the giants.

Halima felt herself trembling like a maiden on her wedding night. It was ridiculous to think for a moment that her true husband Shomari would be among the party. In a time of war, what nation would send its *ncamba*, war leader, as an ambassador? It is true that by all law and honored tradition, the persons of such ambassadors were held to be sacred and inviolate. But no country would ever tempt fate in such a way.

Yet still she trembled.

Now nine men marched into the great hall, past the gauntlet of one hundred spear-toting palace guards. They were giants all, of proud bearing. She had been away from the land of the Abaka so long that the chiseled features of the men seemed identical – every one of them reminded her of Shomari, her beloved. All of them wore the stately white robes and turbans of ambassadors.

Halima recognized their leader. It was venerable Watende, head of the Council of Elders. The gray-bearded old man addressed Olugbodi:

"Noble Olugbodi, whom men called Olugbodi the Trustworthy, King of the People of the Snake, master of Kali and of the ocean, we greet you."

As the old man spoke, Halima let her attention wander among the strong-jawed faces of the warriors of the Abaka. Her eyes settled on the very last of them, the tallest of the men.

He was boldly returning her stare. His eyes were fierce and hot, and before them Halima's heart melted. She felt her knees buckling under her as if they had turned to butter. She had to grip Olugbodi's shoulder to keep from toppling, and stood, swaying.

Shomari!

The words of old Watende barely registered in her brain as he continued to praise Olugbodi.

"Your sons have fought valiantly against us, and they have earned much honor. Many of the mightiest of the Abaka have fallen. But enough blood has been shed from this young generation. There are enough widows. Let us put an end to the killing."

Halima looked back at Shomari, who stood silently in

the back. He wore no kingly emblem or war leader's headdress.

Has he come all this way to see me? she wondered.

Olugbodi listened patiently to the ambassador's speech, and a boyish smile appeared on his plump features. When the old man finished, the king sat forward, considering their group, and stroking his fleshy triple chin.

Then abruptly, he clapped his hands. All around the room spears leapt to the ready in the hands of the warriors of the People of the Snake. The party of the Abaka drew instinctively into a circle.

Olugbodi turned to his slave general, Masomakali. "Take these ruffians and bind them."

As the palace guards converged on the visitors, Shomari pointed angrily at Olugbodi.

"Villain!" he bellowed. He started toward Olugbodi's throne, but a sharp spear poking his belly stopped him in his tracks. He stood there helplessly, as his arms were yanked behind his back and thick ropes were wrapped around him.

Halima turned to Olugbodi in horror.

"You foul, slithering snake. You've defecated on the throne of my father!"

King Olugbodi gave her a stinging blow across the face.

"Go to your room. Go to your room, or you will be taken with your friends to the darkest dungeon."

Halima stood helplessly watching the guards wrestle proud Shomari, and bind the King of the Abaka like a calf for the slaughter. All the while, his black eyes were fixed upon her.

She wanted to call out to him, but to let Olugbodi know that this was the war leader of all the Abaka would seal his fate. With great effort, she held her tongue and backed away, thinking *Oh my love, who has traveled so far and risked so much to find me. I will save you.*

So, the cunning and treacherous King Olugbodi chained the party that came to make peace with him. He ordered Masomakali to torture them and by any means, extract the secret of the pass to the mountains.

Halima, herself imprisoned in her bedchamber, was a wreck. She paced like a caged animal in the room, wringing her hands – helpless to aid her true husband.

Three days passed, and on the third day, Mwendapole came with news. Only he was allowed to see her now, for to the People of the Snake he was but an old fool, a jester to entertain the royals with amusing stories and songs.

"What have you learned?" Halima demanded.

The face of her father's griot was drained of blood. Sadly he told her, "The nine ambassadors of the Abaka have each in turn been tortured – gruesome tortures of the People of the Snake, cruelties inflicted too vile for your ears. But not one has betrayed the secret. Not one has cried out in pain. Already the elder is dead."

"I must see Shomari," Halima said.

Mwendapole shook his head. "Impossible, my queen."

Halima took him by his frail shoulders. "Friend of my father, I must see him."

To slip past the guard posted at the entrance to her chambers, Halima dressed as a servant girl, donning a veil to disguise her features.

Deep into the tunnels beneath the palace, pathways hewn in the stone in antiquity by underground streams running to the sea, Halima and the old griot wandered, until they reached the dungeons where the prisoners were kept. A pair of burly guards with shoulders as broad as water buffalos' stood at the doors.

Mwendapole told the men, "This young girl says these giants raided her village, killed her parents and violated her."

The guards scrutinized Halima.

"She wants only the chance to spit in the face of her

attacker," Mwendapole said. "If she were your sister, would you not grant her that small revenge?"

The bigger guard frowned. "There's not much left to spit upon."

Halima shuddered. The guard threw back a huge bolt and let it creak open. Halima glanced apprehensively at Mwendapole, then ducked into the black chamber.

The cold, dank room stank of sweat and mildew and stale blood. Halima shivered as she stepped forward, unable to see in the darkness. Then there was a sickening smack as she collided with flesh. She heard the rattle of chains – like the death rattle – and scuttled back.

The guard came into the chamber, carrying a torch and throwing a garish light onto the form of a giant who hung upside down by chains from his ankles – his mouth hanging open, black pits where his eyes had been gouged out and his manhood lopped off.

Halima spun and buried her face into the griot's breast. "Shomari!" she cried in anguish.

"Is that the coward who attacked you?" the guard asked. He punched the corpse casually. Halima thought bitterly of the proverb, "What is said over the dead lion's body could not be said to him alive."

Old Mwendapole turned Halima gently so that she faced the dead giant again. "Is it he?" he whispered.

Halima forced herself to look at the face – and saw that although the slain warrior had a chiseled visage like her beloved husband, it was not Shomari. Her heart began to beat again.

"This is not the one," she replied. Weak-kneed, she moved on into the room. The harsh light cast by the guard's torch fell over the faces of the other men. All were dead.

Except the last, the strongest, who still clung to life.

Shomari hung naked from the chains, his broad chest crisscrossed with open, bleeding wounds. His head lolled to one side, like part of a broken doll.

Tears began to stream from Halima's eyes. *Oh my dear husband, what have these jackals done to you*, she thought. Her husband seemed to sense her presence. He stiffened suddenly and groaned as consciousness returned to him. His eyes fluttered open, and as he saw her, a smile appeared on his parched, puffy lips.

Halima stepped close to him, and in the melodious tongue of the mountain people, she said, "My darling foolish love, why did you come here?"

The king of the giants whispered, "I couldn't live without seeing you again, Halima."

Halima was nearly blinded by tears now. "Oh my beloved," she whispered.

Shomari smiled painfully, his black eyes full of warmth. "It seems it's true what the old ones say: 'He who marries beauty, marries trouble.' "

The big guard frowned. "I thought she came to spit on him."

The griot told him, "She is cursing him and rebuking him for his crime against her."

"It doesn't sound like a curse to me. It sounds like the honey talk of lovers," the guard said suspiciously.

Shomari hoarsely ordered his wife, "Go on, spit upon me, wife."

Halima shook her head violently.

"Yes," he insisted. "Among us that is a sign of blessing – like the gentle falling rain."

Halima felt her throat drying up, an empty well. Behind her, the suspicious guard took a step forward and grabbed her arm. But Halima tore away. She threw back her fist and landed a blow in the middle of her husband's chest, so that he swung back like a punching bag.

Then she followed by pummeling him, spluttering in her own language every angry curse she knew. She grabbed hold of Shomari, wrapping her arms around him and burying her face against him, holding him. Both

Mwendapole and the guard had to use all their strength to wrestle her away.

In the language of the Abaka, as they dragged her way, she cried to him, "I will save you, husband!"

Halima immediately sought an audience with the king, Olugbodi. When she entered his private chambers, he was studying a map with his general, Masomakali. On the scroll, little pieces of stone of different colors sat, representing his various armies and those of his adversary.

His expression was so studious that for the first time he seemed to Halima like a real king, not simply a primping peacock.

She got straight to the point. "I wish to free the last of the Abaka ambassadors."

Olugbodi raised his eyebrows mockingly. "Our enemies, my queen?"

"I will tell you what he will never tell you, no matter how you torture him. I will tell you where the path to the mountains to the kingdom of the Abaka lies."

Olugbodi's eyes narrowed into catlike slits, and a smile appeared. He glanced at his three-fingered henchman.

Halima went on firmly. "In return you will free the Abaka."

King Olugbodi spun, turning his back on her, and chuckled with joy. Then he faced her wearing a look of triumph.

"I accept your bargain, Halima – with one additional condition."

Halima grimaced in anticipation.

"You must give yourself to me," the king said with a gleam in his eyes. Halima looked down at the stone floor. Then she steeled herself and nodded morosely.

Olugbodi held up his index finger. "That is not enough," he went on, his voice lowering. "I must see you stripped before me on your knees, begging for my love."

Halima looked up at him, nostrils flaring, blood rushing to her cheeks. *The pig!*

Sternly Olugbodi pressed on. "Or do you prefer to see your Abaka lover unmanned and die a shrieking eunuch?"

Halima met his eyes coolly. "I will do as you wish."

Masomakali grinned a crocodile's sharp-toothed grin.

"There is no shame in it, girl. A cow must graze where it is tied," he hissed.

Olugbodi looked like a fat little boy with a jar of honey. "Masomakali, the map!" he cried. The slave general strode over with the map and laid it out in front of Halima.

Halima felt a torrent of emotion sweep over. Again she felt as if she were in the river, rushing toward the great falls.

In her mind's eye, she saw the peaceful mountain city and the magnificent clouds rolling overhead. She remembered the cruel words of the seer, the old man of the mountain who warned Shomari that she would, for love, someday betray the Abaka. But beneath this clamor of thoughts rang one clear notion: she would save her husband, Shomari. She pointed to the pass on the map.

Masomakali blew up. "The Kalian bitch lies, my lord. Our spies have searched that area. All that's there is an impassable thicket of prickly nyika bushes and bamboo."

Olugbodi looked sharply at Halima. She shot Masomakali a contemptuous glance.

"Beyond those thorns is the pass," she said, "If you had courage you would have found it."

Masomakali scowled.

Olugbodi clapped his palms together in glee. "Prepare our armies to march within seven days, Masomakali."

"Yes, Highness." He hesitated, as if reluctant to leave. Then he hurried out of the chamber.

Halima demanded, "And now you will free the Abaka."

"You forget – you have yet to meet the final condition."

Halima turned to go. "I will prepare myself."

Olugbodi blocked her path and stood there, his fists on his chubby hips.

"I want you as you are now, proud one," he said huskily. "I want your own smells, not some perfume from the bark of a tree or the glands of an animal."

Halima looked away, biting back her anger. She unfastened her dress and let it fall. She unwrapped her headdress, and peeled off her silk loincloth, so that she stood naked before Olugbodi.

She stepped toward the monarch, but he stayed her with a raised hand. "Remember?" he said.

Halima nodded stiffly and forced herself to her knees before King Olugbodi.

Head bowed, she mumbled, "King Olugbodi the Trustworthy, my lord and master, I kneel before you as less than your slave, as a supplicant before her god. I am an empty vessel. I beg for you to take me and fill me."

Afterward, Olugbodi lay on top of Halima, panting, his fat gut pressed against her gently rounded tummy. She was drenched in his sweat, which smelled of cooked pig fat.

He embraced her and gasped in her ear, "I have loved 300 women in my day and none like you. I knew you and I were a pair from the moment I laid my eyes on you. That underneath all that pride was a creature of the jungle. These other women, they make love to have children to take care of them in their old age, when they are sagging crones. But you burn – as I burn."

He caressed her belly. "Oh, I love you, Halima. I want you to bear my sons. I know you have one here – but do not fear, he won't go to the sword. I will rear him as my own; he will be raised in the way of the Snake and he will be a second Olugbodi."

Halima said nothing. But for the first time he looked into her eyes, and saw the revulsion that was there.

He choked with exasperation. "Am I such an ogre?" He took her soft shoulders and shook them. "Do you really hate me so? Are you so much in love with that Abaka?"

Halima shut her eyes.

Olugbodi climbed to his feet, clutching his robe around him with stiff dignity. He said with a mirthless smile, "At least admit you enjoyed our lovemaking."

Halima lay expressionless. Olugbodi shook with anger and shame – as if he were the one who'd been violated. He stomped to the door and threw it open.

"Masomakali!" he hollered.

Halima sat up slowly. "What of the Abaka?" she called. "You gave your word."

Masomakali arrived at the doorway.

Olugbodi told him, "Have the guards keep her here. And have the Abaka put to death."

"No!" Halima screamed. "No, you gave your word!"

Olugbodi turned his back to her. His shoulders rose and fell as he sighed deeply. Then he added, "See that he does not suffer."

He strode out of the chamber, shutting the door behind him.

Halima lay on the floor of the chamber, weeping, curled up like a fetus. Shame overcame her as she thought of how she had allowed Olugbodi to defile her flesh – all in vain.

For her husband still was to perish, and there was nothing that could be done to stop it. All his people were doomed as well because of her. She shook, weeping like a child. She pined for her mother, her father, her great aunt Bimkubwa to hold her, and for the foul stink of Olugbodi to wash away.

Then a gentle hand, the strong hand of a man, touched her bare shoulder. Halima looked up, startled.

She was astounded to see before her the face of Madongo, the sword bearer of her father. She almost cried out in surprise, then embraced him, huddling against his broad chest. She ran her hands over his gleaming bald head.

"How did you get here?" she gasped in astonishment. "Are you Madongo in truth, or the ghost of Madongo?"

He pointed to an opening in the wall of the king's chamber.

"There are hidden passages in the palace running clear to the sea. The knowledge of the tunnels was entrusted only to the most loyal of your father's palace guards," he explained.

"I thought you were dead, dear friend," Halima said, as she fixed her dress modestly about her.

"When Neema and I returned to Kali, we learned Olugbodi had seized the throne. We feared for our lives and went into hiding in Neema's village."

"Why did you come?" Halima asked.

"Word came that you are a prisoner. At the sea I have a small boat waiting to rescue you."

Halima embraced him gratefully. He looked unchanged: his bald head glistening, and powerful body bare except for a fisherman's loincloth.

"Oh, Madongo. You know I am a princess no more, but only a powerless wretch – and yet you came for me."

Madongo raised his sword arm. "For 180 years my fathers have served yours. While I breathe, this arm is yours."

"And never have I needed it more, friend," she said.

To her chambers, Halima quickly summoned Mwendapole, and told him to take two servants and begin the journey to the Silver Mountain. He was to warn the leaders of the Abaka that an army of King Olugbodi was on the way.

"Tell them to wait in ambush in all their numbers in the hidden pass, and there to destroy his armies in one blow," she commanded.

"Do you wish me to join with the Abaka in battle?" the old man queried hesitantly. "I have not held a weapon in many years – in truth, never."

"It is not your battle, friend of my father," Halima told him. I want you to live a long time, so you may teach my son the wisdom of our ancestors." She kissed him gently on the forehead and sped him on his way.

She and the iron-thewed Madongo set off into the secret passageway from the king's chamber, to find the dungeon where her husband Shomari was a prisoner facing death.

They clambered through the pitch-black tunnel, squeezing through the narrow passageways. Even turned sideways, and scuttling like a crab, Halima felt the sharp, jagged stone scraping at her flesh.

227

In front of her, the broad-shouldered warrior had an even rougher time negotiating the corridors. She heard dust crumbling away as he forced his way through. Halima's heart pounded furiously. They were moving so slowly – and each moment brought her husband closer to death.

She cursed herself for the minutes she had wasted with Mwendapole. But she knew her husband would not wish to live if his people were destroyed.

At last she saw a glow up ahead. Madongo stepped out into a hall, and then pulled her after him.

The torch-lit hall, though scarcely wide enough to accommodate two average-sized men at once, was like a wide valley now compared to the secret passage through which they had been scrabbling. They hurried along toward the prison cell.

"Beware of the guard, faithful Madongo," Halima whispered.

Madongo craned his neck cautiously around the corner, then crept, on leopard feet, into the hall to the cell. Halima followed on tiptoes.

The hall was empty now. The door to Shomari's cell was unguarded. Halima felt her jaw clench tightly. *Why would they have left the cell unguarded – unless there was no one alive to guard?*

They approached the cell door solemnly. It stood unbolted. Taking a torch from a bronze holder in the hall, Madongo nudged the door and it swung creaking open.

Halima covered her nose. The chamber smelled of rot and death. And yet the room was empty now – the hacked up carcasses of the giants had been hauled away...

... except for a solitary figure which lay on a slab in the middle of the room, arms crossed, covered by a white shroud. Halima felt her knees begin to give way beneath her.

Madongo strode to the slab, on which a single goblet sat. The goblet was decorated by twisting, intertwined serpents, their fangs bared. He picked up the cup, sniffed it and winced, then hurled it away.

"For killing elephants," he muttered. He leaned forward and pulled back the shroud. Halima saw the face of her husband, Shomari – blue-black, frozen in a grimace, his eyes open and gazing at eternity.

Halima dropped to her knees. Feverish prayers rushed from her lips.

"Mother, Father. All my kin who dwell in the shadows, I plead with you. Do not let this be so. Do not let my husband be swallowed by the abyss. Send him back to me. I beg you!"

As Halima continued to plead and weep, her body convulsing like one with the fever, Madongo rested his ear against the giant's breast, then solemnly rose. He put his fingers to Shomari's throat and almost shivered at the coldness. Finally he put one hand over the mouth of Shomari and felt not one hint of breath.

He turned to Halima. "Princess, I am sorry. We must go now, before you are missed." Then he began to pull the shroud up over the body.

"No! No! No!" Halima shrieked. "It cannot be! It cannot be!"

Madongo started toward her comfortingly – as she shut her eyes, threw back her head and let out a piercing scream like a female baboon whose mate had been slaughtered by hunters. Madongo nervously clapped his broad right hand over her mouth.

Then, from under the shroud, an arm fell. Halima jabbered with excitement, muffled by Madongo's hand, and pointed to Shomari's fingers, which twitched once…then twice. Halima leapt to her feet and rushed to her husband's side. She ripped the shroud away. His eyes were shut now, clenched as if from horrible pain.

"He's alive!" she cried in joy.

Madongo was beside her in an instant. "It will take a

great physician to save him."

"You have doctors in Neema's village?"

"Yes, Princess," Madongo said. "But there is little time."

"Lift him!" she ordered.

Madongo heaved and moaned as he hurried through the tunnel toward the sea with the giant over his shoulder. It was like watching an ant carry a huge crumb of bread. Halima scurried along behind, sloshing through water that swirled around her ankles. Here the stones were smooth, damp and cold. The rank odor of rotting seaweed filled her nostrils.

"The tide is coming in," Madongo warned her, panting.

Indeed, just a few moments later they were waist deep in the frigid seawater. Halima tenderly held the head of her husband, so that it did not sink beneath the water. Madongo was struggling under the great weight of the giant now. Chest heaving, he slowed to a halt and leaned against the slick stone wall of the secret tunnel.

"Princess, I must rest," he murmured.

"The water is rising, Madongo," Halima reminded him. It was lapping at her navel now.

"I cannot bear him," he confessed. "He is like a giant tree."

Halima splashed close to the warrior and looked him in the eyes with ferocity. "Do you truly love me, Madongo?"

He bowed his head. "Yes, you know it."

"Then you must save him – for he is my true heart."

Madongo nodded painfully.

She took the giant's legs. "Go on now!" she ordered.

Together they waded, lurching through the water.

They were neck-deep in sea water when at last light appeared at the end of the tunnel. Halima was gasping for breath, inching forward on tiptoes, trying to keep her nostrils above water.

"I have him, Princess," Madongo shouted. "Swim for

the boat!"

Reluctantly, Halima released her grip on her husband's legs, and let her feet rise from the slippery floor of the tunnel. Thrusting out arm after arm, she swam through the mouth of the tunnel out to the sea.

Huge waves crashed against the jagged rocks around her, battering her and spinning her about. But she forged ahead, drinking in as little of the salt water as she could.

Just ahead she saw a small sailboat, made of reeds lashed together with coconut rope. A sinewy old man was at the helm, fighting the waves and paddling furiously with a long oar. The boat spun about like a toy spiraling down a drain.

Choking and spluttering, Halima cried out to the old fisherman. He fought to turn the boat toward her. She swam, kicking with all her might, battling the powerful waves that sought to hurl her back against the rocks.

A tremendous undertow kept pulling her head under-water, trying to take her down to the depths. She swallowed more and more water, till she felt her belly full of it. At last she reached the boat and the boatman reached for her. She stuck out her hand and she felt the old man's grip – powerful from decades hauling up nets full of fish – take her other wrist and yank her out of the water.

Halima clambered into the boat and knelt on all fours, stomach heaving as she vomited up seawater. Then, still reeling, she lurched to the side of the vessel to look for a sign of Madongo and her husband.

At first, all she saw were black crashing waves and white frothy foam – then she spotted them. Madongo clung with one arm to a jagged boulder near the base of the cliffs. The other brawny arm was locked around the giant's neck, barely keeping his face out of the ocean.

Tall waves slammed over the boulder, threatening to rip the warrior's arm from its socket. Again and again the pair would vanish under the waves – but always the head of faithful Madongo would reappear.

Halima pointed them out to the old man. He handed her an oar, and together they struggled to guide the boat toward the boulder.

Halima had never used an oar before. She'd only lain idly in barges while her father's servants took her out on jaunts for her amusement. But her determination to reach her husband taught her quickly. She stabbed the water again and again with all her might, till her slim arms ached.

At last they pulled alongside the boulder. Madongo, groaning with effort, pushed the giant up as Halima and the boatman each grabbed one elongated arm and pulled as hard as they could.

The small boat turned halfway over, nearly capsizing from his weight, and a rush of cold water ran into the craft. Shomari slid like a huge elephant seal onto the floor of the boat. Waves crashed against the hull, threatening to splinter the fragile reed boat against the rocks.

Madongo braced his feet against the boulders and shoved off, sending the boat careening away from the rocks. Agile as ever, he sprang into the boat, and ripped the oar from Halima's hand. He and the old man began to paddle frantically against the surf, to get the boat clear from the rocks.

"We must raise the sail!" the old man cried in a voice barely audible over the surf.

Madongo pointed to the palace wall, overlooking the cliffs. "The guards will see us!" he yelled back.

"We must, son, or we'll be crushed like eggshells!"

Madongo nodded fearfully. As he and the old man back-paddled furiously, Madongo yelled to Halima, "Princess, you must hoist the sail!"

Halima crawled to the mast. Blinded by waves that splashed across her face, she felt for the rope to raise the sail. Using all her strength, she untied it. The sail slowly unfurled.

Now the boat glided away from the cliffs and across the open water. Halima gave a sigh of relief, and knelt beside her husband.

"Princess, this is Neema's father Chinua," Madongo said.

The old man, who was wrinkled by the sun like a raisin, smiled at her, revealing a mouth checkered with missing teeth.

"Thank you, father of my friend," Halima said.

From the cliffs, a horn blew. In a moment, the cliffs were lined with tiny figures that at this distance looked like crows on a clothesline.

"Row!" Madongo shouted at the old man. The two dug their paddles deep into the water and the boat sped on as a hail of spears and arrows showered down on them.

Halima threw herself on her husband, shielding him. *If this is the end of our journey, let this be how we shall be found*, she thought.

Arrows screamed through the air and splashed into the water like some black hellish rain.

Thunk! One smashed into the bow beside Halima's head. Thunk! Thunk! Thunk!

Madongo howled in pain as a dart hurtled into his thigh. But biting his lip, the burly warrior continued to pull out to sea with the help of the wiry old man.

The arrows rained down around the boat like hungry gulls diving into the sea for fish. Halima lay over her husband, her eyes closed in terror, until the sounds diminished and became gentle, far-off plunks, more like bird droppings plopping in the water.

Finally, they were beyond the range of the city wall. Halima sat up. The old man was panting like a dog, as if his sturdy old heart might now suddenly give out. With a grimace, Madongo wrenched the arrow from his thigh and hurled it away.

She inched forward on her hands and knees on the

rocking boat, unwound her soaking head wrap and wound it around the warrior's broad thigh to staunch the bleeding.

"Are we safe?" Halima asked him.

Madongo shook his head. "Their boats will be after us."

With bloody hands he gripped the paddle and started pulling through the water vigorously. The old man sucked in a deep breath of salty air and followed suit.

Halima looked anxiously over her shoulder and could see behind them what look like a dot in the ocean. Then she realized it was a long boat with two dozen oarsmen armed with spears. The loud beat of a drum set their pace.

"They're coming!" she shrieked.

Madongo and the old fisherman threw all their strength into their paddling, taking long, deep strokes that sent the boat skimming across the water. But behind them, powered by the backs of more than twenty strong black warriors, the vessel of the enemy shot through the water like a shark.

They were roaring a chant in the language of the People of the Snake:

"We are the sons of the snake.
Feed us and live,
But tread on us and perish.
We are the sons of the snake.
Against us none can prevail
For we will rule eternal."

Halima could see that at the head of the craft was the king's snake-eyed henchman, Masomakali. His sharp teeth gleamed with an evil grin of triumph as the long boat bore down on them.

Neema's father panted heavily now, a raspy wheeze of a man about to keel over dead. He stopped paddling, and

the boat skated gently along the surface, slowing to nearly a dead stop. The wind died for a moment, and the boat spiraled about in a slow, purposeless circle. Madongo looked around in wild desperation, like a cornered rodent.

We are doomed, Halima thought – *but not to capture. No, not capture.* She knelt beside her husband, who lay still as death at the bottom of the boat, the faint glow of life ebbing from him. She touched his ice-cold cheek tenderly.

"Wherever you are bound, Shomari, I am with you," she said. She called to Madongo as she snuck his short iron sword from its leather scabbard. She held it before him.

"Madongo, do not let them take us alive," she ordered.

Madongo shook his head in horror. "I knelt at your father's feet and swore to protect you."

"There is no hope, my friend," she insisted.

Madongo looked around frantically, and pointed with excitement to a set of rocks in the distance. The pair of immense boulders jutted out of the water just a few yards apart. Between the boulders a forbidding torrent of waves smashed and swirled chaotically.

"There!" he gasped.

The old man protested. "We'll be crushed fine as flour!"

Madongo turned to Halima. "A small boat could make it. There is our hope, Princess."

Halima nodded. "For the rocks," she ordered. "Let it be our salvation or damnation."

The old man gritted his teeth, and he and Madongo threw their last morsel of strength into a headlong dash for the boulders.

The enemy vessel had pulled up behind them, just two boat lengths to their rear. The bare-chested warriors aboard were already cheering and proclaiming victory. Halima saw that their pursuers were veering away from the rocks, planning to catch them on the other side.

She stood straight up in the rocking boat. "Jackals, are

you not men enough to follow us?" she hollered at them at the top of her small lungs.

Her taunt gave new vigor to her young pursuers. They veered back and put such force into their strokes that their boat was within an arm's reach of them when Chinua's little craft reached the gap between the rocks.

"Get down, Princess – this will be close," Madongo warned. Halima crouched down, huddling against Shomari's stiff form as if his frigid body could still protect her.

Madongo began muttering a fervent prayer as Neema's father guided the craft so that the bow dove precisely midway between the boulders. The boat rocked left, then right, nearly tipping over in each direction. Shomari's immense body almost rolled out of the boat, taking Halima with it.

As the boat rocketed through the gap, she raised her head and saw a jagged black rock passing a nose hair away.

She screamed in terror – but she was not alone. Madongo and the old man let go of their manly pride and took up her fearful scream. They turned it into a warrior's whoop of joy as the boat leapt safely through the perilous gap and into the open sea.

Halima twisted back to see the longboat of their pursuers shoot between the boulders behind them.

The warriors of the snake cried out, a high-pitched battle cry like the screams of an eagle descending on its prey. The swirling current twisted the longboat so its bow arched into the air. The vessel cracked against the rocks, and split in half like a twig.

The war cry of the oarsmen turned into squeals of utter terror and panic as they spilled headlong into the water. Halima shut her eyes, while the roaring waves snuffed out their cries.

The wind carried Halima's own tiny vessel out to sea, as the warriors, thrashing about the ocean like drowning ants, grew smaller and smaller.

Madongo, who was watching grimly, said, "May the Great One in the Sky have mercy on them."

The boat sailed along the coast until darkness settled on the sea and the sky above turned gray as slate. Halima lay, rocked as in a cradle by the gentle waves. As the boat sailed serenely across the moonlit sea, Halima slept with her head on her husband's clammy chest.

Suddenly she realized something was wrong and sat up in alarm. "I can't hear his heart anymore," she cried.

Chinua, who'd been manning the till as Madongo dozed, crouched down beside her. The deep eyes of Shomari stared unseeing at the brilliant round moon.

The old fisherman said in a hushed voice, "He is at the threshold between life and death, Princess – one foot on this side of the river, and the other in the land of shadows."

Halima fought panic. "What can we do?" she demanded.

Said the father of Neema, "I am an old man. I have seen many pass across the river – and none return."

Halima shook her head. "He will come back for me."

Madongo was awake now too, and knelt beside her.

"Call him," he suggested. "Call him back."

Halima knelt in the boat, cradling her husband's head in her lap. She closed her eyes and let the words gush out of her, as gently she sang:

"Leave me tomorrow, love.
Do not ford the river.
Lend me one night, love.
Stay, love, stay."

Tears rolled down her cheeks. It was an old, sappy song Halima had heard 1,000 times. Only now did its meaning ring clear.

Halima felt a gentle tug on her fingers and looked down to see Shomari's hands gripping hers. His eyes too were brimming with tears.

"He is returned," said Chinua, looking up at the sea of stars in amazement. "Praise to the Great One in the Sky! Praise to the Rain Giver!"

CHAPTER 15

REFUGE

M idday the next morning, the boat arrived at Neema's village. Fifty or so beehive-shaped houses with thatched roofs lined the shore, interspersed with palm trees with enormous fan-shaped leaves and dangling coconuts.

The tiny boat was greeted by dozens of youths who swam out and towed it swiftly to shore, dragging it onto the golden sand. Their muscles were strong from swimming, and they wore only simple cotton loincloths.

A stretcher of palm branches was hurried down to the boat. It took four strong men to bear Shomari up from the beach to the house of the healer, Morowa. The people of the village were loyal to Halima's family and they called out welcome, singing her name in praise.

As Halima hurried beside the stretcher, the people of the village ran alongside her, the women throwing flowers at her. They were beautiful people, small and lithe, with joyful voices as clear as tinkling bells. The women of the tiny fishing village wore their hair in tall, intricate, spiked braids decorated with shells and beads, and went naked except for a garment of three broad leaves that covered their loins. They wore simple jewelry fashioned from cowrie shells, coral and pearls.

The stretcher bearing Shomari was rushed into a rectangular house made of bamboo, which stood on stumpy stilts. A herd of tall-legged crabs scuttled underneath it.

Halima attempted to follow. But as she ducked to enter the low doorway, a broad woman the size of a hippo with a heavy, furrowed brow emerged, blocking her way. Unlike the other women, Morowa wore a long skirt and a headdress full of ostrich and vulture feathers.

She held back Halima with one fleshy hand.

"We will heal your husband," Morowa said curtly, and ducked back into the house, pulling the curtain after. Madongo and Chinua, father of Neema, each took one of Halima's arms and restrained her.

"Trust them, Highness," Madongo said gently. "They may not have all the titles of the court physicians, but I've seen the doctors of this village cut a tumor from a boy's brain, and open a woman to deliver her child. I've seen them use their herbs to cure madness and to stop contagion. He is in good hands."

Reluctantly, Halima nodded.

"Come, let me take you to my house. You need food and rest," Madongo said.

As soon as Neema saw Halima approaching on the beach, she ran out of her house and down the shore, squealing like a young girl. She leapt into the arms of her mistress, nearly bowling her over.

The two embraced and kissed and clutched each other joyfully. Neema was dressed like the other women of the village, her bottom bare, although she wore much more jewelry – including all the fine gold pieces Halima gave her. Halima pushed away her handmaiden and looked at her in astonishment. As they hugged, their bellies met and Halima noticed Neema's full tummy and swollen breasts.

Neema proudly ran her hand over her protruding belly.

"My husband Madongo has made me fat with a baby," she announced.

Halima smiled and ran her hand over her own abdomen. Neema brightened even more.

"You also!" she exclaimed. She laughed, still the bright, gay laughter of a child.

Halima chuckled too – for the first time in months, it seemed.

Madongo came up behind Neema and gave her a playful spank. "Woman, save your gossip for the marketplace. The princess is ready to drop from hunger. And so are we – or have you forgotten your husband and your father?"

Neema embraced Madongo and then wiry old Chinua. As she hugged her father, Madongo gave Halima a quick glance, tinted with embarrassment.

So he and Neema were married now. For an awkward, peculiar moment, Halima felt a pang of the old jealousy returning. But just as quickly it subsided. For she had her own husband now, whom she dearly loved.

The princess raised an eyebrow. "So you married my maidservant without my permission, eh?" she said with mock severity.

Madongo and Neema bowed their heads.

"Then I give you permission now, Neema and Madongo," she added with a smile. "And I offer my blessings."

The couple gave a deep sigh of relief.

Madongo's house was a simple bamboo structure. Swallows had built their nests in the thatched roof, and little green lizards scurried along the walls. Fishing tackle and tools hung neatly from pegs inside.

All kneeling cross-legged on the floor, Halima and her hosts ate the soft, gluey flesh of stewed crawfish and sipped *uki*, a drink prepared from sugarcane. Across the way they could hear the beat of the drum and the sound of the *wombi*, the eight-stringed harp the healers played as they worked and sang over Shomari.

After supper, Neema's father bade them good evening.

Neema and Madongo waited up with Halima, late into the night, praying with her for Shomari's recovery. But at last her hosts began to yawn and apologize deeply. The couple lay down, curled together on a bed of palm leaves, and soon they were snoring.

Halima stayed sat bolt upright, listening to the weird, inhuman cries and throbbing drum. Bizarre visions passed through her mind as she drifted back and forth from the realm of the waking to the land of sleep.

In her mind's eye, she saw her husband naked, stretched out on a mat, strange spirals and other markings painted over the length of his elongated frame. The healers swayed over him, chanting and praying for the intercession of the spirits.

Yet again she saw for a moment Shomari standing before her in the shadows, waving to her sadly.

In her dream Shomari was again making love to her. She remembered his bull-like strength and savage passion. His words came back to her, the words he said to her when he went off to war: "Do you think I would leave one such as you? I will always come back to you, Halima."

The door to the bamboo hut swung open and bright orange light streamed across Halima's face. She sat up, blinking, unable to believe it was already morning.

The healer Morowa loomed over her. "Come," she commanded.

Halima scrambled to her feet.

"Follow me, Princess," Morowa said. The beefy woman turned and strode off down the beach. Halima scurried after her, fixing her long skirts about her.

"In all of nature no beast is as cruel as man," the healer said angrily. "No animal would've ravaged a body as those butchers did. The torture would have killed an ordinary man, but he has the strength of a lion."

"Then my husband lives!"

"When they poisoned him they did not consider his

great size. They did not give him enough poison to destroy him."

Joy filling her heart, Halima rushed to the curtained entrance to the healer's house. But Morowa blocked her way and held the curtain shut with one broad hand. She looked at Halima sternly, her dark eyebrows knitting together.

Halima frowned. "What is it you're not telling me?" she demanded.

The medicine woman said nothing and pulled the curtain aside. Halima tore herself from the woman's gaze and ducked into the house. The air was thick with incense. Jars of goat's blood and other medicines sat out on a table.

Shomari lay stretched out on a bed of palm leaves. As in her vision, he was painted with strange markings, crosses and spirals. Halima rushed to him and knelt beside him. He wore a faint smile and raised his right hand weakly to stroke her hair. She felt a warm rush of tears on her cheeks.

"Oh husband, oh husband, I was so afraid," she murmured. She buried her head on Shomari's chest where his wounds had all been finely stitched. His heart beat was powerful now, like a lion's.

His chest rumbled as he told her in his deep, gentle voice, "All the torment I endured was a fair price for this one sweet moment." He ran his long fingers tenderly across her tear-soaked cheek. "The only cruelty is not to see your beauty."

Halima slowly raised her face from Shomari's chest and saw that her husband's eyes were fixed on infinity.

"Oh no," Halima moaned. She covered her face and began to bawl.

"Do not weep for me," Shomari told her. "We of the Abaka have a third eye, an inner eye. Through it we see the whole world, not just shape and color but order and meaning. My inner eye is open now, Halima, and I see so much more now than I could ever see before. I see what a fool I was to send you away. Your place is beside me, always."

He drew Halima toward him and they embraced. She bathed him in hot tears and they nestled together for a few blissful moments. Halima lay on his chest as it rose and fell, listening to the squawking seagulls.

She sat up again.

"Husband, now I must tell you something that will make you send me from you side again." She felt her courage ebbing. She could not say it.

"I am so ashamed. My yearning was so strong; I sacrificed everything to have you again. To save you I sacrificed my flesh to Olugbodi. And to save you, I told him of the mountain pass to your kingdom. Your seer spoke truly – for love of you I did betray your people."

Shomari threw back his head and groaned, an awful roar like a lion thrust through with a spear. Shockwaves of anger and pain erupted from the giant. Halima bowed and began to pull away. Their lives together were at an end, she realized. It was folly to imagine otherwise. At least now she knew he was safe and alive, and at least they had had one precious, untroubled moment.

But Shomari still clung to her with an iron grip that could not be broken. He lay shaking, trying to compose himself.

"The wrongdoing was mine, my wife. The old ones say, 'When the leopard is away, the cubs are eaten.' "

Halima tried to ease his pain. "I sent word to the Abaka. I told them to prepare themselves, and told them to mount an ambush at the pass.

Shomari shook his head. "They will not believe an outsider. I left my younger brother Jumoke to rule in my stead. He is strong and valiant. But he does not have the shrewdness to discern that the warning is true."

He half sat up. "I must go to them," he muttered. As he rose, a spasm shot through him and he fell back, coughing and spitting up blood.

Halima pushed hum gently down. "No. No. Rest, my love."

Shomari nodded. He reached up, took her head and brought it down so it again rested gently upon his chest.

On the beach, Halima knelt in the burning sand. She was dressed like the other women of the village now, wearing three broad leaves strategically placed to shield her loins, a tiny string around her waist holding them on.

Neema squatted behind her, fixing hcr hair into the spiked braids the women of the village wore.

"Now we will truly look like sisters," she said with a bright smile.

Halima gazed out silently over the still ocean as Neema chattered on. "The men will be back from the sea soon. They are emptying their wicker traps of all the lobsters and filling their nets with fish." She added, proudly, "Madongo is fast learning to be a fisherman. The men all admire him. With his strong arms he can drag up a whole net almost by himself."

For six months, Madongo had gone out to sea with the other men and given Neema's parents three quarters of his share of the catch. For among these people it was the custom that when a man had no material possessions to give as a bride price, he must pay instead with the sweat of his brow.

Halima looked at the gulls, which cried out as if in grief as they sailed through the hazy sky.

"I miss braiding this beautiful hair on the velvet cushions of your father's palace," Neema said, running her hands through Halima's locks. "But we can have a good new life here. When your husband is strong again, he will learn to fish and sail as Madongo has."

Halima shook her head. "We cannot stay here, Neema. There will be men of Olugbodi's searching for us, warriors of the People of the Snake."

"But Princess, we are one of hundreds of villages along the seacoast. They will never find us here." Neema suddenly pointed into the distance cheerfully. "Look, Princess – the men are returning."

She still has in her all the joy of a young girl, Halima thought, as she stood, squinting out across the bright blue water. Far in the distance, she could make out two long boats pulling for shore.

Neema prattled on. "Tonight, I will show you how we fry shark meat. You will not believe what a good cook I have become."

Halima stood up next to her, stiffening with fear. Neema ceased her idle chatter, sensing something was wrong.

Halima felt her heart began to race. She reached down and jerked Neema to her feet, pointing to the boats approaching. Hoisted above the sails fluttered a banner depicting a pair of snakes intertwined. It was the flag of the People of the Snake!

From all around the village there went up cries of alarm. Women began to cry for their children, rounding up the naked toddlers who waddled innocently on the beach.

Neema grabbed Halima's arm.

"Princess, we must run to the bushes." They ran a few yards like chickens with their heads cut off, kicking up sand in all directions, and then Halima halted. Neema pulled at her hand frantically, but Halima shook her off.

"I must see to my husband," she declared.

Neema looked at her wide-eyed, quaking in terror. Halima remembered how her servant had been brutally attacked by the squat deserter in the forest and nearly violated. She could not ask her to linger by her side.

Halima told her friend, "You do not have to stay."

She pulled off the turtle-shell pendant, the symbol of her clan, and handed it to the other young woman.

"Keep this with you. Run and hide yourself now, little

sister," she ordered. Neema hesitated, then gave her a grateful look and dashed off into the grass.

Halima turned and ran toward the sick house. When she was a few yards from the sick house, Morowa the healer caught her by the wrist.

"It's too late," she hissed and gestured to the shore, where the enemy boats had arrived. Moving with speed and discipline, two dozen jet-black warriors poured out of the boats – a pair of long, narrow *dhows,* hollowed out tree trunks. The men dragged the boats onto the beach.

They wore the war dress of the People of the Snake, with bands of reptile skin around their bulging biceps and thighs. They jogged up the beach in tight formation, carrying their spears upright.

Like Neema, most of the young, nubile women had run off into the tall grass. At Morowa's signal, the older women and children of the village clustered nervously about Halima, butting her with their bodies until she was hidden at the center of the crowd.

Halima felt a crush of fragrant female flesh jamming around her, and could barely see over the shoulders of those shielding her.

The head of the war party, a barrel-chested young man with a soldierly swagger and peach fuzz on his chin, approached the group. The women chattered anxiously among themselves. The boat captain raised a hand, silencing them for the moment.

"Who speaks for the women of this village?" he called out.

Morowa the healer pushed her way to the front of the crowd.

"I do," she said, crossing her plump arms in front of her.

The warrior turned to her, but spoke loudly enough that all could hear.

"We are here on the business of Olugbodi the

Trustworthy, great King of Kali. You who are his loyal subjects have nothing to fear."

A few skeptical grunts erupted from the crowd.

"Princess Halima, wife of the king, has been kidnapped by Abaka spies. We've been sent to rescue her."

Morowa replied, "We have had no strangers visit the village in many months." There were murmurs of agreement among the women.

Now the boat captain shouted out, "Know that by order of the king, those who harbor these fugitives face death."

Morowa faced the youthful warrior eye to eye. She told him with contempt, "In the days of King Babatunde the Good, young men were not sent out to bully women."

Some of the women laughed, and others cheered Morowa's boldness. "Cowardly boys!" a voice in the back hollered.

Some of the old women bent and came up with fistfuls of sand and hurled them in the faces of the warriors. The young men staggered back in surprise and embarrassment. For a moment, the boat captain looked as befuddled as his men – then he snapped into action.

"You men guard these women!" he cried, waving to one boatload of men. "You others, search every house and all the woods." Warriors who'd piled out of the second boat ran up the beach, dispersing in all directions.

Growling and trying to look as menacing as possible, the remaining young warriors surrounded the women on the beach, poking their fleshy sides tentatively with the points of their spears, as if they were some unfamiliar and possibly dangerous animals.

The herd of women drew back into a tight pack, a few brave ones yelling back slurs upon the warriors' manhood. From behind, Halima felt a hand take her head and push her down, so that she knelt in the sand, well-hidden among the bare legs and feet of the older women of the village.

In a few moments, the other warriors returned,

dragging behind the nubile young women and adolescent girls who had taken refuge in the jungle.

The boat captain sternly examined the features of each of the squirming maidens. *He must have been given a description of me,* Halima thought. Neema was among the fresh set of prisoners. Squinting, Halima could see that she had hidden the turtle pendant before she was snatched.

Good thinking, Neema, Halima thought. For if that pendant had been found, the warriors would not rest until they found her.

Meanwhile, the rest of the warriors returned from the houses. Some carried pots on their heads, others bowls full of cowrie shells, kola nuts and jewelry. Now the women of the village howled in rage, some making as if to lunge past the spears of the men guarding them and attack the looters.

The boat captain sighed. It was evident that this whole exercise was going less smoothly than he had planned.

"We are not pirates," he snapped at his men. "Leave the fishwives their property." He spotted the leader of the second boat and demanded, "Have you searched every house?"

His lieutenant, a tall, skinny youth no more than seventeen, nodded. "All except that one," he said, pointing to the healer's house.

Crouched in the sand, Halima grabbed the thick ankles of the woman in front of her so hard her fingernails bit into the unlucky woman's flesh.

The healer spoke up. "That is a holy place to us, our place of healing. No outsiders are allowed there."

The captain snapped his fingers and pointed to his skinny second in command. The lieutenant and two others started toward the rectangular house.

Morowa shrugged. "There's only one sufferer there now, an old leper."

The warriors stopped in midstride and looked at the boat captain. One man with exceptionally wide nostrils sniffed the air apprehensively.

From the healer's house wafted the distinctive scent of rot. Halima could not imagine what potion Morowa had concocted on such short notice, but it truly had the stink of pestilence-ridden flesh.

The boat captain rolled his eyes. "Go on – she may be lying."

Morowa told him, "Yes, it should be safer now. We have almost cured him. The ointments we have given him will soon help his nose and fingers and feet grow back. If it is the will of the spirits of the sea."

The warriors turned back fearfully toward the boat captain, who ran his hand over his jaw indecisively. Halima began to tremble. In her mind's eye she saw the men charging through the door of the healer's house and burying their spears into her helpless husband's chest.

The boat captain declared, "Men, there has been no such contagion on the coast in a generation. If you're all so frightened by this old fishwife, I myself–"

Suddenly, Neema gave one of the other young women who were lined up beside her a rude shove.

"Stop pushing me!" she barked. The other girl looked at her in confusion for moment – then she understood and charged Neema, tackling her and bringing her down to the ground.

"Bitch!" the other girl screamed. "I know you've been lying with my husband, you adulteress!"

They grappled on the ground, first one on top and then the other.

The tension among the warriors of the People of the Snake broke instantly. They watched guffawing, as the two bare-bottomed girls wrestled, legs entwined, on the burning yellow sand, pummeling one another and tearing at each other's braids.

The exasperated leader of the war party shouted an order, and the warriors – with considerable effort – pried the two clawing she-devils apart. One brawny warrior with a ring through his ear held each of them by the nape of the neck, an arm's length apart. They continued to reach for one another, sharp fingernails outstretched, still snarling curses.

"If this is how their women fight, I do not want to wait here for the men to come home!" he told the boat captain. He nodded toward the sea, where a dozen tiny sails appeared in the horizon.

The young captain threw up his hands in frustration. "Let's go!"

He ordered his men back to the boats. As the strong young men marched down to the boats, all the women, young and old, jeered at them. They bent again for fistfuls of sand and pebbles and hurled them after the men.

The boat captain turned to the crowd beseechingly.

"We are returning to Kali to join the great army of King Olugbodi, which is readying to march. Many of these brave young warriors will fall in battle before our enemies, the Abaka. You should honor them."

Morowa sucked her teeth so loudly the dead could hear it. Others followed suit, and one tough old bird squeezed out a wheezing fart in contempt.

The boat captain strode off a few paces, then turned back to remind them, "The fugitives may come to you. I warn you: Give them no shelter, or others will come and burn your plague-infested village to the ground."

As soon as the warriors climbed into the longboats and pushed off, Halima ran to her friend Neema and helped her up from the ground where the warrior had flung her. She slapped the wet sand off the girl's backside.

"May the Great One in the Sky punish me for ever calling you a fool, Neema. Today you saved my husband's life," Halima said.

Neema smiled proudly as the two young women embraced. Behind them the women and children stood at the water's edge, watching the longboats disappear into the distance. One young girl of about eight began to sing a prayer for the men going into battle. One by one, the women of the village took up the song.

Halima sighed and thought, *Foolish young men with all your pride and anger, killing each other, making widows – when will you lay down your spears forever?*

Fed goat's blood and other medicines, Shomari grew stronger and more vital each day, as if willing himself quickly back to health. Halima was permitted to spend more time with him now. She sang to her husband and fed him, changing the linen bandages on his myriad wounds from time to time.

He listened with a smile to Halima's voice, but she knew he was tormented. For as he lay there, the army of King Olugbodi prepared to march on his people, the noble giants of the Silver Mountain.

On the fifth day of their stay, Halima squatted outside Neema's house, churning butter by briskly shaking a calabash, while beside her, her friend cleaned and gutted a basket of freshly caught fish. She looked up to see up a boy child of about five years old come running.

"Come, come!" he cried urgently, grabbing Halima's arm and pulling her with all his strength. "Madongo says you must come now!"

The two girls scrambled to their feet and chased after

the scampering youngster down the beach to the healer's house.

Halima gasped in amazement. Her husband Shomari stood outside the house, a spear in hand, swaying slightly but standing on his own feet. Chest thrust out and dressed in a fisherman's loincloth, he cut a proud figure, towering more than a foot above the murmuring fishermen and their wives who stood about him, gawking.

Halima rushed over to him. "Husband, husband," she pleaded. "Lie back down."

"I must go," he whispered.

Madongo stood next to her, echoing her appeal. "You are too ill, great warrior," he cried.

"What use will you be to your people dead?" Neema implored, standing beside her mate.

Halima went to him. "Husband, your eyes," she said gently. "Your soldiering days are done."

Shomari shook his head. "I have told you: We of the Abaka have an inner eye and with it we can look deeper than any sighted man."

In a firm but respectful tone, Madongo told him, "Lord, philosophy will not help you against the slings and arrows of the People of the Snake."

Shomari stepped back and in a powerful voice challenged, "Who among you has the strongest arm?"

"No, husband!" Halima cried. "No foolish games. I forbid it!"

"I say, who among you has the surest arm?" the king of the Abaka demanded.

After a few trembling hands pointed him out, Madongo quietly replied, "I, lord. I alone here am trained as a warrior."

Up until now, Shomari had been using the spear to prop himself up, but now he forced the weapon into the hands of the other warrior.

"Go back ten paces and hurl it with all your strength,"

he commanded.

Madongo shook his head vigorously. "I am no murderer."

Shomari grabbed Halima's arm. "If you truly love me, let me prove I am still a man."

Halima looked into his eyes, at once vacant and full of eerie power. She knew that if she did not grant his wish, his love for her would slowly rot away, and in a few years – or perhaps many – ferment wholly into hate.

Grimly, she nodded to Madongo.

The broad-shouldered warrior frowned in distress. Then he bowed obediently, and wearing a look of profound reluctance, backed slowly up. The crowd watched transfixed, some silently mouthing the number of each step as he retreated: One... Two... Three... Four... Five... Six... Seven... Eight... Nine...

"Ten," finished Madongo when he was in place. Wearing a pained look, he set his sights on the blinded warrior-king.

A solemn hush fell over the crowd. It seemed that even the seagulls hovering above ceased their constant cawing. All that remained was the sound of the eternal ebb and flow of the surf.

Madongo planted his feet apart and crouched slightly, poised to throw. Neema, crying, buried her face in Halima's shoulder.

Shomari bellowed, "Your best shot, warrior." Halima gripped Neema's hand as Madongo wet his lips – then hurled the spear.

Halima's heart rose to her throat as the spear swooped through the air like a bird of prey at its target. The weapon zipped past Shomari's ear and crashed into the outer wall of the healer's house behind him, wedging between the tall stalks of bamboo. Her husband didn't flinch. *He must not even have known it was thrown,* Halima thought.

The crowd let out a collective sigh of relief. But Shomari was not pleased. He turned angrily and ripped the spear out of the wall. He cast the weapon back at Madongo and it landed barely a foot before him, kicking up a spray of sand.

"No," Shomari demanded. "Not like a girl. I said your *best* throw, warrior. At my heart."

Halima knew now that before Madongo had aimed to miss – but he could not play that trick a second time. He looked at her, beseechingly.

Halima, feeling faint, whispered to the sword bearer of her father, "You are forgiven."

Madongo nodded gloomily. He took careful aim, then leaned back with all his strength and pitched the spear silently at the heart of Shomari.

The iron dart shot through the air, spiraling with merciless certainty at Shomari's chest. Her husband stood still as a rock. *Oh no, he wants to die*, Halima thought. She fell to her knees, gasping, as women of the village let loose a chorus of high-pitched squeals of horror.

At the very last instant, Shomari stepped from the path of the spear, and with one long-fingered hand snatched it right out of the air. He did this in one fluid movement so graceful it seemed easy, like a trick practiced for years by a juggler in her father's court.

Shomari hoisted the weapon high above his head, waving it triumphantly in the air while he let out a wild whoop of a warrior and jumped up and down, making the earth shake.

The crowd roared in astonishment, and then converged on Shomari with cries of praise.

"Hundreds of years from now, the people of this village will still sing of this day," said Chinua.

Halima threw her arms around her husband, kissing his bare, heaving chest and shutting her eyes in relief.

He looked down at her and growled, "Now, wife, do I have your leave to return to the Silver Mountain – or must I give your friend one more throw at me?"

Halima beamed, swept with pride in him. "Where you go, I will follow," she whispered, happy tears rolling down her cheeks.

CHAPTER 16

THE LAST
BATTLE

*S*o it was that Halima and Shomari set out to return to the land of the Abaka. Madongo and Neema accompanied them. Halima released them from their oaths to her family and told them they were free to remain in the village, but they chose to go with their beloved princess.

That night, in an ancient ceremony, Shomari and Madongo, who had shared in one terrifying moment a bond few men could ever know, sacrificed a sheep. They shared its blood and liver, linking them forever as *gichairo* – blood brothers. From this day forward, they would have all the responsibility and all the rights of true kin.

The people of the fishing village gave the party all the provisions they needed: calabashes of water; smoked fish; jam and honey; flint; shields and spears. The travelers attired themselves in long, nondescript robes that the travelers from scores of different lands wore in those days.

After making a sacrifice of a young goat and saying prayers for a safe journey, they set out at dawn. The people of the village cheered and waved as Halima left the seashore and headed inland, walking three paces behind her husband, as was the custom. Madongo and Neema took up the rear, carrying baskets of food and supplies on their heads.

Along the way, kinfolk of Halima and the others still loyal to her family furnished the party with food and shelter, as they passed from village to village en route to the great Silver Mountain.

On the third day of their journey, they stayed among the cowherds of the lowlands, who were known for breeding big, healthy longhorns. They had suffered in times of drought and survived only because old King Babatunde had sent them grain to feed their cattle. So they loved Halima's family and protected the travelers.

When darkness fell, Halima and Shomari lay together under a large blanket of lion fur in a small, round room beside the granary of the village chief. A torch hung on the wall, filling the room with a dim, flickering light. Madongo and Neema were snoring inside the granary itself.

The animal smell of the fur kept Halima awake. For a while she twisted and turned, unable to sleep, then she ran her delicate fingers over her husband's taut, flat belly.

"Husband, it has been so long since we've made love. I miss the strength of your body," she purred.

Shomari groaned.

"Do your wounds still hurt you, husband?" she asked.

The giant tore her small hand away and clapped it on her midriff.

He chastised her, "My children, my family, my people face slaughter, and you want to talk about lovemaking as if we were newlyweds. I am no randy youth."

Halima felt blood rush to her face and looked away, ashamed. But then she turned back and saw her husband's twitching jaw and knew in her heart there was something amiss. For as it is said, "It is the wife who knows her husband."

"You need to see my prettiness to feel desire – is that

why you do not touch me?" she inquired softly.

Shomari groaned a second time. "My own wife mocks me," he protested. "Today I stumbled in the forest where I used to walk as a lion. Now I need to be led across the river like a doddering old grandfather." He reached for her. "I do not feel like much of a man this night, sweet Halima."

Halima took his hand and ran it across her cheek. She kissed his long fingers.

"You are very much a man to me, Shomari. When you stumble and fall, you rise up again and go on – that to me is a man."

She stood up and doused the torch, pitching the room into absolute blackness.

"Now in this darkness, forget you are blind, Shomari, and make love to me as you did on our wedding night."

She knelt beside him in the darkness and stroked him gently, so that he swelled in her hand. Soon she could hear him taking deep breaths and felt his pelvis begin to rise and fall. He arched up, his manhood pushing through her hands as solid as a stout young tree.

He began to chant her name again and again: "Halima, Halima, Halima."

When he stood straight up, like a spear stuck in the mud, Halima climbed over him and squatted gingerly down. Now, when he parted the petals of her womanhood and entered her it was like she was a virgin being penetrated for the first time.

Halima threw back her head and shrieked. All the pain, all the months of separation that had passed only sweetened their lovemaking now. Jolts of joy and passion shook her to the core.

She rode him, thrashing, hands holding her belly to protect her unborn child from Shomari's powerful animal strokes. Yes, this was taboo – she knew it. But if she could lay with that pig Olugbodi while she was with child, the Great One in the Sky would forgive her for once making love with her own husband.

Blood rushed from her head to her groin, leaving her dizzy and full of wild abandon. All inhibitions fled her as she squirmed and rocked on the immense shaft of the bucking black stallion beneath her.

Soon she was possessed by delicious dreams, and to her mind there came unbidden a crowd of wicked fantasies. She thought of all the men who had passed through her life and in her mind now, each one marched in and took his turn with her.

She dreamed of Madongo, how the sight of his manhood crowded into his loincloth excited her first feelings of passion, and for a few moments it was him rising up into her.

She dreamed of the handsome deserter, who wanted to rape her like an animal on the forest floor and make her his queen in a new country to the north, and for a time it was his greedy hands stroking her breasts.

She dreamed of Hasani, Shomari's virile son, who sought her for her beauty, and next it was his young, powerful body that worked her tirelessly.

She dreamed of Olugbodi, who wanted to possess her even more than he wanted to rule the world, and now it was him taking her in every humiliating way, humbling her and making her love it.

She dreamed of the brave, mysterious caravan master Kamau, and it was he teaching the secret tricks of lovemaking learned in a lifetime of travels.

And she dreamed of her stepson Kokayi, who wished he was a man, and for a moment he was grown up and it was he who held her in his strong, protecting arms.

As she rose and fell on that tall, magnificent column, all these thoughts took hold of her, but they came and left, insignificant passing fancies that dissipated like breath upon a mirror.

In the end there was only one: strong, sure, good

Shomari, the king of the giants, who was all of these men and more. It was he who was in her thoughts as she climaxed once, then again, and then a third time.

"Yes yes yes, Shomari!" she cried as he exploded inside her.

Afterwards they lay clasping each other tightly, both drenched in sweat, panting.

"You have not lost your iron, husband," Halima whispered. He grabbed hold of her and pulled her close, kissing her throat and nuzzling her cheek against his with desperate longing. How sweet this moment was. *If we must die tomorrow, we will be happy*, she thought.

In the distance, they heard the staccato beat of the talking drum.

They sat up in unison, listening intently. Solemnly, Shomari interpreted: "The army of Olugbodi is on the march – 12,000 strong. They are only one day behind us. At dawn, we must take up our trek again and quicken our pace."

The next day they arrived in the town of Ampara, in the hills where the clan of Halima's family lived. To frustrate invaders, the town was completely encircled by a thick hedge of eurobia bush, the leaves of which, when scratched, let out a burning white sap that scalds the skin.

The village sentinel led the visitors safely through a maze-like tunnel into the village interior. Inside were neat rows of houses built of mud and clay. Shaped like vases, the walls were smooth and varnished. They looked to Halima like the work of a potter more than an architect.

Here, according to customs handed down from father to son, the smiths forged unbreakable iron in furnaces that heated to temperatures that rivaled that of the fiercest volcano. The technique was secret, but it was said the smiths mixed droplets of their own blood with the ore, in a bubbling cauldron of molten metal, while saying arcane prayers and incantations over it. Then the strong-backed men beat and hammered the iron into fine spears, plowshares and swords. They traded them to kingdoms all over the continent, for they were legendary for the beauty and durability.

A billowing cloud of yellow and black smoke hovered above the smiths large stone furnaces.

"It stinks here," Neema whispered, holding her broad nose at the sulfurous smell that filled the air. "Like rotten eggs."

"Hush," Halima scolded her. "The welcoming party comes to greet us."

It was crucial that their contact here was successful. For they hoped from among Halima's kin to secure troops to travel with them to the Silver Mountain and reinforce the Abaka.

A group of burly men – biceps huge from wielding blacksmiths' hammers – approached them, holding their long, newly forged spears point forward. The four travelers drew together. Out of the "welcoming party" strode the chief of the village, Halima's cousin Sahale, a middle-aged man with a comfortable paunch.

Madongo spoke up, introducing them. "Sir, this is the Princess Halima, daughter of Babatunde, your kinsman. We –"

"I know who you are," the chief interrupted him. "You are fugitives wanted for treason against the crown."

Halima stepped forward angrily. "I am the daughter of the king of this country. How can I be called a traitor?"

"That is for others to decide," said Chief Sahale. "We

have been told to hold you until troops from the army of King Olugbodi arrive."

Halima stamped her foot into the dusty ground. "We are kin. The blood of my family is in your veins. You cannot betray me!"

The Chief of Ampara replied, "Olugbodi is a good king, prudent and generous. We have prospered under him. By making peace with the Zimbai, he has made the roads safe at last for merchants, so that we can exchange our swords and spears for goods from other lands. He is, of course, himself our best customer. And our taxes are low – only one hundred arrows for each family each year."

Halima shook her head in disbelief. "If you hold us here, my cousin, you condemn us to death."

"That's none of my business," shrugged the chief. His voice sharpening, he commanded, "Throw down your weapons."

The men of the village quickly made a circle around the group. There were at least three dozen of them.

Shomari cried to Chief Sahale, "We will not be disarmed."

The chief waved his hand, pointing to all his men.

"You cannot win."

"Then we will die standing!"

There were mumbled comments of admiration among some of the young men. They spent their days polishing shiny blades, but never in their lives had cause to use them in anger. They only dreamed of battle and glory.

The chief sighed. "All right. Hold onto your weapons. But still we will watch you and keep you here until the troops of Olugbodi arrive."

They were ushered to a small, dingy shed, a place filled with cast-off pieces of metal, twisted and misshapen, like dreams that had gone awry and become nightmares. The four travelers sat on the earthen floor, surrounded by grotesque, half-completed objects. Guards paced outside, making sure they didn't attempt to steal away into the night.

Madongo cast his eyes about their dismal surroundings and ran a hand over his smooth scalp. "It seems we are at the end of our journey."

Neema embraced him, quivering with fear. "What will happen to us?" It was ignoble, Halima knew, but she was sure that by "us," Neema meant Madongo and herself. For Halima and her husband surely faced only one possible fate: quick execution.

Shomari stood up and beckoned his wife, "Halima, sing to us. Give us courage."

Halima sang, with all her heart, an ancient song of her people that had come with her family from the Old Land.

Her strong, brave voice carried outside and across the midnight air:

"This is my land,
This is my native soil,
Do not take me from it,
Or I will die.
This is my mother's breast.
These are my brothers.
Do not make me leave them.
I fear to walk alone."

As she sang on, sharp-eared Shomari whispered to the others, "Listen." Madongo and Neema, craning at the tiny slit of the window, could hear outside a low, soft whistle of a wind instrument accompanying Halima.

"There are many of her kin here," Madongo observed.

"Perhaps they will help us," Neema suggested hopefully.

"We will see," Halima replied, her song complete.

"Now let us sleep, for I think tomorrow will be a hard day."

The next morning they were awakened by the strident beat of war drums. Still sleepy-eyed, they wandered out of the shed into the glaring light of day.

The village square was full of bare-chested warriors in full regalia of the People of the Snake. Most of the townspeople were out as well, to see the confrontation.

Halima shuddered with dread as the three-fingered general of King Olugbodi emerged from the troop of sixty or so warriors. She had hoped he'd drowned.

His eyes gleamed when he spied Halima and the others, as Chief Sahale escorted him to the prisoners. Masomakali stalked in a wide circle around them, sizing them up as though they were cattle meant for slaughter and he was reckoning how many guests they would feed, and who would receive the choicest cuts.

When at last he was face to face with Halima, he leaned in and hissed in the language of the People of the Snake: "You have hurt my beloved master Olugbodi greatly with your betrayal. He pines for you like a lovesick boy. For that you will suffer before you die. Before I and my men are done with you, you will curse the Great One for making you a woman."

Chief Sahale, who stood a few yards back, called out gruffly, "Take them and be gone. We have work to do here."

Halima's mind rebelled against the fate Masomakali decreed for her. She pushed past the three-fingered man and ran out in front of the villagers. She cried out with all the strength of her lungs, "Which of you are my kin?"

She ran to one old woman and gestured at her own cheek. "Mother, do you not recognize this face? These eyes are your eyes!"

She stepped next to a man. "Brother, do you not recognize this chin? This chin is your chin."

She raced over to a slim young girl and held up her delicate hands. "Sister, do you not recognize these hands? These are your hands." She clutched the startled girl's palms for emphasis.

Halima spun and addressed the mob. "My brothers, my sisters, my family, you cannot betray your own flesh!"

There were mumbles of agreement from the crowd. Now some in the town began to protest, "Do not let them take her away! She is our daughter!"

Another shouted, "One lineage is one blood!"

A few dozen people of all ages pushed forward, surrounding Halima's party and shielding them from harm.

Masomakali turned to the village chief, fuming, "You are in charge here. Order them to part."

But now Sahale grew hesitant. "And yet I do not want to see my people divided. For it seems those who are her close kin will protect her, and those who are not her kin will side against her. It will be neighbor pitted against neighbor, and blood spilled on the land today."

He told Masomakali firmly, "I must ask you to take your armed men and go; join the rest of Olugbodi's troops."

A cheer went up from Halima's supporters in the crowd.

"You see – you cannot cook a goat's calf in her mother's milk!" Neema declared triumphantly, crossing her arms.

Masomakali glowered and pointed at the surrounding houses with his deformed hand. "If we leave today, we will return with an army to raze this rodents' den."

A few in the crowd who were not related to Halima protested, and demanded that the princess be turned over to the soldiers.

"Better one dies than the village burns," they shouted.

Shomari strode forward and addressed Sahale. "Noble chief, whose people forge mighty steel that will last 800 years, let us settle this like men. I against this one, who tortured to death eight of my friends, in mortal combat. If I am victorious, you'll give us free passage to the mountains. If I am killed, the rest of these travelers are his."

The potbellied chief nodded, stroking his flabby chin. Then, pleased by this proposal – which spared his people from sharing in the bloodshed – he turned to Masomakali and asked if he would accept the challenge.

The slave general narrowed his eyes, scowling uncertainly. He took in Shomari's huge bulk. The giant was muscled like a champion wrestler from his neck to his toes.

Then Masomakali noticed the blank, glazed appearance of Shomari's eyes, and recognized blindness. His sharpened teeth glimmered like those of a crocodile as he grinned.

"I accept the challenge."

A festive atmosphere seized the town now as people prepared the place in the village square where the fight was to take place. The townsfolk were quite naturally pleased that the matter would be resolved without any of them losing their skin.

The older men sized up the two combatants, arguing and wagering about who would win. Meanwhile, some young men drew a circle in the earth with lamb's blood, and pounded bamboo stakes into the ground around it. The tops of the stakes were then sharpened into points as fine as needles and daubed with poison.

Jugs of cooking oil were poured around the ring. At the commencement of the fight, the liquid was to be set on fire.

Shomari stripped to his loincloth. As Neema greased

down his giant frame, Madongo whispered a rapid-fire stream of advice. "He will be quick and cunning. Expect him to slip up behind you early on."

"Thank you, brother." Shomari embraced the shorter man, and took the chance to whisper, "If I fail, see that my wife does not suffer."

Madongo nodded somberly. Then Shomari hugged Halima and their lips brushed.

"You are my hero," she whispered. "I will always love you."

He smiled – for the first time in so very long – his confident, kingly smile, took up his spear and shield and turned away.

The two men entered the ring of death, slipping between the stakes, and the oiled muscles of their backs shimmering in the scorching sunlight. Halima was dismayed to see that, stripped for action, Masomakali was much more powerfully built than she would have imagined. His body was a mass of tight, gnarly sinew covered with wormlike scars.

Chief Sahale gave a solemn order and a torch was put to the ground. A ring of fire leapt up, hemming the two combatants in.

At the sound of the crackling flame, Shomari crouched instinctively, raising his shield. Masomakali did likewise, and the two began to circle each other, stealthily.

Then all of a sudden, they rushed together like charging bulls. Their buffalo-hide-covered shields struck with the power of lightning bolts colliding. Young women in the crowd screamed and fell back. There was a terrible clang and the two men hopped back.

Halima's heart beat like a sledgehammer falling on an anvil. It pounded as loud as though she were the one standing in the ring of fire, facing death. The combatants circled each other again, shields raised, weaving in wheels within wheels.

Suddenly, Masomakali rushed a second time.

Halima shrieked in warning and blind Shomari braced himself just in time. The shields clashed again with a force that would have battered an ordinary man to the ground.

A broad, suffocating hand clapped over Halima's mouth and she found herself pinned from behind by one of Masomakali's warriors, silencing any further interference.

This time, the combatants' shields clung together, as Masomakali's momentum carried Shomari back. Throwing all his weight into the effort, the slave general propelled Shomari backward toward the burning bamboo stakes. Shomari's bare feet sank into the dust again and again as he stepped back against his will.

No, no, no! Halima thought, overcome by helpless anguish. She watched her husband's broad back move closer and closer to the razor-sharp stakes.

At last Shomari stopped moving and dug into the earth with his heels. Halima saw his bulging thigh muscles grow taut as he steadied himself. Now, step by step he drove his adversary back.

Now, as they crossed the circle in the other direction, Masomakali looked behind him and saw the stakes approaching. His eyes grew large with fear. At the last second he gave way, lowering his shield and stumbling clear.

The two warriors faced each other panting. Shomari caught his breath, then with a sudden burst, thrust out his spear. The iron tip ripped through his adversary's shield as if it were a fig leaf, glancing past Masomakali's cheek and drawing a thin red line of blood. Shomari used his spear to pry the shield out of Masomakali's hand and then – with an almost contemptuous gesture – he flung it out of the ring.

The crowd roared in approval.

Masomakali scurried back, armed only with his spear now, which he clenched anxiously with his three-fingered hand. He looked like a frightened lizard. Shomari stood at the center of the ring, turning his spear this way and that as if through it, like a water finder, he could divine his opponent's position.

On cat feet now, Masomakali stole around behind Shomari and crept in for the kill. Halima sank her teeth into the hand of the warrior restraining her, and struggled in his arms – but she was powerless as a kitten. She could not warn her husband.

Some in the crowd cried out in protest at Masomakali's treachery. But in the hubbub of voices, Shomari couldn't make sense of the words of warning.

He stood motionless as the treacherous Masomakali snuck up close behind him. The slave general's eyes shone like a vulture's descending on carrion. He aimed at the point between Shomari's shoulder blades and threw all his strength into one awful, final lunge.

It was over.

Halima shut her eyes against the bloody sight. She refused to see the weapon tear through her husband's back and come ripping out of his chest like a birthing child.

She heard the bloodthirsty crowd roar in excitement, but still refused, absolutely refused to believe it. "No, no, no," she screeched, going limp in the warrior's arms.

She thought of Shomari lying in the dungeon of Kali, and how she refused to accept his death. How she had prayed and he had returned to her. Again, she refused to believe him dead. Her eyes shut tight, she pictured him darting out of the path of the spear in the nick of time and grabbing hold of his enemy.

Yes, he has the vision of the inner eye, and with it he would see Masomakali creeping behind him, she told herself. *He would have turned and seized him. They would have dropped their spears and grappled like wrestlers. And now, if I open my eyes I will see them spinning together in a savage dance.*

Refusing to see anything else, Halima opened her

eyes… and that is exactly what she saw!

The two men, now unarmed, their spears on the ground, were locked together in a deadly embrace. Each had his hands on the other's throat as they stumbled around and around, each trying to knock the other down. Their nearly naked bodies were covered in blood and sweat and dust.

The crowd was in frenzy – Masomakali's men cheering wildly for the leader, Halima's kin chanting Shomari's name.

It was brute strength against strength, and Masomakali's cunning could not save him now. His eyes were full of animal fright – for he knew he was going to die. In a swift movement, Shomari released his opponent's throat, reached down and took him by the waist. Masomakali's feet left the ground and fluttered, kicking, as Shomari lifted him overhead.

Masomakali screamed in despair, a high-pitched, womanish cry like some shrill bird of the forest. For a moment, Shomari held him aloft as if restrained by pity. Then he brought the enemy down with all his strength, hurling him onto the bamboo stakes.

The spears sheared through Masomakali's body like knives through butter. He writhed for a moment, spitting up blood, impaled in four different places. He shrieked in torment as the flames ate his flesh. Then he was still. His deformed hand hung limp at his side.

Shomari, dripping in blood and sweat, dropped to his knees in the dust. The crowd cheered and converged on the circle, throwing buckets of water to douse the flames, and tearing away the thicket of stakes.

Halima rushed to her husband, who knelt, his chest heaving. He embraced her, burying his face in her bosom.

"Now I know that the Great One in the Sky is with us," he declared. "If we reach home before the army of Olugbodi, I know that I can defeat him."

Halima looked up and saw the Silver Mountain in the distance, awaiting her return.

Before Halima left, Masomakali's second in command among the troops implored her to come back to Kali.

"If we return without you, King Olugbodi will have our heads," he said ruefully. "Without you he is nothing."

Halima, touching her belly, told him, "Give this message to Olugbodi: I will not be back. My son will be back to claim his kingdom."

Traveling all day and throughout the night, they arrived at the foothills of the Silver Mountain by noon the next day.

There they saw that the rambling fields of bamboo that surrounded the pass to the upper reaches of the mountain had been trampled down to nothing. Madongo and Halima exchanged somber looks. They knew the army of Olugbodi had passed this way. Only a huge team of war elephants could have wrought such destruction.

Halima gazed in concern at her husband, whose unseeing eyes were serene. She looked up at the mountainside and wondered what more her own eyes would see before this day was done.

When they reached the pass, they were not surprised to

find the thick, thorny nyika bushes which had hidden it had been torn away. As they entered the narrow pass, they found it eerily still. The stench of death quickly filled their nostrils.

The corpses of warriors of the People of the Snake and of Kali and of the Zimbai filled the pass, lying twisted and intertwined as huge bald vultures sat on their faces, pecking greedily at their eyeballs. *So there was an ambush,* Halima thought. *Perhaps there is hope.*

Neema began to pull away. "Please, Princess, let us go back, please. We will find nothing but death here." Grimly, Halima shook her head.

They wove through the gauntlet of broken bodies, stepping over corpses where there was no room to pass.

"This once I envy you your blindness, blood brother," Madongo said to Shomari.

It was nearly sunset when they finally reached the great gorge that set apart Shomari's kingdom. The rope bridge had been cut by the city's defenders. But to Halima's dismay, she saw that other, temporary bridges had been slung across the ravine by Olugbodi's engineers – and these bridges were still intact.

In the distance they could see Shomari's city. Black smoke rose above it and sparks swam like fireflies through the sooty air. Halima hung her head

Grimly they crossed a bridge and approached the outer gates of the city. The great wooden doors had been shorn from their hinges like a broken jewelry box, and all was silent inside the city except the triumphant call of vultures. High above the shattered city flew the flag of the People of the Snake.

Halima turned to Shomari and took his arm. "Oh, my husband!" she groaned.

Shomari pulled away from her and shambled through the gates like a puppet propelled forward by strings.

Neema began to weep. She pounded on Madongo's

broad chest. "Why? Why do men butcher each other?" she demanded. "Let women rule the world if this is what you must do!"

Halima started after her husband, but Madongo stopped her, suddenly raising his spear. Out of the smoking ruins a single figure crept.

"It is the griot, Mwendapole," Madongo said in surprise. The old man's soot-covered robes were ragged and bloodied, but he was unharmed. He was sinking to the ground from exhaustion, but Halima caught him and kept him steady.

"What happened here, venerable Mwendapole?" she demanded.

The griot replied, "This blood-soaked ground tells the history of this battle better than my poor words, Princess. But let me tell you, men will long remember the bravery of the giants of the mountain – the tall ones that are no more.

"As Princess Halima instructed, I warned the Abaka of an attack and told them to position their forces in the mountain pass. When the armies of Olugbodi arrived, they were ready and pelted them with arrows and spears and finally sticks and stones. But more and more warriors of Kali and the Zimbai and the People of the Snake swarmed into the mountain pass. For King Olugbodi did not care how many men he lost. He would take this mountain.

"The Abaka fought bravely, but numbers were against them, and at last they were overwhelmed at the gates of the city where the final battle was fought. And that was the fiercest – the grandfather of all battles. For 500 years they will sing of the courage of the giants. Each of them brought down ten of the enemy before he went to the spear. But in the end all their courage was for naught.

"I remained hidden, and so I alone survive. All the rest in the city were slain or taken captive or fled into the forest. The *ncamba*, Jumoko, brother of Shomari, was left with only a few dozen men, and they have vanished into the mountains, vowing to fight on against the tyrant Olugbodi."

Mwendapole looked at his feet. "You must think me a great coward."

Madongo shook his head. "The battle was not yours, old one."

Halima pictured her beautiful co-wives and their children. "And the king's family?" she asked, holding her breath.

Mwendapole said, "Even the boy children armed themselves and tried to defend the city, but they were slain. Queen Rashida and all King Shomari's wives took a poisonous asp and let it bite them, so that they would not be taken as slaves."

Halima buried her face in her hands, the enormity of her sinful betrayal of these people filling her with guilt.

"My husband. We must find my husband," she mumbled.

"Yes, we must leave this place," Mwendapole told her. "For the army of Olugbodi is now chasing after the few who escaped. When they return tomorrow, they will raze the city to the ground, sow salt into the earth, and burn all the dead."

They hurried through the charred, broken gates and into the burning city, all choking and bleary-eyed from the thick black smoke that curled through what was now a necropolis. Bodies, blood and severed limbs were everywhere, and hungry flies settled down in droves on the corpses.

In the center of the city, they reached the compound of the king, from which tall flames shot. Halima's heart sank when she saw the body of Shomari's young son Kokayi, who had saved Halima from a lion, lying curled in the doorway. He looked as if he might be asleep – save for the arrow in his heart. The boy died the death of a man.

In his hands he clenched the long spear of his grandfather, which Shomari had given him so long ago.

Halima knelt beside him, weeping. She lifted his head and ran her hands across his features, which were peaceful and angelic, as if he were in a deep, untroubled dream.

Halima shook, shame filling her. "Oh brave Kokayi, your Little Mother has killed you."

From inside the compound Shomari emerged, carrying the body of his first wife. Her stiff body was draped in a long purple mantle, and even in death she had lost none of her proud beauty.

Shomari threw back his head and let loose a roar of anguish that echoed through the streets of the murdered city and shook the sheltering mountain walls. Gently he laid down his queen and staggered to his feet.

"All of you can go," he intoned in a dead, hopeless voice. He bent and pried the spear of his father from the lifeless hands of young Kokayi. "I will stay to face them when they return."

"You will die," Madongo protested.

"Then I will die standing."

Madongo wrapped his hand around his spear. "If you stay, I stay, brother," he insisted.

Shomari hurled the spear away in frustration, then fell to his knees, burying his face in his hands. He pounded his chest with both his fists, then threw them in the air either to beckon the Great One in the Sky or to curse him.

"I am undone," he wept. "I am a king without a country. What is there for me but death?"

Halima crouched beside him, rocking with shame. All this was her doing, she thought. She was the vilest creature on earth, lower than the most degraded prostitute or vilest blasphemer. For it was she who, out of selfishness, had brought death upon this land.

With her treason she had murdered the city. She, who'd been born to serve the people, had put her own passion above all else. She had sacrificed them all for her love of Shomari.

And yet … she knew, in her heart of hearts, that she would make the same choice again. For her, right or wrong, that was the only choice.

Halima stood up, a torrent of emotions welling up within her. She pushed Shomari in his side and wrenched him to his feet.

"Stand up! Stand up like a man!" she cried.

She grabbed his hand and planted it on her belly.

"*This* is your country now, Shomari," she shouted. "I and your child, we are your kingdom, and I demand you defend us."

Halima's sharp words stung Shomari, and he turned to her slowly. Halima remembered that other man whom she and Neema had mocked as a "king without a country." It was the handsome deserter who promised to sweep her away to a new land over the mountain, beside the great river that flowed south to north.

Desperately, she went on, "There is a fertile valley in the north, where the grass is tall and the air is pure, a free land as yet unpeopled. Let us go there, husband, you and I and our friends, and found a new kingdom. For there is nothing for us here or in Kali."

Shomari stared at her with his dead unseeing eyes, as Halima stood trembling, waiting for his reply. He wiped the tears from his sooty face and pointed to the mountain peak, where the crimson sun was falling behind the ice cap.

"Wait for me by the river, wife," he said. "I must climb the mountain face and visit the old man of the mountain, our seer Olushegun. I must seek his wisdom. The army of Olugbodi will not return until after morning light. I will be back by dawn or I will not be back."

Halima embraced him. "If you return I will be there waiting. If you do not return, I will be there waiting," she whispered.

As the giant warrior strode off, the old griot marveled, "He will scale that mountain face alone, in the dead of night?"

"We should have stopped him," Madongo said.

"He has climbed that mountain before and knows every handhold, every foothold. He will reach the mountain peak and he will be back by dawn," Halima told him. "He will come for me."

They waited for Shomari at the rocks by the river, where Halima used to squat alongside the women of the city, washing clothes. In the darkening sky, Neema slept in her husband's arms. The pair decided to come with Halima on the journey – if there were to be a journey – for both of them deeply loved their princess. Of course, Mwendapole announced he would accompany them. For it was his duty to serve her family, as his ancestors had for generations.

Halima leaned against the boulder, her hands resting on her full belly. She could feel the life growing within her; now she was sure she could feel the second tiny heartbeat.

The princess looked at the city, which was still burning, and called to Mwendapole.

"Friend of my father, was it evil that I did? To sacrifice so many for the love of one?"

Mwendapole looked up at the stars. "In time, Olugbodi would have found the pass. Perhaps the Abaka were destined to fall. All kingdoms last but a time, and then they become part of the past," he said gently.

"But what is wrong with me that I should make such a wicked choice?" she demanded. "Now I have condemned us to be wanderers, outcasts all our days. If we begin a new people, what kind of people will a weak creature such as I ever make?"

The old man turned to her and said, "All along yours has been a separate destiny, Halima. You were not destined to follow in the path of your mother, but to lead us to a new place we have never been."

Halima nodded, comforted by the old man's words. She gripped in her palm the gift Kamau the merchant had given her, the Seed of Hope. She considered the legend: that where it was planted a new Golden Age would spring up.

Under the bright stars, she wandered in and out of sleep. Such strange things she saw: her father and mother embracing, reunited in the afterlife; old Bimkubwa giving her milk and bread for a long journey; Rashida kissing her, offering her a dove.

Then she saw a new land by a great, broad river, where wheat grew as tall as an elephant's back. She saw her child, a young, strong, brown boy – Kokayi and yet not Kokayi – running toward her laughing, arms outstretched, crying "Mother!"

Halima's eyes opened.

The mountainside was transformed by the brilliant yellow light of dawn. She felt fully rested now. It was as if the strange sweet dreams had washed away all the pain and tribulations, readying her for a new tomorrow.

She was surprised to see that about forty refugees from the fallen city, mostly women with small children, had drifted into their camp. They were bedraggled and disoriented, like woodland creatures slowly returning to their dens after a forest fire and unable to comprehend that not only their homes but the forest, too, was no more.

They stood about, saying only a few words to each other, still too stunned to weep. What force brought them all to this one spot, Halima could not imagine.

Neema, Mwendapole and Madongo were already on their feet. Madongo, looking around anxiously, helped Halima stand.

"Halima, we must go. It is dawn – soon Olugbodi's army will return."

The fire was out of the city of the Abaka now. It sat peacefully, a single, wispy column of smoke rising from the smoldering ruins.

Halima shook her head. Neema, touching her own

belly, put a fleshy arm around Halima's shoulder.

"Princess, think of your baby."

Halima shook her head again. "My husband will come for me," she told them with supreme confidence.

"Look!" Mwendapole exclaimed. Halima turned and joy filled her heart as she saw Shomari striding toward her. Shomari moved like an older man now, with the sure, slow gait and serenity of a wise man.

As he passed through the small crowd of lost souls, the people all gathered around him, some clinging to his robes with a mix of awe and desperate hope in their eyes.

When Shomari was in the middle of the camp, he turned and addressed them all in a robust voice. "Come, follow me. We have a journey to make, and a new land to people."

He looked at Halima, his deep brown eyes alive again, not with sight but with feeling. He smiled and took her hand. Together, they turned away from the destroyed city, as rain began to fall quietly on the last smoldering embers.

Without a backward glance, they marched off, heading for the other side of the mountain, the far-off valley where their destiny lay. They walked five abreast – Shomari, Halima, Madongo, Neema and Mwendapole – with their followers hurrying behind.

As they left, Halima turned to her husband and asked, "What did the seer say?"

Shomari told her, "The old man of the mountain sat with me and spoke these words: 'Your children will know grandeur and they will know despair. They will walk as kings and they will walk in chains. But they will always have courage, for in them is the blood of titans.' "

THE END

ABOUT THE AUTHOR

C. Michael Forsyth is a graduate of Yale College. He is the author of the critically acclaimed novel *Hour of the Beast* and the children's book *Brothers*. He is a former writer for Weekly World News. You can find out more about his work at http://freedomshammer.com.